SCANDALOUS HEIRESS

Those Notorious Americans, Book 4

CERISE DELAND

COPYRIGHT

W. J. Power Publisher

Photographic art: Hot Damn Designs

Graphic designer: Wicked Smart Designs

ISBN-13: 978-0-9908943-3-9 Digital

ISBN-13: 978-0-9908943-4-6 Print

❀ Created with Vellum

CONTENTS

SCANDALOUS HEIRESS

Money can buy anything, can't it? Those brash Americans--their dollars and charms work wonders. Until they learn that money can buy anything...but love.

She was his ruin.

Ada Hanniford is an oddity. An American heiress, a beauty, she's sowed her wild oats and paid the price in sly rumors. Preferring politics to promenades, gardening to waltzing, she rebuffs the toffs who would seduce her for the fun of it or propose to marry her merely for her millions.

Embracing impending spinsterhood, she's shocked to meet a man who fascinates her with tales his own adventures in exotic lands. She's drawn to him, charmed by his kisses and his sense of honor.

Then one night, he braves society to save her reputation... and in the act, destroys his own.

He was her salvation.

Victor Cole is a survivor. A man who has worked diligently to overcome his lack of title and land, he has finally buried the disgrace of a wife so scandalous he had to sail thousands of miles away to wipe away her stain.

Then he meets Ada Hanniford. She's so natural, so unique, he must court her and kiss her. But would he be wise to claim her? With each word, each sigh, he comes closer to loving her. But when the one man whom he should respect shames her, Victor cannot allow him to sully her. Rescuing her becomes his sole purpose. But to save her means he stirs scandal once more...and destroys his own bright prospects.

How can a man and woman who love each other overcome the slings and arrows of their scandalous pasts and build a life together if no one else can forget their regrettable mistakes?

WILD LILY, BOOK 1
DARING WIDOW, BOOK 2
SWEET SIREN, BOOK 3
SCANDALOUS HEIRESS, Book 4

CERISE DELAND

SUBSCRIBE TO
Cerise's Bon Bons!

PRELUDE I

Caroline, Duchess of Brentwood
Brentwood Hall, Somerset

January 10, 1882

Dearest Victor,

I beg you to reconsider and sail home to Brentwood immediately. I need you to advise your brother. He's determined to finally choose a bride and I daresay his current obsession is utterly unsuitable. Still entangled in that messy business with the Prince of Wales, Richard has not yet proposed to this girl. So there is that.

But you would shudder to know her. Oh, indeed, she is one of those outrageous American girls, flirting with any and all. I see why she appeals to him, her manners so bold, her previous escapades recounted only in whispers. But Richard is determined to have her. A hoyden, she would make a mockery of all of us.

You must make haste, my darling boy, to placate my fears and talk sense into Richard. You are the only one who can, who ever could. He says she's perfect for him. But you know how it will all end. You know in his choice of women, he is less than—shall we say?—prudent. This one is wrong from the eagle look in her eye to her sharp wit. He'd never tolerate her for a moment if her father were not disturbingly wealthy.

And if you don't consider that sufficient motivation to attend me, I urge you to come for Vivienne and Deirdre's sakes. My granddaughters lack a sense of the cultured feminine and I wish to provide it. They approach the time when they must attend boarding school and you must not allow them to remain in that horrid uncivilized country past their age of refinement.

Do come, *mon cher*. I need your help.

With all affection,

Your loving mother

PRELUDE II

Lord Victor Cole
No. 20 Great George Street
Quarter,
United Kingdom of Great Britain and Ireland
Shanghai International Settlement
Jung Kuo, Middle Kingdom of China

February 25, 1882

Dear Mama,

Thank you for your recent missive. Oddly enough, it comes at a very serendipitous moment.

I agree with you about my daughters' need for a bit of English sunshine. To sail at the end of March, I have arranged for my business partner and my Chinese comprador here in Shanghai to assume responsibilities until my return. I've ordered my servants to close my house for the coming year. You will be pleased to learn I've booked passage for the three of us, plus the girls' Chinese nurse, on the _Royal Empress_ out of Hong Kong March 10.

If weather holds, and we encounter no _tai-feng_ around the

horn of India, you might expect to see us in June. Please be advised that I will stop in Joppa and Naples for a few days' each to consult with my factors. I will send you notice of my progress from those ports.

However, please do not take my arrival as any insurance that I might persuade Richard to look elsewhere for a bride. You and I both know how he is—stubborn like Papa.

In the meantime, stave him off any hasty marriage or worse, eloping with her. By the way, does she even like him? I'm certain he likes her dowry. Having heard of these American robber barons and their wily daughters, I imagine she welcomes the prospect of a title to match her friends'. Oh, well. For discussion after I arrive, eh?

My love to you.

Victor

CHAPTER 1

May 30, 1882
Brentwood Hall
Somerset, England

The sound of a woman's laughter rang through him like the tinkling of chimes. Light, fantastical, amusing, Victor felt the trill of it in his bones but focused on his mother's welcome. It had always been so easy to surrender to her crushing hugs.

"Darling, oh, you do look marvelous!" She drew away, grinned at him and patted his cheek. "Such a long sea voyage can debilitate one."

"The carriage from the station in Bath was worse than our ship, I'm afraid." He sank into the cushions of the sofa. He hadn't been so at ease since he left his own house in the British Quarter.

"Oh, horrid, darling, but you're home safe and sound." She let her turquoise eyes feast on him while she hung onto his hands.

Victor let her get her fill. He'd always loved her, his father and siblings and this sprawling Palladian mansion she'd made into a haven. Away from the rush of London, it was quiet. Blissful compared to the cacophony in the streets of Shanghai.

"I'm so relieved you've come. Your Papa is upstairs in his sitting room, waiting to receive you. He's feeling more chipper this morning in anticipation of your arrival."

He squeezed her fingers. "I hurried from London as soon as I got your letter. He's had another turn, has he?"

"Since his poor spell last month, he's become more frail of body as well as of mind." She shook her head, her large eyes hooded and weary. For a woman of fifty-one, she still did not look her age. With hair bright as old gold and eyes of turquoise, she'd always been a vision. That of course was the reason she'd attracted the widowered seventh duke of Brentwood only three months after his first wife's death. To hear them tell the story of their first meeting, they'd fallen in love in an instant in the bank where her father and the duke kept their accounts. Impetuous as the duke was known to be, his second wife matched his impulsiveness. In the next month, he'd proposed and she'd accepted. Against all rules of mourning and decorum, they'd married two months later. Victor himself was the proof of their sexual attraction, his birth coming only months after their wedding.

But his father grew older and his temperament had changed. Victor understood from his mama that his father's recent memory lapses had only increased his rash behaviors and his brother and two younger sisters bemoaned their father's ailment. The man had been a firebrand and they missed his humor and his determination.

"He is much worse." Her lower lip quivered, but she fought her tears. The fragrance of roses wafted into the conservatory from the open glass doors.

So did the sound of that young woman laughing...and she did so with young children. His own, he would wager.

"Tell me about his attacks." Victor was eager to learn about the man he'd revered all his life, unhappy to note the discussion concerned that man's failing health. He didn't want to insult his father, nor antagonize him. The first he'd never had reason to do, but his mother had written him that the second was now easy to do. "What does the doctor say? I must know before I talk with him."

"He seems to have moments when he is simply not with us. He stares into space, then suddenly returns, remembering bits of conversation from minutes before he drifted away. If you ask him about such lapses, he turns irritable. So you must be attentive to your conversation when he seems suddenly not to hear you."

"Very well. I will."

"He has a proposition for you."

Victor sighed and brushed a speck of lint from his trousers. "The Welsh farms again? I don't want to debate taking them over for him. I am no estate manager, Mama." He'd gone to Shanghai years ago to make what fortune he could from business. *That and to escape the detritus of Alicia's scandals.*

His mother patted his hand and her marvelous eyes twinkled. "Not that. Something else."

He detected skullduggery, not unusual for his parents. "What have you and he concocted?"

"He will tell you. Swore me to secrecy, he did. When you go up, he'll present it."

He shook his head. "I don't care to argue with him."

"Then don't. Listen to him." She shook back her hair, her tiny pearl earrings dancing in the sunlight. "You'll be intrigued."

Will I? Few prospects catch my imagination. A long sleep by a quiet cove is the one that might. "For your sake, I'll try to be."

"Not just for my sake, but yours as well. The girls too. I'm so glad you sent the girls up to us while you finished your meetings in London. They've been a delight. To your father. Me. And Richard."

"Ha-ha!" shouted a woman from the garden. "I see you, Viv. You are out!"

"No, no, no!" squealed his oldest daughter.

Gales of laughter filled the conservatory.

"Ah, Deirdre! I can fiiiind you," called another female.

"Who's out there with the girls?" he asked, pleased that his daughters were having fun. The first young woman whose laughter drew him was not the only one in the mayhem outside.

His mother leaned close, her conspiratorial expression also desperate. "Richard's choice and her friend."

He girded himself to greet the candidate to be the next marchioness of Ridgemont. She'd have beauty to match her money, no doubt about it. Richard would take no less. "I'm ready to meet them both."

"Ah, here's tea," his mother announced as Fawkes the butler appeared from the main house with a tray. "I assume you're starved."

"I am," he said with pleasure that he was about to eat. "Most especially for Cook's lemon curd and raspberry tarts."

"Cook," said the elderly butler as he gingerly bent to place the tray on the table before Victor's mother, "made them first thing this morning for you, sir."

"I shall come down later to give her my thanks," he said with a wink at the man he'd known all his life.

"She'll appreciate that, sir." The servant squinted through his rimless glasses, focusing on his duties to finish the tea presentation. "Will there be anything else, Your Grace?"

"No, Fawkes." She lifted the glass dome over a plate of tea sandwiches and shortbread cookies. "I see you've given us the items the girls adore."

"Cook likes to please them, too, ma'am." The man excused himself and with careful steps, backed away.

After he closed the door behind him, Victor sat back while his mother poured for him. "Fawkes seems to suffer from failing vision."

"He does," his mother said and handed him his cup and saucer. "He won't admit it. I've asked Doctor Weeks to look in on him whenever he comes to visit your father. Glasses help but do not solve the problems age creates. I use them now myself."

"I do too. To read." He sipped his tea and waited while his mother served herself.

"Oh? When did that become necessary?"

"A few months ago. Reading Mandarin calligraphy requires a sharp eye for the delicacy of the strokes. Miss one and you've misinterpreted so badly that you've insulted someone you wished to praise."

"Poor dear."

"Oh, Mama, thank all under heaven, not poor at all."

"What you were meant to do there," she said with pride, her chin high.

"Exactly."

"How well have you done? Forgive my boldness to ask. Your father simply tells me you are your own man. 'Good fellow. Solid.'"

"I'm proud to say I've made a surprising fortune in Shanghai. I've enough to travel this year and next if I like. Profit enough to improve the house in Hanover Square for Viv, Deirdre and myself." His Chinese laborers dubbed him *tai-pan*, though he was less wealthy by half than most foreigners

5

in the international settlement. "My reading glasses damage only my vanity."

She sniffed. "At thirty-one, you shouldn't need spectacles."

"Nor you, my dear, at fifty-one."

"You flatter me. Keep doing that."

"I know where my bread is buttered."

"Rascal." She drank her own tea. "I hope you sent up all your trunks from London. I need you to stay with us, Victor. For the girls' sake, for your father and me. A ray of sunshine."

"I have brought all our belongings with me. For an extended stay, yes. Hanover Square receives a fresh coat of paint and new upholstery in the public rooms. To tell you the truth, I relish the prospect of summer in the country." *Here, but most especially in the cottage near Brighton, quiet and secluded.* "The girls, I know will be charmed by you and Father. They need you and that perspective on family, I believe."

"And I'm thrilled to provide it. Your papa, even as ill-possessed of all his wits as he is, does too."

Victor could see the strain apparent in the lines near her eyes. "But Richard worries you."

"He does. He is...not himself at times."

His half-brother had always shown a wild streak. Impulsive, aggressive and stunningly self-centered, Richard nonetheless managed to charm as many with his generosity and his *savoir-faire*. "Perhaps he is in love. That changes a man."

His mother fixed him with the stark look of reproof that alerted all in the family to her earnest intent. "He is changed. But not, I fear, by love."

Alarm shot through him. Richard had dealt with bouts of mania when he'd been at Cambridge. One May, Victor had had to calm him by forcibly bundling him off to the Lake Country. Whatever Richard's symptoms now, he didn't wish to be burdened with the knowledge of them so soon after his arrival home. A holiday was in order. Rides in the forest, visits with old friends. Soft breezes on his face as he read a few new books which he could never get in Shanghai. Still, his mother needed him and he would rally to the cause. He always did. Victor set his teeth and brushed the crease in his trousers. "You've set me a great task."

"You always were the one to soothe us all. The one to solve our riddles. Our desperate situations."

He sipped his tea. *Would that I had been as successful solving my own challenges.* "You're much too confident."

She lifted a shoulder. "And you know that I have reason to be. Did you not dissuade your brother years ago from eloping with that draper's daughter?"

"He can be head-strong. But he's not foolhardy. He wouldn't have married her."

"She had a girlish beauty to commend her." His mother arched two pale, finely plucked brows.

He laughed. "My dear, she was endowed with many attributes, none of which was a dowry."

"Precisely."

"Add to that, I've no idea what's happening with the price of land or your production here, but I would wager, when Richard marries, he'd welcome a suitable marriage settlement made of sterling. Deliverable to his bank each year on January first."

His mother nodded in agreement. "He tells me we're doing well here. In the black. Which is more than I can say for many whom we know and love. He does not tell me of his own finances at Ridgemont. So I worry. But whatever his balance sheet—" she said with an index finger in the air, "he merits an heiress with suitable *accoutrement*."

"Indeed he does." As the heir to their father, the seventh duke of the venerable centuries' old title of Brentwood, Richard was the marquess of Ridgemont with lands of his own and income in his own right. In addition, Richard had always done a fine job of handling his shares of an export-import company dealing out of Bombay. "His foreign company brings him good profit."

"Still? He will not tell me." His mother's lips thinned.

"I know Richard's agent, Chiang Hsing-li in Shanghai. He's shrewd and careful. I have checked Chiang's books for Richard's share in the Woochow Tea Company at least once a year for the past three, and he seems more honest than many." Other British investors in Woochow might not be so fortunate, but Victor knew Richard was getting a fair deal from his agent in Shanghai. Westerners in the China trade knew that every respected Chinese agent took 'squeeze' to supplement his income. From what Victor had estimated, Chiang's take averaged two percent, significantly lower than the ten to fifteen that many stole.

The duchess stared at him. "That comforts me. But he's in quite a stew with this latest scandal. He has hinted to me that he needs a significant amount of cash. I am appalled at the rumors. And I am so glad you're here to help."

Victor stifled his sigh. No rest for the weary. Not yet. "Is Richard here? I didn't have a chance to ask Fawkes when I came in." *Too taken with absorbing the sights and fragrances of home.*

"He went down to Bath four days ago to speak with his estate manager there. Urgent business of some sort. He promised he'd be home for dinner tonight or early in the morning. Our other guests arrive beginning tomorrow afternoon."

"Fine. And how long is this house party?"

"Five days. Richard insists." His mother leaned close and lowered her voice. "I fear he'll make an offer to this girl and use the party as the occasion to announce it."

"What of the girl's parents? Has he gotten her father's approval?"

She cast a wary eye toward the door. "That's the other thing. Neither one has arrived. Her father remains in London to negotiate some business venture and her mother declined, saying she was indisposed."

"Odd."

"Darling, they're Americans. You've been away too long and cannot imagine what they do and don't."

He snorted. "Sweetheart, I know Americans. I've dealt with quite a few in Shanghai and they are not cave men."

The sound of laughter drifted inside.

His mother tipped her head toward the door. "She's come and brought along her friend, who added her family's official chaperone."

"Oh? A good solution."

"No, no, no. A French woman. A countess of some forgotten place."

"Mama, you're being unfair now." He feigned a grimace at her.

She shrugged. "I know. You're right. But wait until you meet her. Victor, this union must not happen."

"Don't worry. Please. I'll have a chat with her. See if she favors our Richard and suits him."

"She won't."

But if her money does, that's the end of it. "Let's be candid, Mama. If she loves him and can overlook his recent problems, she may be the very woman he needs. Have you any indication of that?"

She inhaled and sat back, her imploring gaze on him. "She is forthright, I'll say that for her. But I am glad you have hit the nail on the head with his scandals. I am so ashamed. Your father and I caused, I thought, enough of an uproar when we married during his year of mourning for his wife. But that was the worst we ever did and much forgiven by society. But this. This is horrid."

Victor did not blink an eye. With nary a breath, his mother swept past his own scandals. Or rather his wife's.

She put down her cup and saucer to the tea table. "What do you know of this uproar?"

He exhaled. No way around it, he'd have to discuss the issue that plagued his mother. "Only rumors. The earl of Howitch's son, John, outlined the matter to me when I dined with him in Naples a few weeks ago. From what I know, it is more fluff than substance." *At least the lady is not with child.*

"Sleeping with Wales's mistress." His mother fairly seethed. "Good heavens, was he using his head?"

Another part of his anatomy. Victor frowned. "He does not continue to see her, I understand."

His mother sagged. "True, but it is all so very sordid."

As infidelity always is.

"I am so relieved to confide in you. You have no idea. I have no one to converse with. Your father does not wish to discuss this. Nor does he wish to discuss his views of Richard's choice of bride. I doubt your father can recognize that the girl is the hellion she truly is."

"Tell me why Richard thinks he loves her." *Why he thinks any young woman would take him, given his recent peccadillo with the wife of the duke of Dundalk.*

"You know how he is, darling." She waved a hand to appear carefree, but Victor saw the furrow of her brows. "Quick to choose."

"Just like the rest of us." He pursed his lips. "Would we were all as happy with our choices."

"Stop that," she scolded him. "You will find a young lady you adore. You've been so long without a companion, you've forgotten how to look for one."

"Mama, I'm not cut from the cloth of a husband."

"Of course you are. Most in the family prove it. Your father and I have been supremely happy. Your sister, Augustine is still infatuated with her husband John after four years. Catherine loves her Colin, the same. She told us last week, they're to have an addition to their three in December."

"I will congratulate them when I see them." His two younger sisters had met and fallen in love with their future husbands in much the same slapdash fashion as their parents. So had he with his wife. The difference was that Victor's inamorata had proven to be a witch. However, his older half-brother Richard, the marquess of Ridgemont, had yet to fall in love with anyone. In lust, yes. Often. And always with the wrong sort. Why should this latest one be any different? "Tell me more about her, Mama. The sooner, the better. The voices outside," he said as he tipped his head toward the garden, "include said young lady, I assume?"

"They do. You will meet her and not understand why he is so infatuated."

"She's American."

"Yes."

"Boldness may be what he needs. And from the sounds of it she likes children."

His mother lifted a shoulder. "She does. But rumor says she has fifty thousand as her marriage portion. God in heaven knows what the monthly earnings are off that."

Impressed, he heard her awe at the enormity of the lady's dowry. A princely sum, worthy of a marquess, no doubt. "That's quite a tick to owe one's tailor."

She mashed her lips together. "He owes no such amount to his tailor. His solicitors, on the other hand, may require a king's ransom to get him out from under this latest legal action."

Victor arched his brows. "That bad?"

"I have not asked him. He does not tell. Rumors say Dundalk will wring every penny from him."

"And a new wife would remedy the financial issue and end the whispers."

"They would," his mother said with resignation in her voice.

"So we will assume she loves him and he her. After all," he said and put his cup and saucer down on the table. "There must be more than her money for him to consider a leg shackle. At thirty-three, he's getting long in the tooth."

His mother winced. "She's...passable."

"Pass—" Putting his napkin to his mouth, he wanted to guffaw. Richard would never even glance at any woman who wasn't incomparable. Dull, American, uneducated. Lascivious, adulterous, unprincipled. Without thought, he'd take each to his bed if he fancied their faces or forms. But plain or ugly? Neither merited a moment's fascination for him.

"Ah, let's go in now!" Called one young lady to her companion and his daughters.

"Here they come," his mother whispered. "Gird yourself. Your girls have been starved for you and the two ladies can be whirlwinds."

He began to rise to his feet.

In a rush of giggles, wispy white muslin and exclamations of delight, four beings dashed in front of him. Two jumped up and down. The other two, taller and willowy, stood behind the younger, grinning and wide-eyed as if they'd never seen a man before. In the shadows, stood the girls' amah, young demure Wu-lai.

"Papa! Papa!" His two chicks barreled into him before he could find his balance. They fell in a heap to the sofa. They were kissing his cheeks, and hugging him as if they'd squeeze the stuffing from him.

"Oh, Papa!" crooned his oldest, Vivienne as she gazed up at him with a grin so like his own. "We're so glad you've come. We've had such a good time."

"We have!" said six-year-old Deirdre with the earnest turquoise eyes resembling her grandmother's and his own. She smelled of roses, like the red bud in her hand. "You'll like our new friends. Grandmama likes them."

He cupped Deirdre's cheek and then his oldest girl's. He kissed them on the crowns of their shining strawberry blonde heads. "You must introduce me, then, shouldn't you?"

"Oh," said his oldest in serious rebuttable, "we cannot, Papa. Grandmama must introduce you, mustn't you, Ma'am?"

His mother chuckled. "You can see what good influence I've had, Victor, that I've managed to teach them rules of etiquette in the two weeks you were in London."

"Wu-lai does not know rules of the English, Grandmama," Vivienne said with concern. "We will teach her the right things. I promise."

Wu-lai, his children's Chinese nursemaid, had come with them to England. At fifteen, she was the daughter of the *comprador* to his factory in the port of Shanghai. Bright, she had learned English quickly in his household school for his servants in the British quarter. When he decided to return to England, he'd asked her if she would like to accompany them. When she agreed, he was overjoyed he'd have help to care for his children on the long trip from China home.

Disentangling himself from his girls, he faced the two young ladies who had laughed and played in the garden. And he was riveted by their appearance.

His mother began her formal introductions.

He registered the formalities of her words.

"Miss Esmerelda Moore, may I present my son, Lord Victor Cole, lately of Shanghai, China. Here to stay in England forever, we do hope. Don't we, girls?"

His children echoed his mother's sentiments.

But his head buzzed.

His eyes filled with the vision before him. One young lady, plain and pleasant.

"How do you do, Miss Moore," he said, bowing slightly. "I am delighted to meet you." *You, with your brown hair and round little face.*

"And this is her good friend from New York and Baltimore, the youngest daughter of Killian Hanniford of Hanniford Companies. I think you wrote last year that you've heard of his businesses? Yes? May I present Miss Ada Hanniford."

"Yes, indeed. How do you do, Miss Hanniford." *How do you do? With that open smile, that riot of glistening cinnamon hair and jolly blue eyes, you fare quite well, I'd imagine. A princess among commoners.*

Forthright, open, up to the occasion, she beamed at him. American in every frank, refreshing way. She was a froth of confections, plush pink lips, rosy cheeks and spotless ivory complexion. He could imbibe all the sweetness of her and never tire of the sight. Or the desire to taste her perfections.

She dropped a quick curtsey. As she rose, she locked her lovely eyes on his. "I am delighted to meet you, Lord Victor."

"The delight is mine." *I see why Richard wants every scintillating, voluptuous inch of you...and why he mustn't have you.*

He would take you, use you, despoil you. And rob you of that spontaneity which takes my breath and makes me wonder if I can ever regain it.

CHAPTER 2

Ada Hanniford curtsied to the tall, somber gentleman who inclined his head in greeting to her and to her best friend, Esmerelda. From his piercing gaze to his stoic bearing, he was no man about town, no charmer of young ladies, no nobleman in search of an afternoon chat or a dalliance. He was all power, contained, reserved. A man who knew his own worth. And cold.

Good. I am so tired of men who look for the main chance. To despoil the uncouth American girl with a cut, a compliment or a tumble.

She extended her hand and he took it. His fingers strong, his grasp quick, he seized her own, then dropped her offering as if it were hot coal.

Still, his eyes—a lighter shade of his mother's fierce turquoise—pinned her to him.

"I am delighted to meet you, Lord Victor," she said in her affable mode. She smiled broadly. He was, after all, another person to examine, to probe, to learn. Not, thank heaven, a suitor.

What a welcome relief. She was bored to death of men

who wished to pursue her and had nothing on offer but puppy-dog looks of love.

"Your mother has told us you have just come home from Shanghai," said Ezzie. "We are ever so interested in your experiences."

I am, certainly.

"I'd be delighted to tell you about the city and the empire," he said.

"Please," said his mother extending a hand toward the two wing chairs, "will you sit for a few minutes?"

"Of course," said Ezzie who always liked the pleasure of meeting a new man. Over the years that Ezzie and Ada had been friends and traversed English society, Ezzie had been the first to plumb the depths of men's characters. Ada had been the one they chased. But Ada had relished her friend's abilities to draw out the true nature of the noblemen who sought brides among the American heiresses even as they denigrated them for their provinciality.

Ada wished to sit and watch Ezzie lure this reserved creature from his shell.

Her friend practically cooed at Lord Victor. "I'd love to stay."

"As would I." Ada nodded and sat.

"May we go to our rooms, please, Miss Hanniford?" Vivienne asked Ada, grabbing hold of her hand to force her attention on her.

Ada noted how Victor's eyes widened at his daughter's request of her.

Deirdre whined. "I want to stay."

"No, Dee," Viv insisted. "They want to talk."

"I want Papa to see the garden. The chrysamums." She set her chin and whirled to face her father. "Grandmama has chrysamums. Miss Hanniford says they'll be big like ours."

He reached over to chuck his daughter under her chin.

"Those plants were from our gardens at home so they will grow big and strong."

"And smell good," she added.

He nodded. "And smell wonderful."

"Miss Hanniford pinched them to make them big."

"Did she?" He ran his fingers through the little girl's golden red tresses. "She is wise to do that."

Ada admired his care of his children. In that, he reminded her of her own father. But she had become attached to the little girls these past few days. She played with them. Archery. Croquet. Blind man's bluff. *Yes, I love them. They crave attention.*

"What do you think, Miss Hanniford?" He stilled her with the gravity of his gaze on hers. "Should Viv and Dee stay with us?"

"I defer to you and the duchess, my lord."

"Yes, do go, my dears," said the duchess with an approving nod at Ada. "We will see you at tea."

The two girls, perfectly mannered, had been welcome at afternoon repast the previous three days that Ada and Ezzie had visited here at the Hall. This largesse toward children Ada thought most wonderful, as the two had lovely manners and were adept at conversation far above their years.

"You'll be at tea, Papa?" asked Deirdre.

"I won't come unless you do," Viv said to him with a pout.

Ada smiled at both girls. She understood now they inherited the red in their thick hair from their father. Their marvelous eyes and pure complexion came from their paternal grandmother, the duchess. If they possessed any traits of their deceased mother, it was not apparent to Ada.

"I will, indeed," he said and gathered them both close in his arms. "Do go. Wu-lai, please take them for a bath."

"Ouuu," said the youngest. "No, I—"

"We will," said the oldest with sharp reproof to her young sister. "Come along, Dee." At that she pulled on her father's coat and he bent for a kiss on the cheek from her and his other child.

The four adults settled into their seats.

As the duchess poured tea, she began an introduction of her son with information she'd not imparted to Ezzie and Ada before this. He owned a factory in Shanghai and imported all manner of household goods to Great Britain and the Continent. "And he is here in England to solidify arrangements for publication of his first book."

Ada liked novels. "What is it you've written, my lord?"

"It's rather dry, I'm afraid. You might not be interested, Miss Hanniford."

His mother raised one brow at him.

He demurred.

"Do tell me anyway," she insisted. *Impertinent fellow. You won't fend me off.*

"I've written a description of the practices of the Chinese traders in the treaty port of Shanghai."

"It's a guide, isn't it, Victor?" his mother encouraged as she handed over tea cups and saucers to Ada and Ezzie.

Ezzie cocked her head. "Do the Chinese deal so very different from our methods?"

"Indeed. Their culture demands their mandarins—their government officials—stay aloof from merchants."

"Why is that?" Ezzie was surprised.

"They value education above all," Ada put in what she'd learned from discussions with her father, her brother Pierce. "They follow Confucius, a wise man who wrote many centuries ago. He put forward a set of principles that honors right thinking and rues those who work with money," Ada dare not move as she warmed to the unsettling heat of Lord Victor's stare. "They need those who willingly work with foreigners. Especially merchantmen."

"Yes," he said with a lingering consideration of her eyes and her lips.

She shifted in her chair. *If his gaze was hot, he remained cold, frozen in his treatment of her.* She liked men who warmed to her. Were open to her. And most were. Most wanted something from her, her approval, her affection, her body. Most moved closer.

But this man glanced away.

"You have a term for them, don't you? These agents?" She acted as if she had not noticed his disregard, as if butter would melt in her mouth. These facts about the Chinese she'd gleaned from discussions with her father, who owned a world-wide shipping company, and Pierce, her older brother, who had dealings in Bombay and Shanghai.

"We do." Victor Cole turned his attention toward her once more. His mouth thin, he did not appear happy about her knowledge. Was he one of those who thought women brainless ninnies?

"A *comprador*, is it?" She wanted to crow, triumphant.

"Indeed, it is."

"You have one?" Ezzie asked, not to be outdone, since her father had trade in China and Japan.

"I do. I am pleased to say he has been in my employ for more than three years."

"You like him?" Ezzie asked as she raised her teacup. "Personally?"

"I do. His entire family, in fact. Wu-lai, whom you've met, is his oldest daughter."

Petite soft-spoken Wu-lai acted as a nurse maid to the two little girls. With her good command of English, she'd told Ezzie and her that she was fifteen years old. Wu-lai, Ada happily noted, was different from many women in her native land. Ada had heard her family discuss the Chinese practice of foot-binding, bending back the toes of a baby girl into her heels, crippling women physically and emotionally, making them dependent on their fathers and husbands. "It's unusual for a young woman to travel abroad. I understand the Chinese are very protective, even backward, in treatment of their daughters."

"My man is very progressive. He knows much about the West because he comes from a large family of Chinese agents. He is a third generation *howqua*."

"A *howqua?*" she asked him, irritated he cited a term she did not know. "What is that?"

"When Westerners opened the ports to trade with the Chinese nearly a century ago, we needed Chinese men who wanted to learn English and French and German so that they could translate to their Chinese officials and the coolies. These translators learned Western business methods and formed a class of business leaders to deal with us."

"I see," she said. "A comprador is a new type of *howqua*. And your agent allowed you to bring his daughter to Britain. Good of him."

"It was. Without her father's approval to allow her to travel with me, I would not have been able to bring my children home with me. I'm grateful to her."

"And in return she can learn much about Britain to tell her father."

He took up his tea cup. "And teach her family about us. The best way to learn a new culture is to live in it."

"I agree," she said, recalling how she'd suffered the intricacies of proper address at school in Connecticut and after she'd arrived in England four years ago. "I spent months learning when to curtsy and when not."

"And how to use a fish fork!" Ezzie giggled.

The duchess blinked, not amused. "I say, my dear, I'm eager to learn what news you have of ending the illegal opium trade. It's vile. We should not be a party to such debauchery."

Ada understood the dynamics of the trade of the poppy. Taken by the British East India Company to treaty ports along the Chinese Empire's coast, the drug was sold to balance exports of cotton, silks and porcelain. Only in this way did the British merchants make a profit. The upshot was that thousands of Chinese had become addicted, smoking the powdered and liquid poppy in opium dens, ingesting it or eating it. Exported in large quantities around the world by British merchants, opium killed millions around the world.

"It's now in cough syrup and tonics for every ailment," Ada said.

"Surely not!" proclaimed the duchess. "Victor, is that not illegal?"

Lord Victor stared at Ada with startled eyes. Appreciative eyes. Then he focused on his mother. "I'm afraid not, Mama."

"Miss Hanniford, how do you know this?"

"My sister," she offered and put her tea to the table.

"The duchess of Seton," Her Grace added in an aside to inform her son. "How comes your sister to know this?"

"She's very attentive to the health of her tenants. The duke, her husband, encourages her in this and has established dispensaries at all his estates. Lily has learned that many of the tonics that chemists dispense contain opium. Laudanum, for one. Too often used by women for various maladies. And for babies, the 'quieting syrups' have strong quantities of the drug. Lily claims that's why so many infants do not eat, fail to thrive and simply waste away."

"Dear me," said the duchess with a hand to the lace fichu at her throat. "I did not know this. Did you, Victor?"

He had stared at Ada, hanging on each word throughout her explanation. Making her tingle. Making her twitch. "I do. Miss Hanniford is correct, Mama. Opium debilitates the body in any quantity. The trade must be stopped."

"I thought we could no longer export it," the duchess said.

"Wasn't that a condition of the treaty after the Second Opium War?"

Victor narrowed his eyes, looking rueful. "We can't, but we have arrangements with other countries to ship it for us."

"Who?" his mother asked, indignant.

"Us," said Ada.

The duchess drew back, a hand to her throat. "No."

Ada nodded. "Not Hanniford Companies. My father and brother refuse. But other American traders traffic in it."

"Miss Hanniford is right, Mama."

Ada glanced at him, grateful for the confirmation, yet questioning why she should so value it from him.

The duchess was aghast. "Oh, but I had no idea of this. How is it that you both know and I don't?"

"It's not a topic discussed in public much, is it?" asked Ezzie.

All three turned to her.

"My father talks of it. Of those who transport it. It is lucrative."

Ada did not stop the grin from forming on her lips. "But how do we stop it? That's the question. Isn't it?"

Ezzie tipped her head to and fro. "I'd say we need a politician who takes it up as his cause."

The duchess nodded, a smile wreathing her face at Ezzie's words.

His turquoise eyes gleaming, Victor seemed to struggle to hold back a grin.

Ada didn't. "How right you are."

"Nothing will happen without some moral conscience in Parliament," Ezzie said.

"I had no idea you were interested in politics," said the duchess.

"I am. I know it isn't considered a fine thing for a young woman. An unmarried woman. And an American." Ezzie smiled to herself as if she were a conspirator and slowly sipped her tea.

Ada took up her friend's banner. "Ezzie is not only a realist, she is also modest. I will sing her praises. At balls and dinners, she's talked with a few members of Parliament about the matter."

"Few are interested," Ezzie said with a twist of her lips.

"And no wonder why," said Victor. "Most of them have family or friends who make their living from the China trade."

"Precisely," said Ezzie. "Lord Ridgemont—your son, Ma'am, and your brother, sir—is interested in supporting a bill to end the evils of opium's import."

Victor stirred, sitting forward. "Miss Moore, you've spoken with my brother Richard about this issue?"

"I have."

"My, my," said the duchess with some surprise and delight, "how good of you. What did Richard say?"

"He has discussed it with his father who agrees with him."

"Well, well," said the duchess, tapping a fore finger to her lips. "Intriguing."

Ada wondered to what degree Richard's interest would bring any results. He was not a sitting peer, but a gadabout. His father, the Duke of Brentwood was a sitting peer in the House of Lords but he had not budged from this house—according to all accounts of his wife and his oldest son—in over a year. Any legislation he might advocate was no more significant than words on the wind.

"We must speak of this to your father, Victor," said the duchess. "In the meantime, do tell us, Victor, what progress is there in London with your book?"

"I've signed a contract with Williams and Hastings. It's to be published in the autumn."

"Congratulations," said all three women in turn.

"A reputable publisher," said Ada with a suitable nod of approval.

"I think so," he agreed.

"My step-sister will publish her first novel through them in August."

"She is to be congratulated and for one so young, too," said the duchess.

"It's a great coup," said Ezzie. "For a woman to publish a book. Rare, isn't it? We're all very proud of Camille."

"I'm sure you're delighted for her," his lordship said. "Cornell Hastings is eager to publish fiction. Very popular."

"And very profitable," Ada added with a grin.

He focused those striking eyes on her lips. "What sort of fiction does your step-sister write?"

Ada felt the prickle of his interest. Daringly handsome with those bright eyes and auburn hair, he was not for her. He was too sedate. Too reserved. She needed a man who lived and breathed...and played. "Camille pens gothic romances, my lord. Dark castles, tormented men locked away in their dreary rooms. In need of a woman to love them."

He laughed shortly. "Your step-sister? Forgive me. I am out of society. I do not know her."

"Camille Bereston, sir. She's the daughter of my father's wife, the former Lady Savage."

"You may not remember her, my dear," said the duchess to her son. "Olivia Bereston? No? She's the widow of Lord Savage who died many years ago. And Camille is her daughter. Lady Savage, or as she is now, Mrs Killian Hanniford, married Miss Hanniford's father a few years ago."

"I see," he said with an appraising look at Ada.

If he knew about her step-mother's previous marriage and Camille's father, he took his time not allowing any indication of his view of it to cross his face.

Ada understood from her father that Olivia—or Liv, as

everyone in the family called her—had suffered some sort of despair in her first marriage. Whatever it was, her daughter Camille had loved her father and remembered him sweetly. If the duchess and her son Victor knew of Liv's discomfiture, Ada didn't wish to be reminded of it. Nor to learn of it. Whatever the problem had been, it no longer existed. Liv and her father were delightfully matched and very much in love. One son and another baby due this autumn proved that. Unconventional as their marriage so late in life might be, they adored each other. One day, Ada might have the same. But truth was, in the past four years, she'd met every eligible bachelor in Great Britain and had found no one who appealed. At twenty-two, she was fast becoming that most noble creature. A spinster.

She wished to turn the tables. "How long do you plan to remain in England, my lord?"

He tipped his head, winsome in his uncertainty. "I've not decided. Much depends on how this book debuts. And I have business interests I must settle here."

It was impolite to ask details of that. So Ada nodded and let that rest.

But Ezzie did not. "What products do you import, my lord?"

Ada suppressed a smile and drank the rest of her tea.

"Porcelain and fabrics. My latest victory is a partnership with an ancient Japanese samurai family, the Hagamura, who manufacture fine silk. This past winter, I started to sell their wares out of Kyoto."

"Do you have an office there?" Ada asked.

Once more in his eyes she saw surprise. Dear heavens. Did the man think all women were dolts?

"Not yet. If the orders grow larger, I may find it necessary."

His mother reached across to grasp one of his hands. "No.

Please do not tell me you will return there? It is so very uncivilized. Oh, Victor."

He squeezed her hand. "Please don't, Mama. This is a topic for another time."

"No, it isn't, Victor. How could you do that? And your girls. They would live in that heathen culture. You cannot for their sakes do this!"

"Mama, I haven't made any decision yet."

"But—but your house in Hanover Square. You refurbish it."

"I do. For us while we are here."

"And your offices in the City?" The lady was beside herself.

Ada found it odd. She had witnessed the duchess's concern for the failing health of her husband. Did the lady not rely on her oldest son to help her in her time of need...or was this son the more reliable one? Ada examined his exquisite tailoring, the absolute one-eighty degree of his pearl stickpin, the precise fold of his cravat, the neat cut of his curly auburn hair. *My.* How she'd like to run her fingers through its wealth.

She swallowed hard on that surprising desire.

"I visited my staff there last week," he said trying to console her with a pat of her fingers. "I simply haven't made any decisions yet. Please understand."

She sniffed. "I don't. I need you. Your father does too, Victor. You cannot leave me."

Ada stared at this second son, surprised. The duchess favored this child as more necessary to her peace of mind than her oldest son, Richard. Oh, true. Richard, Lord Ridgemont, was her step-son. But still. Did not most families rely on the oldest and heir to provide the backbone of stability when their father grew infirm?

"I understand your feelings, Mama," Victor went on. "But

I know Richard will be your bulwark if and when you need him."

"I doubt—" The woman caught herself. "Forgive me," she said to Ada and Ezzie.

Ada threw her a compassionate smile. "I understand, Your Grace. You've only just had the chance to greet your son here this afternoon. And much needs to be discussed. We intrude. Ezzie, what do you say that we retire for the afternoon?"

She got to her feet and gave a small curtsy to mother and son. "Wonderful to meet you at last, sir. Thank you for the insights on trade with China. And thank you, Your Grace, for tea."

Ezzie rose and excused herself with the same fond wishes.

CHAPTER 3

"**D**ear Christ!" exclaimed Ezzie in one of her natural outbursts as she fell back against Ada's sitting room door and giggled. "Was that not awkward? And intriguing? To think! China and Japan! I should like to go, wouldn't you?"

Never. "I read about them. Or hear tales. That's enough."

"Oh, you'd go if he went with you."

"I doubt it."

"Don't be coy, Ade. Is Lord Victor Cole not the most fiendishly handsome man you've met in months?"

No. Years. "I don't like him."

"Oh, the devil in a nightshirt! Ada! Those eyes." She rolled her eyes at her. "Those arms." She made a boxer's fist. "His shoulders." She sighed. "I could just get lost in him. I'd go with him to China! Japan! Hell, even!"

"Stop!" Ada chuckled and strolled into her sitting room.

"And his girls would be fun."

They would. "He wouldn't."

"You can't know."

"I do." *He hasn't laughed in years.* "The way he looks at us."

"How do you mean?"

Ada pulled the bell for her maid. "He thinks we're more foreign than his Chinese friends."

"Ba! You don't know that." Ezzie wrapped her arms around her torso. "I could marry Victor Cole. He's so much more intriguing than Richard, don't you think?"

Better looking. But too somber. Ada hated to spread gossip, but there was no other way to object than to reveal some of what Liv had shared with her. "My step-mother told me he has skeletons in his closet that are uglier than Richard's."

"Oh, delicious. I bet he was a rogue in his youth."

On the contrary. "He was a paragon."

"What? Well, where's the rub?"

Ada gave in to share more. "Liv says he married badly."

"His poor dead wife?" Ezzie plunked in the chair opposite her and stared wide-eyed at her. "Tell me everything."

Ada licked her lips. She should have kept quiet. "They married young. His wife was newly debuted at court and set the world on fire with her beauty."

"And?" Ezzie prodded. "So? Come on."

"She had affairs, Ezzie. Lots of them."

"No! Really?" She slapped a hand to her chest. "She slept with others when she had *him in her bed?*"

He was a spectacular piece of manhood, but if he was as cold to his wife as he'd been to them today, Ada couldn't blame the woman for seeking comfort where she might.

"She must've been mad." Ezzie mused. "Utterly crazy to be so brazen. But—but the girls...oh my. They aren't, you know...are they? They look like him and his mother. Oh, Ada. Why didn't you tell me before?"

"Rumors are not polite to spread. My step-mother and Camille were hurt by so many. Lily and Julian, too, might have topped the scale. Most especially my father has suffered for misconceptions of his character. Even you and I had our time at the trough."

"Oh, piffle! That little tidbit in Cherbourg years ago?"

"Enough people learned of it to give you and me a reputation." *So that Perry Drummond thought he could ruin me a little more.*

Ezzie sat back, repentance on her sweet round face. "I forgot. I'm sorry. Of course, you're right. It's my fault. Lord Drummond wouldn't have been so forward with you if it hadn't been for our escapade in Cherbourg."

She clutched Ezzie's hand. "Not your doing at all. I encouraged Drummond's kisses." *That he did it as a lark was the worst betrayal. What I get for believing in romance.*

Ezzie sighed. "I wonder if I can truly trust any man. They always seem to have rough edges."

"We all do. Men and women. The sticking point is, that some don't care to acknowledge their own. Or reform."

Her friend sighed. "But I do like Victor as much as Richard."

Ezzie could find good in the devil. "I'm sure he's worthy of that, Ez."

"What if *I* set my hopes on him?" Ezzie sounded half-kidding.

"You might." Ada opened a hand as if to say, *why not?* Ezzie wasn't formally engaged to Richard Cole yet. If the infamous Marquess of Ridgemont was not yet ready to ask her the right question, many in town expected him to propose to her. Yes, if she preferred Lord Victor, her change of heart might cause a ruckus. But must she wait forever for a man who up to now was taking his sweet time? He'd even indulged in an affair these past nine months that left London atwitter. Not in such a big hurry was the notorious Ridgemont. "No one says you can't. Or shouldn't."

"I won't if you like him, Ade."

"But I don't." *That's all I'd need—a man with his own scandalous past.* "He'll live abroad and I don't care to leave Britain. So there you have it!"

Ezzie bit her lower lip. "I feel desperately sorry for him."

"He seems to have recovered." *Recovered to the point that he's indifferent to women.*

Ezzie thought on that a minute. "Do you think so?"

"It had to have hurt him. Men cannot stand that sort of thing. In olden times, they clamped their wives in chastity belts."

"I bet he wished he had done that." Ezzie frowned.

"I would've liked to know him before his wife did him in." Ada would give him the benefit of the doubt that he'd once had red blood flowing through his veins.

"Hear, hear! He's no iceberg, Ada. Look how he loves his children. And his mother."

"That he does." The man was not a cold fish through and through.

"I could love him."

Ada examined her friend. She loved Ezzie's spontaneity, her willingness to love freely and without reservation. But she questioned what, if any, instinctive discretion Ezzie possessed. "What about Richard?"

Ezzie demurred, raising her shoulders and sighing into the cushions. "Well, of course."

Which meant what? Ezzie knew about Richard's recent scandalous seduction of the Prince of Wales's mistress, a married woman—and she didn't care about Richard's peccadilloes. She'd been taught by her mother to care only about catching an English nobleman of means and title. Ada had yet to meet Richard Cole so she couldn't speak from first-hand knowledge of the man, but she'd agreed to this house party at Ezzie's insistence.

"I need your perspective, Ada," she'd pleaded with her for

weeks. "I like him, despite what gossips say. And you know that over the years, I've had few prospects. Not any my mother would bless. I've got to pursue this with Richard. My mother would send me to the jungles of Brazil if I didn't. A duchess is what she wants of me."

For the past few months Ada had tried to dissuade Ezzie from her fixation on the marquess. She couldn't talk any sense into her nor could she point to any other man who might be interested in Ezzie and therefore be a proper suitor. So then, against the force of Esmerelda Moore's battleship mother, logic had little sway.

Add to that, even though Richard had not yet approached her parents for permission nor begun the discussions of finances for her dowry, pin money and widow's portion, he had indeed all but notified society he intended to ask for her hand. By Ezzie's own accounts, he had kissed her often in public. In private, he had put his lips to other more scandalous part of her body. His hands, too, if Ada interpreted her friend's blushes correctly. That alone defined him morally and ethically as her betrothed, even if society knew nothing of that intrusive behavior.

So of what challenge was Richard's brother, this cool fellow who appeared like a genie from a distant land? He was probably cut from the same cloth as his brother. The younger learned from the older, wasn't that the way of it? Birds of a feather and all that.

Ada was there to help her friend see reason. About men, money, and British society, God rest their aristocratic souls. "You know nothing of this brother, Ezzie."

"True, of course. I should focus on Richard," Ezzie admitted.

"Exactly. It's not Victor who will propose to you this week."

"You're right, Ade. Damn it. I must make my mother happy and marry Richard."

❧

Fawkes led the way up the central staircase toward his father's master chambers.

Delighted to be away from effervescent Ada Hanniford and her friend, Esmerelda, Victor wished to run up the steps. But Fawkes moved with such hesitancy that Victor's sympathies went to the man who'd been a devoted servant all these years. Now was the time to offer him retirement to one of the little cottages in the village.

This house was a complex machine and Fawkes had organized it to the minute since a year before Victor's grandfather died. Originally built by the fourth duke in seventeen ten, Brentwood Hall had been renovated in the early eighteen hundreds with Palladian influences by Robert Adam and landscapers who gave the old Bath stone beauty longer wings, more bed chambers and little nooks and crannies where one could escape. As a child Victor had charged through the empty bedrooms playing hide and seek with Richard and their sisters. Augustine and Catherine would wiggle into unique places like the plate cupboard in the still room or the linen cabinet in their mother's downstairs bathroom. Richard was always easy to discover, huddled in a closet or storage room.

"Your father had a good night's sleep," the butler told him as he followed him down the hall. "He seems very alert this morning, so says his footman, Hanks."

"Hanks is his caretaker?" That man, the youngest son of the previous vicar in the parish, was a bit slow but gentle and kind.

"He is, a good man indeed, sir. Takes care of every need

His Grace requires."

"I see. Thank you. I will express my own gratitude," he said as the butler opened the door to his father's sitting room.

The sixty-nine-year-old hunched into his overstuffed Chippendale close to the wine-red marble fireplace. His father's hair, once coal black, was now white as parchment. His eyes, once forest green, stared up at him in faded jade. Sadness clogged Victor's throat, but he grinned at the man who could be ridged as stone, but sweet as an Austen hero to those he loved.

"Good morning, Papa." Victor took his father's thin blue-veined hand and leaned over to kiss him on both thin cheeks. "I am so happy to see you so well."

The man's lips spread in a generous smile. "Rascal. Get on with you. I am not well. But you are. And I am glad of it. Sit. Sit. Sit."

Victor dragged the nearest chair closer, a large uphol-stered piece that matched his father's. In the morning light, Victor saw how much he'd changed since he'd left for China more than four years ago. His jowls sagged and his broad shoulders sloped into his thinning torso.

"Saw your mother, I imagine."

"I did."

"She told you I am not well. But I am. At least, this morning, I have my wits. Sharp as a bell. But." He lifted a gnarled forefinger and it shook. "It goes. So we will do this quickly. Save the details of my infirmities for later when we've run the gauntlet."

A tall dark man approached to stand beside his father.

"Hanks, come closer. Meet my second son. Victor Arthur Sunderland Cole."

The man inclined his head and put his face into the sunlight. Both he and Victor gave no indication that they knew each other well. Had done all their lives.

But Victor warmed in satisfaction at the thought of Hanks as caretaker of his father. While the man had the battered face and crooked nose of a boxer, he was broader than Victor and had arms like tree trunks. He could easily carry his father from chair to bed or bath.

"How do you do, Hanks. Thank you."

"Aye, my lord." In his hands, he held a knitted afghan. "Would you care for this, Your Grace?"

"No, no, you may go, Hanks. I'll have Lord Victor call for you when we're done."

With that, the big man bowed himself away to close the hall door behind him.

"Now. Tell me about Deirdre. She has recovered?"

Last summer, Victor's youngest had suffered a life-threatening bout of typhoid fever. Careful nursing by his staff, most especially Wu-lai and her mother, had brought his daughter back from the throes of death. He was most grateful. His girls were his charms against fire, flood and disaster. Every time he suffered a setback, each of them had brought him laughter and release from pain. If he ever lost either, he would surely crumble to dust. Wu-lai's mother said they were the reincarnation of his two grandmothers come to save him from himself. Privately, he laughed at that since only one person had ever bested him and she, thankfully, had gone to her own just rewards, fiery as they surely were. He also questioned much about religion so that the Buddhist principle of one returning to life as a higher or lesser being was difficult for him to accept.

"She has. She seems healthier than before. And Vivienne never showed any signs of the disease. I watch them closely."

"You were right to bring them home. Here we have better sanitary conditions than in that hideous country."

That was not necessarily true. Cities and villages here were still riddled with typhoid, a disease brought on by poor drainage of wastes. The disease that had felled Queen Victoria's beloved husband Albert more than twenty years ago still raged in this country and in Europe. But Victor wasn't about to argue with his father today or any day. He was too frail. Time too short.

"Your mother tells me you wrote that you visited with your staff in the City."

"I did. They continue to do a superb job of records. Ordering. Invoices. I am pleased."

"Not many men can say that about a group whom they hired five years ago and who work without their master's supervision."

"I'm pleased at their ethics, sir." *I try to chose all with whom I associate very carefully.*

"As well you should be. Tell me your status. Income to date this year. Losses. What are they?"

Victor sat back in his chair, proud to tell him. "Well sir, we pay ourselves and staff their salaries regularly, and this year perhaps a bonus, too."

"Last year?" He peered at him, impatient, licking his lips. His father had forgotten that Victor sent him records every six months. "Tell me. I must know."

His father wanted a report on the health of his export-import business and he deserved it. "I've turned your initial investment in me and mine into a growing concern, sir. We sold more than three million pounds worth of Chinese imports last year in Britain alone. Nearly the same in France and Germany. Hunger for silks and porcelain is not so great in Italy or Spain. Camphor too to kill insects and stabilize perfumes."

His father barked in laughter. "Good choices. Where does it come from?"

"Our ships load it in south Asian ports. Very profitable."

His father sat silent for an overly long time. When he

rallied, he said, "And your manager here in the City? What's his name?"

"MacIntyre. Frederick MacIntyre. Good man."

"A Scotsman with an eye for numbers as I recall."

Victor laughed. "Show him a column of figures and within a blink, he's added them up for you."

The old duke frowned, his eyes straying and returning to Victor. "Keep him."

"I will, sir." He leaned forward, elbows to his knees, and searched his father's eyes. Victor sought to keep him focused. "What is it you want to discuss, Papa?" *Tell me before you cannot.*

"I have a problem. I want you to fix it for me. For your mother and Richard, too."

If his father wanted him to dissuade Richard of proposing to the lovely American, he'd have a difficult time of it. She struck him with her frankness, her vibrant complexion and an odd interest in world affairs. He knew Richard well enough to predict that he'd enjoy her, consume her and never let her go. Her vivacity was a lure to any man who wanted a young and nubile creature in his bed. By making her his legal wife, Richard could possess her body and soul.

"If you mean to have me warn Richard from marrying the American girl, I doubt I can."

"I don't want to dissuade him."

So his mother was alone in this. Unusual, that. But then his mother was more the social creature, his father the realist. Still, Victor had to test the older man's resolve. "She has a sharp tongue to match her mind."

"He likes that in her. She'll poke him in the ribs when he strays. Keep him straight."

Could anyone do that?

His father glanced away, lost in thought, and tapped the arm of his chair. "He'll marry. Must. At last. I want him to get on with it. Quickly. I'll not be here much longer and I want matters settled before I depart. You seem set. Recovered well. Financially too. But you are not happy, are you?"

Victor bristled.

"I do not wish to offend, my boy. I will say what I mean. Allow me that."

"Yes, sir." Folding his hands, Victor quelled the riot inside him. His father saw too much. Took license to be blunt because of his age. But Victor could not argue with him at this point in his life. Truth be told, he hoped for as much largesse from his own children when he grew old. "Well then. What is it?"

"I make you a proposition."

The clock on the mantel struck the hour. As it bonged the last note of three, his father said, "I re-wrote my will a while ago. Can't remember when. Hear me. Hear me. I bequeath you the old dower house of your maternal grand-mother in Brighton."

The house by the sea. Tears stung his eyes. How kind of this man to give him the very place he'd always loved.

"I've hired a team to go in, clean it, whitewash it, repair the floor, add a new bathroom, the latest plumbing, no more of that cistern washing, you know. Electricity, too, and a new stove in the kitchen. You'll have to hire a gardener to weed out that old vegetable patch. I leave the furnishings to you and yours. I put in two household staff. Butler, maid. Hired by the month. Yours to keep or not."

The gift stunned him. "Father, I'm grateful but—"

"Hear me out."

Sick or well, one did not argue with the seventh duke of Brentwood. Not even a beloved son.

"I had Monroe before me here last week." For more than twenty years, Charles Monroe had been his father's estate manager for this property as well as two smaller ones, in

Sussex and in Dorset. "I changed my will and my asset allocations. I assign to you ten thousand a year, beginning now. Runs the house in Brighton. Pays for five, maybe six staff wages. So. All this. It's yours."

The enormity of the gift stunned him. The duke had always been generous to him, kind even in his darkest days five years ago. Victor had never been a recipient of his father's wrath. Nor had his father ever demanded things of him which he did not wish to give. But this...*this* was an enormous bequest that could change his life completely. If...if he remained in England. "You want me to stay. Not return to Shanghai."

"Let your *howqua* run it in Shanghai. Let your Frederick MacIntyre run it from the City. I want you to do something else for me. For your children. Your mother. Even Richard would benefit from it. Yes. Yes, he would. He needs your friendship, example of your steady hand. But this would benefit you."

"Yes but—" How could he do this? He shot to his feet, ire ringing in his head. He'd worked so hard to build a business and now this tore his work asunder. "You want me to become a gentleman farmer?"

"No, by God!"

"What?" He couldn't contain his shock, his confusion and an odd compelling joy. "I—I can't, sir, can't retire to the country. Can't fail to participate in the business that I built from a mere idea."

"You can!"

"Ten thousand a year might run a modest household, but I wish to give my daughters a good life, dowries, educations, all worthy of their name. I am grateful for your gift, sir, but it is not enough." The look of despair on his father's face crushed his anger, but did nothing for his conflict over the offer. Cursing silently, he whirled to place both hands upon the mantle. "I've never thought about returning here, remaining here."

"I expected you to say that. I can imagine it must not be easy to forget what happened here. But she's gone. And it has been many years."

Six since I learned of her perfidy. Five since I left, took her with me though I longed to throw her overboard, or...smother her in her bed.

"Victor, people forget."

He faced his father. "Why would you ask this of me? Papa, I was in hell here and only too happy to get out. The scandal robbed me of wits and hope. Why would I remain in England now that I've a growing concern in Shanghai?"

"Because I need you. Britain does."

Victor put both hands to his hips and leaned toward his father. "Oh, Papa. Please do not be grandiose with me."

"Victor, I want you to do what you were destined to do."

He winced. That dream died years ago. "No."

"You argue with me? Do not!" The old man threw out an arm. Spittle ran down his chin.

Roiled, yet mindful of his father's delicate condition, Victor held his tongue.

"I want you to...to...run...run. Parliament. Parliament, yes. Yes, that's..."

Victor saw his father's attention wander to the window, then back.

"See here, my boy." The duke licked his lips. "Our man for Brighton and Hove has contracted consumption. He will not live. We own that seat, Victor. We must keep it. You are our man."

Victor stepped back to his chair and sank into it. "I don't understand why you think I would be best for it. Not after my years abroad. Once perhaps, but now?"

"Yes, now. Because abroad you have learned the values of

trade and commerce. You will help to secure the Empire."

He opened his mouth to object.

But his father put up a trembling hand. "You understand issues of naval arms and geographic demands. So many of these home grown idiots in Parliament have no earthly idea what they speak of. I want a strong Britain. But I want an intelligent Britain. Not a war-monger. Not a saber-rattler."

The stab of Victor's youthful criticisms of older politicians pierced him. "You remember my own words?"

"I do," his father said with gravity. "Consider them. You do us more good here than you do in Shanghai. And you serve not only your family but also your country."

Victor cocked a brow. "And that one other entity?"

"Indeed," the duke gave a sharp laugh. "You serve yourself. The little boy who wanted to stand up in the green and address the townsfolk about unfair pay to coal miners."

"That little boy has seen so much of the world now to know he was naive."

"He's not any longer, is he?"

No. When he attended school, he believed in endless growth and possibilities. When married at the tender age of twenty-two, he believed in love at first sight, happily ever after, marriages filled with love, an honest wife. He believed in armies that fought for viable reason, men that conducted business based on honesty and ethics, where graft did not exist, hatred did not bring more malice and people could live in peace.

But when he discovered his wife had taken lovers, many of them since the time she was sixteen, when he learned that his man of business was one of her amours, when he found that the man had cheated him not only of his wife but also of ten percent of his income, Victor had fought with his demons not to murder his wife and her latest lover.

His father had saved him. Talked sense to him. Given him

seed money to leave England, travel far to the ends of the earth. Encouraged him to take his faithless wife with him and squire her away from the society that had nurtured her vain adultery. His father had truly saved him.

And as time passed, he had saved himself.

Why should he return here?

His father considered him gravely. "That last reason is the best one. The most important one."

Victor didn't wish to hear him say it.

"From the age of ten, you wanted to sit in Parliament. Debate rules and ethics. Vote on budgets. Make laws you could be proud of. You wanted to sit in Parliament, Victor, and now at last, here is your opportunity."

"Why now? There will be no general election soon." But his father most likely understood current political issues better than he. The duke had friends. Dear god. Legions of them who would feed him news, gossip, trends.

"You can use the time. So begin. Build a group of friends, supporters. Your day will come. The current prime minister makes grave mistakes, especially in regard to colonies."

"I know it. When I stopped in Naples, John Drummond told me Gladstone has sent ships to Egypt."

His father scoffed. "Yet he says he's not enlarging the empire."

"But he is." Tempted to accept his father's offer, he ached with the pain of wanting what he was once denied by the taint of an unfaithful wife. Outraged that he'd given up his fondest ambition for circumstances not of his own doing, he glimpsed a new horizon and yearned to walk it. But he'd built his company in Shanghai, made a small fortune and the benefit from it he would not toss easily aside. "I must think on it."

"There'll be no finer chance than this, Victor. Take it."

CHAPTER 4

Ada sprinted down the main staircase the next morning at seven.

No one stirred early in this household. She'd been first up the past few days. Today, from the looks of the empty foyer and salon, she'd catch worms again.

She'd awakened fewer than thirty minutes ago and sprung from her bed. She pulled the cord for her maid, intent on doing her morning ablutions quickly to escape the house and let the brisk air along the river blow some sense into her brain. She'd spent the night, tossing and turning and fuming over Victor Cole.

She wrinkled her nose. He might be beautiful, sculpted in form and firm in body, but he was carved from marble. More than cold, he was rude. Sitting next to him last night at table, she'd done her duty by her hostess and host, her family and her breeding. She'd talked to the man. Correction, she'd talked *at* him. He, straw man that he was, found it proper to speak to her in the fewest possible words.

Yes, Miss Hanniford.

No, Miss Hanniford.

I do like riding.
I do like my fish.
I long for dessert.

She'd wanted to pinch his thigh, tickle his ribs, wave a magic wand to awaken him from his apparent nap, pound his chest, breathe life into him. By time for the chocolate mousse and peach compote, she'd prayed to sprout wings and fly from the room. Only the remove of the ladies for tea and the gentlemen for their brandy and cigars saved her. By heavens, had they offered, she would have lit up an ugly brown stick and downed an ounce of cognac herself. She needed sustenance after the wasteland of the previous two hours.

If she had to sit next to him again this evening, she would bite him on one of his marvelously broad shoulders. If that didn't work, she'd remove her spleen with a fish fork. More fun certainly. Get his attention, one would wager. Anything to see him startle, perhaps even see him bleed like a living creature.

Worse, she had the distinct impression that his mother watched over them from her place at head of the table like the hen she was. If the duchess surmised that Lord Victor might possibly be interested in her, the lady needed glasses and a full bottle of French liquor to clear her head.

Ada sailed into the breakfast room, grinning that no one was about.

"Good morning, Miss Hanniford." Fawkes the butler appeared from the hall. Could he see through walls? "You are up very early again. Like it?"

"Good morning, Fawkes. I do indeed like the morning." *And the solitude.* "I've heard so much from the duchess about the path along the river, I plan to enjoy it myself."

"Will you walk or ride?" he asked as he came forward to pull out a chair for her. "I can have the groom prepare a horse for you."

"I'll walk. Thank you." *God, when would she remember it was not good form to thank servants?* "I like to ride occasionally, but prefer to go with a companion. Horses are not, shall we say, my favorite animal."

"I understand, Miss." He suppressed a smile. "Will you have your usual coffee?"

"Thank you, Fawkes, I will."

"Wonderful. And shall I serve you or do you prefer to choose from the sideboard yourself?"

She'd always hoped to diminish the work servants had to do for her. All their fussing seemed so unnecessary. Rather like stuffing a turkey for Christmas dinner. The bird was good as he was. No farce required. "I shall serve myself, thank you."

"Very well." He began to back away.

"One thought, Fawkes?"

"Yes, Miss?"

She hadn't asked for this previously, but she was sorely out of touch and needed a distraction from brooding over Victor Cole. "Since no one else is awake, I wonder if I might read the newspapers, please?"

Surprise lined his bushy brow. "Of course you may. Only Lord Victor has been down and seen them already. I was pressing them for the next...er...gentleman, but I can give them to you."

"I am most appreciative." *So, His High and Mighty Lordship has already passed through this portal. Fabulous.*

She pressed her hands along the smooth linen of her napkin and sat back to contemplate the joys of the morning that awaited her. Peace. So rare at a house party. The deluge of other guests would begin tomorrow. So, too, Richard would arrive today, having finished with his business. She'd begin to examine the marquess and decide what to say to her best friend about her intended groom. She'd have time these next few days to view him in person. From what she'd read of him, he was a young roué. No suitable match for sweet Ezzie. Yesterday, the duchess informed them that he had promised to escort them both to the theatre in Bath tonight. Ada shut her eyes, praying that Richards' brother would not volunteer to be her escort. To endure his indifference was worse than having to thwart five suitors with bad breath and groping hands.

Murmurs from the central hall had her turning to see who might be up and about. *Please, let it be a servant. A maid. A—*

Damn.

Victor.

His tall, elegant frame paused in mid-step on the threshold to the breakfast room. His turquoise eyes met hers and held.

"Miss Hanniford." He nodded.

"Lord Victor." She did the same.

"You are awake early."

"I am."

"You slept well?"

"Fairly."

"Not enough fresh air here, yet, I would gather?" He walked over to the other side of the circular table, using a cloisonné walking stick she'd not noticed yesterday, put his hands to the back of a chair and actually smiled at her.

Did he break his mouth to do that?

This morning he was dressed more casually than when she'd sat beside him at supper. Last night, he'd worn formal attire, a black swallowtail coat and white cravat, a pearl and jade stickpin that added luster to his tanned complexion and did a poor job of distracting her from his appealing lips and perfect sculpted jaw. Today, he wore tweed, a brown shot with dark green that turned his skin even more hale and hearty. The only sign of an infirmity was his beautifully decorated cane.

"Do you mind if I join you?"

Why? "Not at all."

Fawkes appeared with the coffee urn in one hand and a set of papers over his arm. At Victor's side, he paused, his brows high in curiosity. "My lord? You've returned from your ride."

"I have, Fawkes."

Ada set her teeth.

"Is that coffee?" he asked the butler. "I'd like a cup myself."

Ada's hope for solitude withered.

"But I read the papers," he said to the servant.

"I've brought the *Bath Chronicle* for Miss Hanniford." As Fawkes poured for her, she saw Victor's surprise. If she'd been ten and green and unschooled in decorum, she would have chuckled when the butler added, "I still have yesterday's London papers, sir. Did you wish to see them?"

"No. That's fine, Fawkes. My mistake."

Ada took the folded news sheets from the man and placed them by her right hand.

"Read the papers often, do you, Miss Hanniford?"

"Daily."

As Fawkes fetched a cup and saucer from the sideboard, Victor gazed at her with a mellow expression. A new look for him.

"I'm glad you're here this morning, Miss Hanniford."

She let her brows rise to ask the obvious question.

Fawkes poured for him and set before him another place setting.

Victor put both hands to the table's edge and leaned forward. "I dare say I owe you an apology."

If she agreed with him, she might insult him. As he had her. So she waited.

"This is awkward."

Indeed.

"I was a bit off last night."

"Off?" She barely suppressed her guffaw.

"There is no excuse for it. I was preoccupied, unsettled."

She would let him drift.

He lifted his hands. "I was an ass."

She grinned at his apt term.

He cocked a brow. "I've hit a chord, have I?"

She acknowledged that with a nod.

He snorted. "I see you are treating me to my own medicine."

"Discretion is salve itself."

"So true. And I see the errors of my ways."

"Good." She rose from her chair to head to the sideboard.

She heard him push back his chair and take a few steps. He came to stand behind her. So close, she could inhale the fragrance of grass and hay, the woods where he'd walked or ridden. She moved along to choose her bacon, her egg.

"Miss Hanniford," he said in a duly apologetic tone, "I'd like to make amends. Have a suitable conversation."

She looked over her shoulder, and there he was, too near. His cologne of bergamot mixing with the sweet aromas of crushed chlorophyll and spring breezes. She swallowed deeply, returning to consider the potato dish before her. "And what would you like to discuss?"

"You."

She whipped her head around to face him once again. "Hardly an intriguing topic for one so well traveled and educated."

"You hoist me on my own petard, Miss Hanniford. I was rude to you last night. Ridiculously so."

"Unworthy of you, I'd say." She wanted to chastise him for being so nasty to her, when all night long she'd seen nothing but how jovial he was with his children and his mother. Loving, kind. "I didn't merit your lack of manners, sir."

"I agree. And I'd like to change your impression of me. More, I'd like to hear about your views of laudanum and soothing syrups. I'd like to know more about your family. And you."

Why? She delved into his gaze, searching for that answer. He'd hurt her. She'd no intention to let him off lightly. She did not suffer fools. So she carried her full plate back to the table and allowed him to assist her by pushing in her chair.

But he sat down next to her.

Turned full to face her.

His cologne, the grasses, his nearness swamped her.

She'd not allow any man who did not like her to discomfit her. There were so many eligible men out in society who would give their right arm to sit beside her at dinner. Many who had proposed titles, houses, jewels and undying love. This man had wasted the chance to even be civil to her. So why she should be attracted to him ate at her good nature. "I'd like to eat my breakfast, sir."

"Do, please. I simply want to say that I am very sorry for last night. If you'll permit me to attempt a conversation."

That burned the porridge. "*Do* you talk? Do you use more than one word answers? I have no evidence of such, sir. I have only your indifference and it grated on my nerves. I did not sleep well thinking I could have changed it all. Drawn you out. Amused you somehow. But I conclude I am not to blame. Nor am I without charms. Or so my family and friends would say."

"So would my mother."

"And others."

"Men, I'm sure." He grinned. At an expression that lifted his features from handsome to mesmerizing, his glee made her gape at him.

"You're right." She recovered sanity and took up her fork and knife.

"I can see why. I'd like to enjoy what they have."

Why? "Sir. I think now you're being bold."

"I'd like to be kind, Miss Hanniford."

"I might consider allowing it," she said, mellowing to his persistence.

"Perhaps after you've eaten, your disposition will improve."

"Two cups of coffee, more like it," she said with a snicker and reached for said beverage.

"Do you mind if I join you?"

Stubborn man.

"I thought you'd eaten earlier."

"I did. But I could do it again in good company. May I?"

Arguing never was her forte. "If you can leave off with this apology business and let me dine and drink and read in silence."

"I can do that."

She gave him the full power of a forgiving smile. "Your trial begins now."

He wrinkled his brows in feigned laughter. "And after breakfast?"

"What of it?" She had to torment him, didn't she?

"May I take you riding?"

"No."

"Oh." He was dejected. Dare she say he appeared to sulk?

"Horses hate me."

"Oh. Well, then, can we walk?"

"We could. Along the river."

"I see."

"I've not been. You can describe the flora and fauna, sir."

"Wonderful. You like them?"

Oh, he could chatter on, couldn't he? "Like what?"

"Flora? Fauna?"

She lifted her gaze and considered the heavy crystal chandelier. He was deliciously easy to play with. "Flora."

"Not fauna?"

"Only birds."

He got this maddeningly searing look to his large turquoise eyes. "Very well. Birds and flowers."

"Tell me how you import 'crysamums'."

He chuckled. "Deirdre simply cannot pronounce it."

"Not 'camellas', either."

"I shall be happy to tell you about both."

"Marvelous. Now, if you don't mind?" She pointed to her breakfast plate.

He pressed his lips together. His marvelous firm lips. Blinking, she nodded. Happy as a clam, she tucked into her bacon.

He sipped his coffee...and watched her.

She paused, her fork and knife in the air.

He gave her a wide-eyed grin.

Impertinent cuss. She sighed, surrendering her peace as another thought struck her.

"We'll need a maid," she told him. Comtesse de Chaumont, the widowed Frenchwoman who was the Hanniford family's friend and ladies' companion, would not arise until eleven. Ada would not wake her to walk with them. The woman would like Victor. But then, Chaumont liked any eligible man. "As chaperone."

"Ah. Of course. Forgot, rules of society. Fawkes can find one who is finished with her morning chores. When you're finished eating."

"Good. But for now?"

"Yes?" He brightened, eager and ready to do her bidding.

She wanted to giggle at his ebullience, his turnaround from self-declared ass to dashing young man. "Do be quiet and let me dine and drink and read."

"At your service, Miss Hanniford." He pressed two fingers to his lips to seal them.

She rolled her eyes at him, then ate her breakfast and read her paper in utter silence.

She folded her paper, drained her coffee cup and got to her feet.

"Finished?" he asked, eager to go, ready to smile with her and tell her about flowers, birds, bees, or anything at all.

"I am." She made her way to the foyer and the grand staircase.

He followed.

Ada Hanniford had spunk and he'd been such a fool to waste last evening shutting her out of his consciousness. He couldn't. Even though he'd wanted to brood about his past and ponder his new opportunity to stay at home, she'd cut through all his thoughts. Last night, as yesterday when he'd met her, she didn't merely breathe, she blazed with life. To close her out was to ignore the sun.

Cursing his silliness, he'd walked the floor of his bedroom last night for more than an hour. Few women—very few women—had ever done that to him. Much to his dismay, testing his loyalty to his brother, he'd admitted to himself that he needed to sit closer to the fire she ignited. And if he could kill his jealousy, he'd assured himself there'd be no harm of it. Surely, if she was to be Richard's wife, they should have a friendship. And he had to make amends.

Truth be told, he was more himself now that he had apologized and been the proper gentleman.

Of course, what he longed to do with her was far from proper and not gentlemanly at all. But he could control those urges. The ones that came in waves to cup her cheek, brush his thumb over her lips, or sweep her up into his embrace and press her lush body to his own.

But no. She was Richard's already. He could accept it, even though he'd envy his brother the joy of her. Best to make good family relations in any case.

During her breakfast, he'd chastised himself over and over as he'd watched her eat and drink and read. She was lovely, natural, fresh. Why was it no intelligent man had snapped her up before this? She was no ingénue. Neither was her friend, Esmerelda. They appeared a few years beyond a debutante's first blush. The only reason behind her continued spinster-hood must be that she had not found a man to suit her.

But then, was Richard the best she could do?

That was impossible. She could crook her little finger and have anyone. *Any one.*

Ah. Unless she had marks against her character, just as Richard did. Was that why she appealed to his half-brother?

She didn't seem like the type to have been sullied by any careless man. She was too wise. Too strident in her own opinions.

But what the hell did it matter? He was not here to analyze or support her in her choice of husband. His purpose was to advise his brother on his choice and if he approved, to get acquainted with his future sister-in-law.

That was his duty.

He fingered his walking stick as Ada took the first stair up to the next floor.

He'd asked Fawkes to send them a housemaid as chap-erone and the butler had promised one would come to the foyer within minutes.

"I'll be only a moment." Ada pointed upward. "I'll need my shawl."

"Best to wear a bonnet," Victor said. "The sun will be strong today."

Horses clattered along the drive. Shouts of the driver rang in the air.

Ada paused, her face toward the lower level and the foyer. "The guests aren't due to arrive until tomorrow."

"And not this early in the morning, either. Unseemly to appear before the afternoon."

Fawkes hurried from the breakfast room and took the stairs down. "I understand it's your brother, sir."

"Richard? Up from Bath so early?" *Odd for my brother to rally before ten in the morning.*

"Yes, sir." Fawkes gained the last step and opened the door just in time to allow Richard to walk in.

"Good heavens!" His dark-haired jovial half-brother glanced up and around to spy him before he got his hat or coat off. Laughing, he made straight for Victor, arms wide. They met mid-way on the stairs. "I say, it's wonderful to see you, Victor. Had a good voyage? The girls, too?"

"We have." He hugged the man, as thrilled to see his childhood friend as ever he was. They'd shared so much, less than two years apart in age. But sharing youth and boarding school, as they'd grown into young men at Eton, they'd grown apart. Richard to all number of questionable friends and pastimes of gambling and whoring. Victor to his books and sporting. Still, part of Richard, the generous man who gave willingly to any and all, he loved dearly. "I'm glad to see you again, Richard. Very glad."

His brother framed his face with both hands and shook him to and fro. "Fabulous. You are not a day older. China does well by you, eh?"

"It does." *Better than your lifestyle has done for you, I see.*

Richard stilled and gazed beyond him. "And who, pray tell, is this?"

CHAPTER 5

What a fool he'd been. Thinking, *assuming* that Richard intended to propose to Ada Hanniford when all along, he'd planned this elaborate house party with his mother and all of them present to ask Esmerelda Moore to marry him.

"Marvelous to meet you, Miss Hanniford." After Victor had done the formal honors, Richard practically purred as he bent over her hand. "I will enjoy getting to know you more intimately. Ezzie's friend is always mine. I should have come home sooner, eh?"

Ada smiled but said not a word to that inference.

Richard took her in. Her eyes, her hair, her lips. "Yes, well." He cleared his throat. "Do forgive me, Miss Hanniford. Only for the moment, please. Then I shall sit down for a long chat. But I must see my father, first. You understand, I'm sure. Is he up and dressed, do you know, Victor?"

"He is. I visited with him before dawn." *As I always do. As you never do.*

"Will you join me?" Richard asked him, one eyelid twitching.

Why? "I've plans for the morning."

Ada folded her hands before her. *She must wish to escape us.*

"Please do, Victor."

"Is something the matter?"

"Oh, a little thing you could help me with."

A woman. Money.

With grace, Ada curtsied. "I shall retire. See you later at luncheon, I assume," she said to both but her clear blue eyes rested in Victor's.

"But we're to walk, Miss Hanniford," Victor put in before she turned away. "I promised and we shall. Fawkes is to have the maid here in a few minutes." *Hell and gone.* He sounded like a boy eager to capture his sweetheart.

"Certainly, if you would like to join me still, Lord Victor, I'd welcome that."

"Give me a few minutes, will you? I'll speak with my brother a minute."

"Where are you two going?" Richard arched a black brow. His tone held a hint of the risqué. "Some place delightful, I hope."

Did she bristle at his brother's implication?

"We're taking a stroll along the river," he told Richard, his tone even to him, unnecessarily sharp.

"Ah. Good idea! I shall join you both. After this, yes, Miss Hanniford? You don't mind if I take Victor with me for a few minutes do you?"

I mind.

"Of course not," she said, but her gaze rested in Victor's where he saw her concern for him.

Not to worry. I know how to deal with him.

Victor followed Richard into his father's sitting room, flexing his fingers fighting frustration. Seeking some peace in his soul, he breathed deeply. His meditation exercises with his *lao shi* deserted him. He brimmed, full of emotions, too conflicted. He'd have to sit on the floor in his bedroom this afternoon to seek his *tao*. Hating what he was when he was consumed with negative *chi*, he had perfected techniques in the past two years that brought him serenity. Except for the last twenty hours since he'd heard his father's proposition and burned at the nearness of gorgeous, outspoken, tempting, Ada Hanniford.

"Hello, Father!" Richard hailed him as they entered.

"That you, Richard?" their father squinted up at his oldest son. In the corner by the inglenook and raging fire, his father sat in his same large red upholstered Chippendale chair. He put out a shaking hand and repeated his question.

"I am here, Father," Richard announced and bussed his father on his wrinkled cheek.

"Home."

"Yes, home." Richard took a seat in a nearby chair and beamed at the man. One person Richard adored was their father.

Victor preferred to stand and took up his stance by the mantle.

"Victor's come home," the duke said to his oldest son in his crackly voice.

"I see he has. He looks wonderful, too, don't you think?"

"He's taller than when he left. How can that be, eh?"

Victor frowned. Was his father of clear mind this morning?

Richard lifted a shoulder. "Good Chinese food, perhaps?"

"I'm cold." The duke picked at his trousers. "Are you cold, Richard?"

"No, Father. It's actually rather stifling in here."

Victor lifted a throw from the bed and took it to lay over

his father's lap. Then he assumed the remaining chair near his sire.

"You went to—to where?"

"Bath, father."

"Bath? To...to see...whom?"

"One of my men, Father. We have a problem with a dam that broke in spring rains and I needed to inquire as to funds to shore it up." Richard shot Victor a glance that belied the truth of this.

"And have you enough?"

"Nearly so." Richard's dark eyes warned Victor that this was not the case. "We'll have to use monies from Ridgemont to pay the workers." Ridgemont was Richard's larger estate north of London.

"Don't you have enough...enough...?"

Victor saw greater evidence of his mother's warning that his father's clarity of mind was unpredictable.

Richard waited for his father to complete the sentence.

Victor filled in. "Enough money from that property to pay for repairs?"

"What? What?" His father frowned. "No, no. You are to marry and get the money, eh? That American gel. What's her name?"

"Esmerelda, Father." Richard sat back, matter-of-fact about this. "Esmerelda Moore."

"Sounds Spanish to me. Is she Spanish? Why would you marry a girl from Spain, my boy?"

"No, Father. She is American. From New York, I think."

You think?

"Rich?" the duke asked.

"Yes."

"How much?" His father leaned forward. Never a man to count money above character, this query surprised Victor. "Her dowry?"

"Rumors say fifty thousand. Twenty for her widow's portion."

A damned fortune.

The old man gave a long loud laugh. "That's it."

The subject repulsed Victor. Though he himself had bene-fitted from Alicia's funds, he hated the medieval concept that a wife must come with money to recommend her. He rose to go. "Forgive me, I should leave."

His father frowned at him. "Stay, Victor. Sit. You must know about your brother's plans."

Why? He's not my keeper and I will not be his. "This is more his business, Papa."

"But you must know. Sit." His father motioned him toward the chair and out of respect, he took it. "Richard is in terrible debt. Tell him, have you?" He pressed his oldest boy.

"No, sir." Richard's eyes met Victor's and in them, he saw a plea to leave off this topic.

He shrugged, little he could do if their father wished to have this out.

"Land values are down," said the duke with a scathing look at Richard. "Fewer tenants paying their rent. Declining dividends, and on top of it all, Richard took another loan against his unentailed land!"

Shocked at his father's sudden acuity on Richard's finances, Victor shot an inquisitive look at his brother.

Richard only pursed his lips and shook his head.

The duke grumbled about his oldest's follies. "But Victor got a decent dowry from Alicia. Twenty thousand, was it?"

Victor inhaled, rebelling at this reference to his dead spendthrift wife. "Twenty-five, it was."

"Hmm. Hmm. Good sum. Richard, have you talked to her father yet?"

"No, I've not."

"Why not?" The duke grew puzzled.

Richard licked his lips and ran two hands through his black hair, then leaned toward the duke. "It's a delicate matter, Father. Let me do it in my own way and time."

"You don't need more wild oats. If that's what you wait for."

"I'd like to go to her with no debts."

Ah. Here's the rub. Victor sat back to wait.

"Reason why many marry is to have no debts, boy."

Richard inhaled. He hated being called a boy. Yet in many ways, especially in regard to money and women, had he not always been?

"You bring her to heal. Have her father sign the forms. Why dally?"

"I have a problem. A big one. I must fix it soon."

What was it? A woman. A gambling debt. Solicitor's fees for this latest conflict about the mistress of the Prince of Wales. Victor folded his hands and crossed one leg over the other.

"I need to borrow two thousand from you," Richard told his father.

Not asking. Telling. Victor turned to consider the fire.

"Borrow? Or take?"

No doubt about it, his father was sharp as a razor at the moment. *Thank god.*

"Borrow. Definitely. I promise you."

His father let out a snort. "No."

"Sir—"

"I said no, Richard."

"I must have it to pay a doctor—"

"Are you ill?" The duke leaned forward and examined Richard's face.

"No, Papa. But it's for a friend."

The old man fell backward in his chair, his regard of his oldest son clear and accusative. "Who's the friend?"

Richard did his best to suppress a squirm. "Sir—"

The old man harrumphed. "A woman."

"If I'm to marry, sir, I cannot have this lady pester—"

"*Is* she a lady?" the duke asked, narrowing his watery eyes to slits. "Doubt it. Has your package, doesn't she?"

Richard had the grace to look sheepish. "Yes."

Old angers burst like fireworks inside Victor. A woman who needed an abortion lest she present her husband with another man's child was a nightmare he'd outgrown. Here it was, now his brother's...and Richard was the perpetrator. He stared at this man, learning him anew. His stomach clenching, he tasted bile.

The duke cursed. "First this business with bedding Wales' mistress right under his nose, now a by-blow! Is it Dundalk's wife who's pregnant?"

Richard swallowed hard. "Yes."

Victor shot from his chair.

Their father banged his fist on his armrest. "You fool! He can bring charges."

A legal case. 'Criminal conversation' accusing Richard of adultery with Dundalk's wife. That would mean an open trial. Scandal that would live for decades. And so would the illegitimate child. Victor could not bear the violence of his memories. He strode to the window, pulled wide the drapes to peer out on the wasteland that he might have faced with Alicia. But she'd aborted the baby in question, nearly dying, and they'd survived that particular scandal.

"He won't do that, Father, I tell you," Richard said with all penitence. "He doesn't know she's pregnant. Besides, it can't be mine. She says it is, but it's Wales' brat. He's had her more than I have!"

Victor faced his brother of whom in early youth, he had once been proud. Once. But still. Once.

The duke shook his head. Waved his finger at his oldest.

Sputtered and caught his spittle, then asked, "What in hell do you do all day, man?"

Richard blanched. "I will marry soon. For you. For us. I must clear my name first. This will do it."

"No. No money. Pay for her abortion yourself. Get out." The old man slumped in his chair. "Go."

Victor heard the tone implying their father was through with this audience. Catching Richard's eye, he rose and led Richard away.

As Victor closed the door behind him, his father called out, "And you will not ask your mother for it. I forbid it."

"Come talk with me, Vic?"

"No. My answer is no, Richard." Victor was the last person on earth who would give Richard a 'loan' to cover his mistakes. He'd fought too hard for too long to earn a decent living. He'd not throw it away on his brother's mistakes. *Let him figure out how to save himself as I did when scandal stalked my door.*

❧

Searching for patience, Ada raised her face to the sunlight dappled through the trees. This gaggle of fellow walkers straggling along behind her was not what she'd envisioned for her morning walk.

It was past ten. The sun was growing warm. She'd discarded her bonnet. Would that she could as easily discard Madame Chaumont, who had surprised her by her readiness to accompany her. So too had Victor's two daughters caught her and Chaumont as they descended the main stairs. They plus their nursemaid, the young Chinese girl whose name was Wu-lai, wanted to tag along.

Victor had taken Ada's arm when first they left the house. But his brother had maneuvered himself to her other side. As the little girls called and commented to their father, Victor had left her to tend to them.

Richard's proprietary attitude in the foyer upon arrival had chafed her. She usually delighted in making new acquaintances. Even if he was reputed to be a rogue, she had been ready to draw her own conclusions about his character. Everyone deserved that, she believed. But that beginning did not bode well and she wished to have Victor back beside her. But he was well occupied.

Wu-lai, a delicate creature, quiet and demure, spoke English to Victor's girls. He in return spoke a mix of English and Chinese, all in an attempt to teach the maid and his daughters new words of both languages. That patience, that willingness to educate all of them, warmed Ada. She'd had a few teachers who had nurtured her own interest in a few subjects, botany foremost among them. A good teacher was a jewel to be treasured.

Beside Wu-lai, Madame Chaumont waited solemnly. This morning, she hung back with the girls and that was unusual for the countess. She'd joined the Hanniford family when first Killian had come abroad with Lily and Marianne nearly five years ago. Ada, at the time, was still in finishing school in Connecticut and had not sailed for Europe until she had commenced in June eighteen-seventy-eight. She'd arrived with their older brother Pierce days before Lily married Julian Ash. On their wedding morning, Julian had been a marquess, but hours later, upon the sudden death of his father, the duke of Seton, Julian had inherited the man's titles and estates. Chaumont, who had been hired by Ada's father, had stayed with them these many years, first shepherding Lily, then their cousin Marianne and finally Ada through the rigors of European customs and manners. Through it all, Chaumont had been loyal even as she searched for a husband among the many men she met. But she had not found one she loved. A pretty blonde in her mid-thirties, perhaps a bit too eager to enchant a man, the French woman was aging. Today, she moved slowly, her skin ashen. Ada frowned, wondering if she were ill.

She beckoned Chaumont, hoping she might join her, but the lady gave a small shake of her head and slid her gaze toward Victor.

He was her next target?

No. Ada whirled away. *Please don't want her.*

"Up there." Richard pointed toward a nest high in a budding oak. "We're about to have a cast of woodpeckers banging on the trees."

"Any idea when?" Grateful for the diversion, she craned her neck but through the thick foliage, was not able to see more.

"None. Like birds, do you?"

She shrugged. "As long as they don't eat crops, yes. Do you?"

He talked about the value of birds. "Buzzards are especially useful. Eating detritus and depositing the remains everywhere."

"Hmmm. Bat guano."

He choked on laughter. "You know about that?"

"I do. Importing it made quite a few men wealthy. The soil here needs the added enrichment."

"Yes," he said with a scowl. "I missed that investment."

He rattled on about the importance of catching a wave of a new product before any and all spoil the fun and take all the proceeds. She listened, polite but assessing him.

Despite gossip she'd heard of him, he possessed the finest manners. Still, those alone could not quell the unease she felt beside him. He walked too closely to her, put a hand now and then to her forearm and grinned much too broadly. He was a fox, wily, aggressive. She would show him that she was not his rabbit.

"Your family is well-known in England," he said as they strolled along the river's edge. "Your father quite successful here in shipping and trade. Railroads, too. Your brother Pierce buys up land as if he intends to become an Englishman."

She ignored his leading statement. "My father and brother have a golden touch."

"Even your older sister married the Duke of Seton. And your cousin? Forgive me as I've forgotten her name. She married a German baron, isn't that so?"

"A Frenchman." *A duc. A prince of the Bourbon blood. Bonapartes' too.* "The sculptor Remy."

Richard snapped his fingers. "Ah, yes! And she's that artist —what is her name?—who paints only women and children."

"She is Marianne Duquesne, using her maiden name professionally."

"And what do you do, Miss Hanniford?"

I plant. I cultivate. "I design gardens."

"Charming. Any one I might have seen?"

"My step-mother's and my sister's."

"I should love to view them."

Angling for an invitation?

"And when you are not planting and pruning, what do you do?"

"Everyone assumes I search for a husband."

"Ha! And do you?" His dark brown eyes twinkled.

"At my leisure."

He laughed, throwing back his head. "You've had a good go at it. Three years?"

He knew how long. The same number of years Ezzie had been in Europe. "Four."

"Your papa is not in a hurry to see you wed?"

"My papa believes marriage should be more than a contractual arrangement."

"Ah, you Americans. Love is the elixir."

"That plus companionship and mutual interests."

He picked up a rock, stopped and threw it across the rushing river. "It's fine to marry where you will when you have the luxury to look beyond the bank balance. Some of us do not have that freedom."

Some of us assume too much freedom.

"I understand your father earned his fortune by running the Union shipping lines. Some say he sold African men."

That stiffened her spine. "The first is true. The second, not."

"No?"

This man could be so rude. She was delighted to correct him. "He ran the blockade for the Confederates, running cotton to this country for a few planters, but he stopped early in the war."

"I see. Why? If it was profitable?"

"Because by selling their cotton and importing rifles to the South, he contributed to the continuation of the war. He didn't want that. Especially because he does not support slavery."

"So he didn't sell slaves himself?"

"Never. In fact, on one trip, he saved all aboard a sinking slaver and set the whole lot free in the next port."

Richard paused and nodded. "A good man. So what they say, that Killian Hanniford is notorious, is wrong."

"I would say so. I suppose your belief has to rest on whether you take all gossip as truth?"

"You have it right there." He picked up another rock and threw it into the water. "I believe everyone is entitled to their mistakes."

Mistake. A small word for a rather gargantuan sin of taking another man's wife to your bed.

"Do that again." Victor walked up to them, pointing to the river.

Ada sagged in relief that he'd left Chaumont. Unkind as that was, jealousy was not an emotion she had ever experienced. She smiled at Victor, happy that he'd come to her side to free her of this dastardly conversation.

"What? Think you can best me, old man?" Richard said. Hovering over Ada, he let his eyes dance. "Skipping rocks was a game we often played."

"And bet money on," said Victor with a wide-eyed look at her.

"Bet me now," Richard said.

"Ten pounds I can get three." Victor lifted his chin.

"Double that!" Richard laughed.

"Triple that," she said.

Richard grimaced. "Oh, no. You jest, don't you?"

"Never," she grinned at him.

Victor narrowed his eyes at her. "I'm good. I'll bet you that. Richard?"

"Well, hel—" At the sight of Vivienne and Deirdre, Richard swallowed his words. "Yes. Let's."

"Wonderful," she challenged them with a toss of her head. Then she bent to pick up an appropriately sized rock or two and weigh them in her hand. "We'll see."

She made her way closer to the river and chose her spot. "Come on! No dallying, you two."

The brothers stared at each other.

Richard grumbled. "Easiest money I've made in a year."

"Easiest money I'll take from you in three," Victor said with a clap on his arm.

Men. Ada wiggled her nose. "You're first," she said to Richard. "Then you."

"Ladies should go first," Victor said with a nefarious grin.

"Ba! You two, are laggards," Richard said and with deliberate action, threw his stone. The stone skipped two times... and died in the water.

Jubilant, Victor chuckled and stepped like an emperor to his chosen spot on the grassy bank. He threw. His stone skipped three times, plunged to its rest, and he crowed.

Vivienne and Deirdre now stood just behind him and they clapped. "Yay, for Papa!"

"Miss Hanniford!" He hailed her with a smug nod. "Step up, please."

"I prefer..."—she pointed to her spot and her stance —"right here."

"If you must," he said and folded his arms. "Deliver when ready."

She considered the force of the current, the flat stones she'd chosen, bent to look at the height of each in relation to the other, stood...and threw her rock. One. Two. Three. Four. Five.

She arched up, smiling at the sky, and turned to preen at the two men.

"I do believe I've won thirty pounds from each of you." She dusted off her hands. "A good day."

Vivienne ran up to her.

Deirdre grabbed her wrist. "Can you teach us to do that, Miss Hanniford?"

Victor, Wu-lai and even Chaumont were biting back grins.

"I will indeed. Tomorrow morning? After breakfast."

The girls jumped up and down.

Victor stepped toward her.

Richard fell in beside her as the group turned for the house. "I presume you'll teach them more than skipping rocks."

"So they don't challenge you?" she countered.

Victor crowed.

Richard's brown eyes clouded at her sharp tone, but he turned to his brother. "Care to lose to your own daughters?"

"I wish to play with any rival who gives me a challenge, Richard."

Ada bit her lip. Victor Cole had struck the proper blow to his brother. He was a good man, unafraid to compete ethically. That was more than she could say for his older brother.

❧

"Where have you been?" Ezzie rose from her *chaise longue* in her sitting room to greet Ada. In her dark rose dressing gown, her chocolate brown hair flowing in shining waves over her shoulders, she was loveliest *en dishabille*. Only the concern lining her brow marred her beauty. "I've been frantic waiting to talk to you."

"I went walking along the river. An entire horde of us, I must say."

"Poor Ade. I know how you hate crowds." Ezzie gave a little giggle. "Richard went too, I understand? My maid had it from the butler."

"He did." *I wish he'd stayed home to greet you properly.* Ada pushed up the sleeves of her white linen blouse and brushed her hands down her new robin's egg blue skirt. She'd bathed and changed for luncheon, hungry for food...and to see Victor again. "He did."

Ezzie nibbled on her lower lip. "When did he arrive?"

"Early. Very early. Eight o'clock."

"Odd for him to be up like that. When we were at the Isleys' house party in November, when I met him, he never rose until noon or after."

Ada sank into the overstuffed chair opposite her. "This is his party to make it official with you. So he's eager to get on with it." *Although he doesn't behave like a man ready to make the final commitment.*

"Did he ask about me?"

Not a word. "Oh, he must've known you were abed."

"How is he? Do you like him? Did he ask you how you and I met? Or if his mother likes me any better than she did at the Isleys' or..."

Ada reached over and grabbed her fingers. "Darling. Don't. You'll make yourself a wreck. When you come down for luncheon, you and he will see each other and you can ask him all this yourself. All will be well." *I hope it will.*

Ezzie flounced onto the green settee in a swish of rose organza and frustration. "I had a letter from my mother in the morning's post."

From the bleakness in her sweet brown eyes, this news was not good.

"How is her health? Better, I do hope."

"No. Nor is Daddy coming. Can you imagine? My mother says I am to conclude my own dowry arrangements! *Who* does that?"

Fathers. Solicitors. Estate managers. Never the bride.

"What am I do, Ade? This looks so awful. No parents. As if I am a foundling or illegitimate. A bastard daughter, whom they cannot wait to get rid of. And here is Richard, one day soon to be a duke. For Christ's sake, what a mess." She rubbed her forehead. "What am I to do?"

"You will tell him that your mother is ill and your father mired in business. It happens." *Although I've never heard of such, we cannot drag the two of them here.* "You and I will put a good face on it and march onward. Richard will propose, you will accept and as your mother instructs, you will set the details."

"Oh! I could never never do that."

Ada scrounged for hope, facts. "Yes, you can."

"How?"

How? What would Papa do? Or Pierce? My step-mother Olivia? Or...or Lily or Marianne if either of them were widowed. "With witnesses. Me...and...and Chaumont. And the butler Fawkes. We need a man."

"You are crazy. Who would call that legal?"

Ada stared at her friend, determined. "I will. You will. Chaumont will."

"Oh, it will never work."

"Not if we don't try, Ezzie." *We will. You must.*

Ezzie waved her off. "What if he doesn't ask?"

He must. "He's come this far."

Ezzie shot up from her settee and marched to the window, hands to the sill. "He's down there, talking with his mother in the garden. Oh, hell. He must know. She must be telling him that my mother has not come."

"The duchess knows your mother will not arrive?"

"Mother wrote that she sent a note to her. With apologies, as if that matters."

Her Grace, the duchess of Brentwood, stood on ceremony with any and all...except it seemed with her son, Victor.

Ezzie shook her head. "What if Richard insists on meeting Papa? What if he takes their absence as reason not to make an offer?"

The society sheets are filled with all the ways Ridgemont could outrage society more than he already has. "He'd be a cad not to do it now."

Ezzie whirled around to face her. "Darling Ada, *he is a cad*."

Ada sucked in a breath.

"Meanwhile, I am not without a few brains."

"That's the right idea."

She crossed her arms. "What if he thinks my parents have decided I'm not good enough for him?"

"Oh, no, Ezzie. If there's any thought along that line it's that he thinks they've decided *he's* not good enough for *you*."

Ezzie squeezed shut her eyes. "I want him."

To that, Ada had no appropriate response.

"One thing's for certain."

"Yes?"

"He must want my dowry."

There it was, the factor that tied every heiress in knots and bound quite a few into lifelong bondage to a man they hated. Even some young women who had no money but standing, like her brother-in-law Julian's sister Elanna, were forced to endure marriage to a man they loathed. That woman, wed to an older richer man four years ago because she had no dowry to commend her, created a scandal when she had left him more than two years ago. She lived alone in London. Her husband had demanded their baby son remain with him—and Elanna had agreed. Whispers hinted that she had taken a lover. Ada had even witnessed her husband, the earl of Carbury, accost her one afternoon in Half Moon Street, demanding she return home. Elanna had laughed in his face and marched away. On countless occasions, Julian had tried to talk sense into his sister, but she refused at every turn. He was at a loss for any remedy to their estrangement. But Ada's entire family had observed numerous explosive scenes of Carbury's resentment and Elanna's refusal to return to her husband and child.

No matter the cost to her pride or her future happiness, Ezzie could not be dissuaded from her hope to wed Richard. If money could buy him, she'd purchase him. "If that's all he wants, then you have the right to make him discuss it."

"Money?"

"Why not? He'll be using yours. Why should you not learn how?"

"But I don't care how."

"Of course you do. He must use it on you. Your children. Your house. Your—"

"My pride." Her friend threw up her hands. "Don't you see, Ade? I want him to want *me*. My problem is he seems to want *everyone!*"

"You don't have to accept him." *Or consign yourself to a life half-lived with a man who will never be faithful.*

"And just whom would I marry, hmm?"

"Ezzie, please."

"You and I have met every single man in the British Isles under age sixty with teeth still in their head and walking upright. Not one has asked for my hand. Not one!"

"You are young."

"Twenty-two. Nearly done for. Stick a lily in my hand."

Ada laughed.

And thank God, so did Ezzie.

"If I were brave, I'd ask you how many have asked your father for your hand." Her friend grinned at her through tears glistening in her eyes. "But to make me feel better, you'd lie."

Proud of her friend's fortitude, Ada reflected on the six men who had approached her father and been rejected. After the third suitor had left their house on Piccadilly with a hang-dog look, she asked him why he didn't ask her thoughts on any of them.

"I'll know when you fall in love," he'd said, "before you tell me who the man is."

She'd laughed it off. "You assume I'll be that obvious?"

He'd chuckled. "Everyone is."

"Won't tell me, will you?" Ezzie pouted.

No. "More important than the number would be my answer."

"I know, I know. However many there were, you didn't want any of them."

"Precisely."

"And when you do find him, would you negotiate your own contract?"

Ada snorted. *Now that you mention it...*"It's my right to set my own terms for the rest of my life."

"But even if you do, the law might not uphold you."

"That new one Parliament negotiates just might be my saving grace. Yours too." She'd take better note of the new terms that allowed a married British woman to own property in her own right.

"If men observe it." Ezzie wrinkled her nose.

"Can a man ignore the law? I doubt it, Ezz."

Her friend mashed her lips together. "I don't want to have to bargain with the man I love."

Is Richard lovable? "But he'll benefit from your money, why not demand he give you what you want?"

"I could and risk losing him." Ezzie sank to the settee once more. "I bet by the end of this party, he'll want you."

A chill ran up her spine but she did not move. She wouldn't allow this man to shame her friend. Or to use her to do it.

CHAPTER 6

Victor watched Ada take her croquet stick from the rack and make her way toward the first hoop. Richard, curse him, stepped up right beside her, too close behind her, advising her on how to hit the ball.

Bright woman, she shot him a look that could freeze a man in the jungle. "I've played this before, sir. Move aside."

No doubt about it. Miss Ada Hanniford, late of New York and Baltimore, had spotted Richard's game...and she didn't play it. His half-brother had been eliminated.

She hit her ball and sent it in a straight line to the next hoop.

Victor rejoiced and walked over to queue his ball.

Three days into this charade of a house party, Richard did not dance attendance on Esmerelda Moore. One of their other guests, another school chum of Victor's, Sir James Edgecombe appeared to find Esmerelda delightful and she flirted with him, inviting all his attentions. Richard noticed, but did not indicate he cared. Instead, he hung like a puppy dog on the heels of Ada Hanniford.

Victor rebelled at his brother's advances. Choking on anger at Richard's sexual misconduct, he determined to protect her. Jealous for the first time in his life, he stayed close to Ada and caused her to stifle many a smile. Richard, seeing his game, turned mean and aggressive.

The other twenty-two guests shared sly glances and refrained from public comment. The elders muttered to each other of Richard's behavior. The younger were watchful if discreet, most being friends of his and Richard's from school. One was an old pal of Victor's, George, Lord Pinkhurst now married to an acquaintance of Ezzie and Ada, an American heiress from New York.

Meanwhile, Victor watched over his brother like a sentinel at the gate of hell. Ada was no novice at protecting herself. She played cards or croquet, charades or dice with the cool head of a practiced gambler. She seemed able to predict Richard's approach and his next moves to back her into corners or monopolize her attention. Yet, she turned him aside and escaped him all too easily. Richard caught her in the foil but could not best her.

But Victor found himself in need of her smile, her humor, the roll of her eyes as his brother attempted another invasion of her person. The man was rather insufferable. She restrained herself out of good manners and slid away from him on any occasion as if he had the plague.

Undeterred, however, Richard plowed on.

And Ezzie? Dear woman. Esmerelda Moore, late of New York, and armed with fifty thousand of her daddy's dollars, did not blink an eye. She smiled, she laughed, she conversed, she played cards and whatever else with as much aplomb as Ada. That she was flattered by Edgecombe's attentions suited her. Victor could even say she welcomed that man's regard. To her credit, she showed nary a sign that she was jealous of her friend Ada. She trusted her friend implicitly.

And rightly so.

Amusing to watch, Ada rejected Richard at every turn. His ardent glances, his hand to hers lingering too long, returning to try again. He had set his cap for her. His leading words as he engaged her in conversation in the drawing room, his solicitous attentions to provide her with her shawl for a walk on the veranda, his decision to rise early just to catch her to himself at breakfast. Of course, he didn't get her alone.

Victor was there. He made a point to be.

Truth was, however, she didn't need him to protect her from him.

"Take your shot, dear boy!" Richard waggled a finger at him to hit the ball.

"Give it a proper whack, would you, please, Victor?" Ada asked, her crystal blue gaze meeting his with meaning and laughter. He and she had begun to address each other by their given names that first afternoon after they had all walked along the river. He welcomed the familiarity. She was American and used to such informal address. Richard, he knew, disapproved of such friendly behavior.

But Victor gladly called her Ada. He liked her name, strong as she, fluid and bright. He liked the way her lips formed as she called him by his own name. *Victor*, she'd utter in dulcet tones that struck the harshness from the consonants and brushed his senses with desires he hadn't felt in years.

Victor, do tell me about Shanghai.

Victor, do tell me about your business.

Victor, he wished she'd say, *do kiss me*.

"Victor?" She called to him, her eyes sliding to one side to indicate Ezzie next to her and Richard who gloated over a good move of his ball down the grassy lane.

He understood her. Implicitly. Her dislike of his brother's attentions. Her concern for her friend. Her affinity—yes, he'd say it—her appreciation of *him*.

He'd never been any woman's Sir Galahad. But hers, he was happy to be. Long a man of athletic inclinations, from riding to cricket to tennis, Victor was happy to show up his brother. Taking overlong to examine the angles, to mentally measure the distances by which to knock his brother out of the running, he crouched and bent and pondered.

"Good god, dear boy!" Richard cried, his hand to his hip. His brother had even dressed for the game. Wishing to impress Ada, he looked foppish in white trousers, white shirt and yellow sweater. "Get on with it. If you're about to pound my ball, please do it."

Victor glared at him. In his words stood risqué meanings. So be it. *Let me show you,* dear boy, *you must not pursue a lady who finds you unprincipled.*

He struck it straight and hard. And rejoiced at how far it traveled and so true, add to that.

"I say, Cole," his friend George Pinkhurst approached and hit him on the shoulder. They'd been at Eton together and Pinkie had gone on to inherit his father's barony. Married to the American Priscilla van de Putte a few years ago, he seemed more dour than he had as a youth, as if he'd had his wings clipped. Marriage had soured Victor on connubial bliss so he was not surprised at George's distaste for it.

"You're doing well at that bloody boring game."

"Thanks," he said as Ezzie came round to deliver her own ball. Edgecombe followed her. "Come to advise me on my form?"

"I think you need me." Pinkie took a drink of his whisky.

"How so?"

"I've watched this little farce for days." George waggled a finger at Ada and Richard.

Victor's indignation at his brother got the better of his wish to remain silent. "She's not about to let Ridgemont win."

"And you?" Pinkie took another swig. "Will you let him?"

Victor let out a breath. If Pinkie detected his interest, others would. His mother, given her dislike of American heiresses in general, would be the worst. That set his teeth on edge.

Pinkie drained his glass. "Demmed nuisance these country parties." He squinted as he surveyed the guests to this illustrious gathering. "Forced fun."

Lord George Pinkhurst of Selkirk had always been a regular man, a good friend to any and all, full of fun, but balanced, and good looking with his tow-headed crop of thick hair and lean athletic build. Pinkie had often confided that one day he had to marry—and he'd do it for money. His two-thousand-five-hundred a year income was eaten by taxes and a leaky roof over the family manor. He needed a fortune and he'd found one. But now Pinkie was the worse for wear, the sparkle in his eyes gone, his jaw going to jowls and his belly to pot at the young age of thirty-one.

Victor lowered his head, the two of them downcast as mourners at a gravesite. "What's wrong?"

"I hate my days." Pinkie nodded toward the rose bushes where stood his wife.

The hopelessness he heard in his friend's words drove a spike through his heart. Victor knew too painfully what a burden a bad marriage was. Wishing he was wrong, he tried another track. "Are you well?"

"About to have a child. So, yes. Well enough for *that*."

Victor took in the sight of the man's wife. The American heiress stood laughing with his mother, the duchess. Lady Pinkhurst had brilliant red hair and a hearty chuckle, care-free, a bit too much so. "Congratulations. That's good news."

His friend licked his lips. "My mother thinks so."

"Victor!" Richard called to him. "We've gone round again. Come take your turn!"

Two hands on her hips, Ada turned to glare at Victor. He knew it as a signal for help.

"You're in trouble, old man," Pinkie said with a sad laugh. "I remember that look."

Had Pinkie ever been in love with Ada? "How's that?"

"I courted her sister, Lily. Married Seton, she did. Before I could do anything to advance my cause. Good woman, Lily. This one seems to be turning out well, too."

"Wasn't she...*well*...before?" Victor could not imagine Ada being anything other than her stalwart self.

"She had a wild streak. They had a few incidents with her, but nothing to totally ruin her. You know what I mean."

Victor nodded, appreciating the fact that Ada had sewn her oats and was now the strong woman he admired. *So unlike Alicia.*

"I need another. Join me?" Pinkie turned toward the footman who held a tray of whiskies for the men.

"Victor?" Richard grew peeved.

"In a minute!" he called and pressed his lips together in apology to Ada. She could, for a few minutes, take care of herself.

She rolled her eyes.

"She's as lovely as her sister. I wouldn't, if I were you, let her get away."

"Oh, I'm not—"

Pinkie chuckled and put up a palm. "Please! I've had two of these. But I can still see clearly, Cole. She's got guts. No guile. Not in any way like Alicia."

None who knew him mentioned his late unmourned wife. "I see that." *Have from the first moment I met her.*

Pinkie snorted. "Do you? What else might you see? The way Ada looks at him? Then you? Really, old man. Or should I call you 'dear boy' like he does? He's the boy. To play Ezzie

Moore for a fool like this? Everyone knows he was to ask for her. And she takes his betrayal well, albeit with Edgecombe's unwitting assistance. Still. Ezzie is a really sweet woman. Got a raw mouth on her and I hope to God that she uses it to give your brother the comeuppance he deserves. In public, would be best."

Victor took in the crowd on the lawn. A few nodded toward Richard attempting to put his arms around Ada to waylay her. Anger buzzed inside him like a hive of bees. "He wants her."

"Will you stand for it?"

"I'm not interested in marriage."

His friend blew air through his lips. "Hell with you then! Let him have her. One more woman he ruins. Then good Ada Hanniford will be fit for no one, not a marquess—and certainly not you."

❧

Ada shrugged off Richard's embrace. "Sir. Do stop this. I am not to be mauled."

"Oh, come now, Ada."

She dropped her mallet...upon his toes.

He yelped and hopped on one foot.

"Apply whisky to that," she told him as she felt rather than saw those in the garden notice his pain. Pleased at her ploy, she picked up her skirts and marched through the rose bower toward the house.

Arrogant, insufferable, rude, insolent cuss. Were there enough names to call him? His unwanted attentions were a disgrace.

Ezzie, sweet soul, did not bat an eyelash. *Thank heavens for Edgecombe.*

"Ada!"

She whirled at the sound of Victor's voice.

Tears sprang to her eyes and dribbled down her cheeks. She dashed them away. Why was she a watering pot now? And why would *he* come to her? He was no more interested in her than a monk.

"Wait! Wait!" He ran up to her and took her elbow. "Are you...*Oh, god.* You're crying. I'll kill him!"

She gulped and swung away in a swish of pink linen and white ribbons. "Hog tie him."

He circled an arm around her waist and carried her two steps into the hollow of the maze. The thick fragrances of red and white roses swam through her head as he sank one hand to her nape and pulled her flush against him. "Darling Ada. I'll see to him."

"Don't call attention to him. It's bad enough."

"He needs rebuke."

The comfort of his embrace washed over her like a wave. She was a glutton for affection from someone she lo... "Please don't."

He held her gently, unraveling all her anger. Nestling into his body, she tucked her head under his chin and let him stroke her back. Let herself ponder the reasons why she should enjoy this. Him. When she didn't allow any man that liberty.

"Did he accost you?" he asked, his dark voice a hushed caress. He raised her chin. "You must tell me. I am for you, honestly I am."

Fear made her shiver. "I wouldn't tell you if he did. I'd have to marry him! And I won't. I *will not*. He makes a spectacle of his interest in me. While I have none in him. None. And I would never shame Ezzie."

"I know." He thumbed away one of her tears. "I trust you, whereas I am acquainted with my brother who merits no trust at all."

She bit her quivering lower lip, remaining close to absorb every iota of his tenderness. "Thank you. But we must not stand here like this. If your brother raises questions about my behavior, this will sound an alarm. I'll not have it."

He knit his brows, stepped backward and shook his head. "As much as one can apologize for another, I do for him. You do not deserve this."

"Then leave me," she beseeched him and nodded toward the path to one side that would lead him back to the party. "Take that route."

His face fell and he raised his arms in a helpless gesture. "If I must."

"You are a good man," she had to say it.

He swallowed hard and took one of her hands to kiss the back. "And you are a noble woman."

Gratitude for his kindnesses ran through her. "I'm honored you think me so."

His turquoise eyes flashed with need and regret. "Would that I could honor you more."

She stared at him. Paralyzed with a ray of hope he might care for her, she wrestled with a hot desire.

He reached for her and she went like one mesmerized into his arms. Pressed to the iron contours of his marvelous body, she saw on his face a ferocity, an affection that she'd never glimpsed on the face of any other man. "Would that I could offer for you, darling."

The shock of his words shot to her heart.

But the shock of his lips on her own blasted all else from her world. She reeled and clung to him, his lips—lush and hot —his tongue—probing and sweet—his hand, a rough brand upon her spine as he crushed her closer.

She moaned, his need her own. This was what she'd wanted. He was who she'd sought in countless ballrooms, endless gardens.

He broke away like lightning. Staring at her, steadying her on her feet, he grew solemn. "I'm sorry. I—"

But she wasn't done. She leaned against him, hand to his chest, up on her toes, greedy for more of him. "Victor," she pleaded, her voice hoarse with discovery, "kiss me again."

Groaning, he clamped her close and swung her further back into the shelter of the roses. He cupped her face with both hands and kissed her with the smoldering passion that their first kiss briefly defined. Kissed her again with a soft mold of her lips and a tender sigh. "Ada," he called to her between sweet little pecks, "Ada, Ada, I've wanted to do this since that first afternoon."

She ran her fingers up into his hair and anchored him so that she might kiss him with all the ardor he aroused in her. And when at last, she tore her mouth from his, she saw in his smoldering dark eyes that in passion, Victor Cole was a delectable rogue. So unlike the cool creature who could lure her with a look, or the sweet man who apologized with humor. He was a danger to her impetuous soul. She could kiss him forever and never tire. Allow him all sorts of freedoms and live to pay dearly for each one, then call the trespasses her bliss.

She needed air. And sanity. Others were too near. Ruin too close.

She pushed away.

"I must go," she told him, pushing curls of hair up into her pins, straightening her lace fichu and brushing at her skirt.

But when she turned, there stood Ezzie and Edgecombe.

Both gaped and chuckled.

Ada stepped backward and Victor's hands were upon her shoulders. "How long—?"

"It doesn't matter," said Sir James Edgecombe with a sparkle in his forest green eyes.

"We won't tell," Ezzie said with a wink at Ada.

Grateful to her friend, embarrassed at being caught, fitful that she craved more kisses from Victor and would never have them, Ada growled, grabbed up her skirts and ran.

CHAPTER 7

"Why won't you talk to me about him?"

Ada looked at her pretty friend, so glorious in her formal finery of pearls to complement her spring green organza gown and beguiling blush. She had avoided Ezzie for the past day and a half, unwilling to confess the madness that had overcome her for Lord Victor Cole. She would not here, either, this last night of this house party.

Ezzie and she stood to one side in Brentwood Hall's grand dining room. The guests swirled around them as the band played the second waltz. In this crowd, Ada would smile and nod, but she would not have a serious discussion about her shocking need to kiss a man she'd met only days ago. "There is nothing to say, Ezzie."

"You were kissing!" Ezzie insisted.

And that's all there will ever be between us.

"Ade, you don't kiss just anyone. You never have!"

Servants had cleared the furniture to make way for the guests the duke and duchess had invited to attend their annual summer ball. The village squire, the vicar and his wife, the lords and ladies from nearby estates came and swelled the numbers of the house guests to more than eighty for this event.

Tearing her gaze from the alluring sight of Victor in black swallowtail and crystal white cravat waltzing past her with his mother in his arms, Ada put on a bright smile. "Whereas you could be more eloquent about your blossoming relationship with Sir James Edgecombe."

"Hmm," she said with a little cat-that-ate-the-cream shiver. "I could, couldn't I? He has become my friend."

"More than, if you found your way to the rose bower with him."

"Ha!" Ezzie raised her fan and fluttered it at her bosom. "As if you yourself have nothing to say for that location!"

Incoherent with fright that her seclusion with Victor would result in gossip and ridicule, especially for her family, Ada had resisted commenting on the subject of her scintillating exploration of Victor's ability to kiss.

Ezzie sighed. Her fan continued to stir up a breeze. "I shall dance with James, should he ask."

So it was 'James', was it? Serve Richard right to lose Ezzie. At his own party. "Good manners to do so."

"More than once, too. Just think, this elaborate house party for nothing."

Ada caught a glimpse of Victor. *Not for nothing, this party. For the knowledge that there is a man in this world I could treasure, I should be grateful.*

"My mother will be pleased. Not a marquess in my pocket, but an earl will do."

Ada was confused. "I thought we addressed him as 'Sir' James Edgecombe?"

"We did. Rightly so. Did you know he is the heir to an earldom?"

"Is he?" she asked, overjoyed for her friend who was driven by her parents to marry up.

"I forget his uncle's exact title. It doesn't matter."

"Doesn't—?" Ada put a hand to her throat. "Fabulous. You don't care. Imagine that. This means, my dear, you are smitten!"

"Let us not be hasty. James might *not* be smitten."

"Pish-tosh. I'd say that's the word I like for his expression when he looks at you."

"Hmmm. I would agree." Ezzie giggled and lifted her fan to be discreet about it. "I'm enchanted."

They both laughed.

Ezzie met Ada's eyes and led her to consider Richard not far from them talking with Madame Chaumont. "I am shocked that your *Madame* does not appear to like him. I thought she tried to charm every eligible creature."

Ada turned to one side to lower her voice. "I'm shocked too. But I fear something is not right with her. And yes, more than her disinterest in an eligible man. I asked her the other day if she's ill, but she denied it."

"Now that you mention it, she is...subdued."

And ashen. "When I return home, I'll tell my step-mother to talk with her. She'll confide in Liv. Everyone does."

"You-know-who hasn't come near me, you realize," Ezzie said, snapping together the sticks of her ivory fan in her gloved hands. "He won't ask for my hand."

Ada reached for her wrist and squeezed in sympathy. "Think of it as a blessing."

"That's the word I heard Victor say to him this morning."

"What? What do you mean?"

"I was passing the library and the door was ajar. After my breakfast, I was on my way to my room and I heard them arguing."

Ada hadn't seen either Victor or Richard at breakfast or when she'd taken Vivienne and Deirdre to practice their archery skills. This afternoon, she'd been relieved she hadn't seen them. Now she worried that Victor and Richard might have argued and she was the cause. "What about?"

"I don't recall the exact words, but they fought over money. Victor refuses to give his brother a loan. Richard resents it."

Good for Victor.

"Then they argued about me. I was terrible to listen but I had to."

Ada leaned closer. "What did they say?"

"Victor took up for me. Says I am a gem and Richard is an...ahem...his exact word is...ass."

Ada grinned. "I have it on good authority Victor likes that word."

"Apt," Ezzie said with a triumphant flutter of her fan.

"Just so."

The waltz ended. The dancers paused, moved to the edge of the chalked floor and dispersed to their chaperones or to find new partners.

Would Victor dance again? As one of the hosts, he should. But whom would he choose? She followed his movements with narrowed eyes...but he disappeared in the throng.

"Did you know that Victor returns to Shanghai before Christmas?"

Ada's mouth dropped open.

"So you didn't." Ezzie's fan went up and she put it to use. "I'm sorry. I thought you needed to know."

I do. Did. Don't. Shouldn't care. "How did you learn that?"

"The argument."

"I see," she said, her heart so heavy she wanted to dissolve into the parquet floorboards. Her gaze drifted to the man in question. He bowed to his mother and put her hand in Richard's.

"He thinks he must go despite the winter weather."

"That's a shame," she said as he strode toward her, his appealing turquoise eyes fixed on her like a magnet.

Chaumont appeared at their sides. "I shall sit. Pardon me, but I must. *Mademoiselle* Moore, will you join me?" she asked as Victor stood before them and bowed.

But Sir James Edgecombe appeared at Victor's side, eager as a schoolboy, his attention on Ezzie.

"May I have this dance?" Victor asked Ada.

Edgecombe did the same for Ezzie.

Ada gave her hand to Victor.

As he led her out, his strong fingers drawing her forward, he said, "I've not waltzed in many years, you'll forgive my awkwardness if I step on your toes, Ada."

"I saw you with your mother, sir," she managed, "and I think you do quite well."

They faced each other while the orchestra chose their next piece.

"You look magnificent in that red gown." She barely got out her thanks when he said, "How are you? What did you do today? Aside from play with my girls."

"I took a walk along the river."

"I thought you might." He flowed closer, his voice lower, more intimate. "I wanted to search for you, join you there but I...didn't."

Hurt, insulted that he hadn't, she had to stun him. "When do you return to Shanghai?"

He blinked. "I planned originally to return next spring."

"But now?"

He winced. "I talk of late autumn."

"Isn't it dangerous to travel in winter storms?" Yes, she was angry, sad. She had come to care for him and he was leaving England. *Why had she assumed he was here to stay?* Foolish.

The orchestra began another Viennese waltz, a sweeping Strauss she adored.

He drew her hand in his, his other around her waist, his heat a soothing balm to her sorrow. "How do you know?"

"Does it matter?"

"No." He locked his remarkable blue-green eyes on hers. "I should have told you. My intention was never to remain, but to return."

She fumed. "It doesn't matter."

"It does. I should have told you."

"Ezzie overheard you arguing with your brother." Did she sound as childish, as petulant as she felt? *Oh, the disgrace of it.* Tears stung her eyes and she wanted to yell at him like a fish-wife for leaving her. *Why must you live so far away?*

The music began and he stepped into first position with her. "Oh, darling, don't cry. I'll explain. I— Hell. We're in the soup now. Dance with me."

She gulped back the urge to sob because the warmth of his embrace was too cool to match the flames inside her. His strength compelled her to move with him, but the inches, the chasm between them grew wider as her heart rebelled against his future loss.

The rigors of the waltz demanded her attention. She'd always loved to dance but somehow she'd never been any good at it. Clumsy, out of rhythm, she hated that she might not match him. To spite him, she bit off her words. "I'll never waltz again."

"Ada, please."

She met his gaze, appalled to see tears cloud his marvelous eyes.

"Finish this. Then we'll talk."

Compelled by propriety to stay on the floor, she flowed with him. "*Then* I'm going to kick you in the shins."

He barked in laughter. "And I'm going to kiss you again."

"Not if you're leaving England for Shanghai, you're not."

"Ada, sweetheart. What if I kiss you and you persuade me to remain until the spring?"

"I won't let you," she told him. "And I won't persuade you." *You'll still leave and I won't go with you.*

His gaze, searing and soothing to her pride, caressed her lips. "I don't believe you."

As the music swelled, they went into the chase and any discussion grew impossible. Her heartbeat picked up a tempo of excitement and pain. He was leaving. Going so very far. She'd never see him again. And there was no point to crave his kisses or his embrace. No future for her fascination with him. No hope she might spend lazy afternoons in rose bowers kissing his delectable lips and reclining in his comforting arms.

Thank god the music died.

He led her back to Chaumont who sat talking with his mother, the duchess.

"Mama, Madame Chaumont," he said to them, his grip firmly on Ada's hand, "forgive me if I leave you for a few minutes. Miss Hanniford and I must talk. In private. I hope you will permit me?" He pointedly looked at the Frenchwoman.

"For a moment, only, *Monsieur* Cole."

The duchess smiled at Ada with such compassion, she feared the woman knew what was amiss between her son and her. How, why, Ada had not the time to conjure. She was near to breaking with sorrow and she had to run free of Victor and his loss.

"Here," he said and led her along the far wall to the doorway to the foyer. "No one sees us leaving. Come now. The library."

He hurried her along in the lead, his hand holding hers. At the doors to the library, he flung one wide and drew her in behind him. Shutting the door, he still held her hand and put it to his firm cheek.

She shouldn't be here at all. There was no point. But his caresses, his kisses? Oh, she yearned for them like flowers need sun.

"I've wanted to kiss you all evening." He brushed his mouth on hers. Hot, sweet, smelling of spirits, his lips were irresistible.

At his confession, she gasped and wound her arms around his broad shoulders.

He hauled her against him, the planes of his body cupping the curves of her own in a desire she'd felt in every muscle every nerve of her body. She kissed him, her lips full on his, wild and wanton.

She flung back her head and pushed away. This must end. "I don't want you. I don't want this."

He pressed against her. Two hands to the shelves behind her, he blocked her retreat and leaned down. His gaze, his breath, his mouth overwhelming her with his seductive intent, he gave her a lazy grin. "I say you do. I say you want me as much as I want you."

He cupped her shoulders and brought her up so that he kissed her, took the breath from her body, the reason from her mind. He broke their hold with a gasp. "I've told myself for days I must not have you. That you were fire to my ice. Salt to my wounds. But you are salve to them. Lovely and witty and strong, but so tender. I want you. And I'm a mad man growling with delight that my brother will not have you. Not have you *ever*. Because you are so wise. You don't want him. You want me. And do not deny it."

"I wish I could." She kissed him once more. "I can't explain my sudden attraction except...except for your honor and your care of your family." She let the tears fall then, cascading silently down her cheeks. She quivered as she stared at him.

Sweet man. Daring, too. She cupped his jaw and peered into those unusual eyes that would haunt her years after she abandoned him tonight. "That's more than enough for some. Even for many who've known someone they care for mere days."

"Grant me days more for us to get to know each other."

"No."

"Darling," he whispered and put his lips to the hollow beneath her ear. "I only said I'd return to China in the fall because I wanted you so desperately after yesterday in the garden—"

"Forget that."

"No!" He grasped her chin, lifted her face for his searing kiss. "No. I can't. And you haven't either. I feared yesterday that I could care for you so much that I'd lose myself..."

She sank backward to the shelves. This was a deeper tenderness—a wound—in him she had not glimpsed. What was it? His wife? "I would never hurt you."

He kissed her again, a rousing claim of lips and tongue and breath. "God, yes, I know that."

She put a hand to his chest to keep him a safer distance. "I don't know what you're telling me."

"I planned never to care for another woman." He squeezed shut his eyes. "I chose quickly. Poorly. That kind of hell lives with you. I told Richard I'd go abroad sooner because I thought to finish my business here and travel far from you. I warned myself not to go near you tonight or ever after. But you draw me. You smile or you frown and I am drawn."

"Stop please."

"I wanted you to have a good man to pursue you. A young man with no failures that shrouded him."

She hugged him, sad that he'd criticize himself. "You are a good man, a young man."

He laughed as if to deny that. Then he ran his fingers along her temple to her chin. "Old. Jaded, but still. I can't ignore you or how you illuminate any room, any conversation. You are quite the most refreshing young woman. I'd like to come to London, take you riding in my landau and meet your family. Say you will receive me."

At the mention of her family, she sobered. This was the crux of her problem, her conflict with his proposal to court her. Her joy in her growing extended family—from her sister Lily and her husband and their two sons, to her cousin Marianne in Paris and her husband Remy and son, to her brother Pierce, and her father and his new wife Liv with her daughter Camille and their new son and another baby due in September—she loved them all. And for years, bitter years, she'd been alone, denied the comfort of their company. The hollow ache she'd abhorred—the one she felt all those years away from them when they lived in Baltimore and Texas and she'd been cloistered in Connecticut—rose up like a spectre to haunt her.

She shook her head. "No."

Stunned, Victor cocked his head. "What?"

"I cannot receive you." She caught back scalding tears. "Do not call."

All light left his face.

She had shattered him.

"If you've heard rumors of my wife—"

"No, I...it's nothing to do with her. It's me." She seized a breath. "I love my family. They are quite wonderful. And I'd never dream to leave them to travel to the other end of the world. Not in the autumn. Not..."

"Even in the spring?"

"No. I—I'm sorry. I cannot. As you could not move beyond your own challenge, this is mine."

She left him, headed for the door, grateful he didn't waylay her. But there, she paused. "I have a favor to ask."

"Anything."

Against her better judgment, she faced him and he slowly turned toward her. "I will leave in the morning. Chaumont comes too, of course. Ezzie may come with me."

"Where?"

"London. We're going to my family. Ezzie likes mine, prefers it to her own."

"I'm sorry, Ada."

"I'm fairly certain Ezzie will leave with me, but in case she doesn't, protect her please."

Surprise etched his brows. "Why wouldn't she go?"

"Oh, Victor. She wants Richard. Or she thinks she does." She waved a hand. "Her mother for years has pushed her toward getting a husband and Ezzie thinks she's incapable of finding another beau."

"But she has. Edgecombe has a very reputable character."

"I've not met him before but nonetheless, I would agree with you."

He stepped closer. "Right you are to leave."

Against all logic, she wished she could stay, become his. His to embrace, his to kiss, his to treasure.

"I will miss you, Ada."

That tested her will to remain. But fear prevailed. "Goodbye, Victor. I will remember you with fondness. You possess every quality of a man I could adore."

CHAPTER 8

London, England

"You've been most kind, sir." Ada thanked the porter for hailing a cab outside the railway station. He'd hauled all her trunks and Chaumont's too on his lorry from the tracks to the street.

"Number One-ten Piccadilly," she told the driver. She'd given Chaumont anxious moments on the train from Bath. A right mess, snorting at an insult at Richard's behavior and aflame with Victor's ardent declarations, she'd brooded all the way back to London.

It had been a bittersweet morning.

She'd risen earlier than her usual seven, but that was not early enough to avoid seeing Victor as she finished her breakfast.

As he walked toward her, she made to rise and escape. She hated arguing.

"Please," he said with a hand up. Dressed in his tweeds, his auburn curls windblown, he looked as if he'd been out walking. In truth, he appeared as sad as she, what with his bleary eyes and somber tone. "Do finish."

"I am," she said but kept her seat.

He seized her hand and pressed it to his waistcoat. Beneath the heavy wool, his heart thumped madly. "I'm coming to London. I will call."

She opened her mouth, ready to refuse him when his mother appeared.

"No, please, Miss Hanniford. Do not rise." From her casual cotton day gown and simply styled hair, she'd dressed quickly. Most women of her rank and age would break their fast in their rooms on trays. Yet here was the Duchess of Brentwood so early in her own dining room—and noting with her keen gaze how her son released her hand. "I've come to say a few words and tell you how I've enjoyed your company."

Ada could not in good manners express her surprise at the lady's compliment. She'd had the distinct impression that the duchess did not care for Ezzie or her or any Americans at all. "Thank you, Your Grace."

The duchess took her place at the end of the table.

The butler hovered, looking decidedly uneasy at this abnormal appearance of his mistress. Butlers— all staff, it was said—knew everything that went on in a household. This one was as discreet as any. Indeed it was what he was paid for. And so dutiful as he was, he ignored them all and asked his mistress, "Ma'am, what may I serve you?"

"Coffee, Fawkes. I understand, Miss Hanniford, from Victor that you must leave us early. A shame, that. But I do understand your reasoning."

Do you? Ada checked Victor's expression, but she read only sadness there. What had he told his mother?

"I regret my older son's actions and hope you will not think poorly of us all."

Ada fingered her coffee cup. "I do not, Your Grace."

"I've told my husband about you and Richard's action. His Grace sends his apologies for any challenges while you visited."

"That's kind of him."

"And he wishes that he could tell you himself. But his illness, you see, prevents that. So we will hope the future will bring us together again when all of us are brighter and more fit."

"Yes, thank you. I did enjoy myself and I'm pleased I've had this opportunity to tell you so in person. I regret I must leave early, but it's best."

"Of course, it is," the lady said.

Ada rose and gave a small curtsy.

"Do return to us someday soon."

Ada expressed her thanks, but could not in good conscience accept that last invitation. With a parting glance at Victor, Ada adjourned to her rooms. With her luggage locked and ready for the footmen to take downstairs, she emerged from her own rooms and knocked on Ezzie's door.

Ezzie, up before her usual mid-morning time, sat on the *chaise longue* in a pink flowered dressing gown. The maid whom the duchess had assigned to Ezzie dipped in homage.

"Thank you, Mary. I appreciate your help this morning," Ezzie told her. With that, the girl curtsied and left them to talk privately.

"I will miss you," Ezzie said with a forlorn look as she sat forward. "I don't know how well I can carry this off without you."

"You can," Ada insisted and bent to kiss her cheek. "It's only one more day. But I cannot bear to stay. And you will do well here. Sir James really likes you. I see it. You feel it, too."

"I don't have him yet," Ezzie pointed out. "If you stay, I'll have you to help me negotiate my dowry. With anyone!"

Refusing to fault Ezzie for using that to keep her here,

Ada knew Richard would not stop at his attempted seduction of her. "If I stay, I will not be happy. Nor will you. Edgecombe is the man who is worthy of you, Ez."

Nothing for it. Ezzie had to learn to navigate society and men by herself. Either as a marchioness or a countess, Ezzie would feel the pressures as well as the freedom of her position.

In the end, Ezzie had agreed, hugged Ada to her chest and with tears in her eyes, bid her safe journey.

The hansom cab idled at the broad front steps of the London residence of Killian Hanniford. Chaumont fished in her reticule for money to pay the man as Ada stepped out to the sidewalk. She inhaled the marvelous air. So close to Hyde Park, the breezes carried fragrances of trees and grasses. London in the springtime, especially in the early afternoon, was more than pleasant. The winter snows and rains cleansed unhealthy aromas wafting from the Thames. So early in the day, it was even possible to see clearly. The fog and the danger of it as dusk fell changed the atmosphere of the town from the Palladian bustling beauty of it at noon to a shrouded nightmare in the dark.

She climbed the steps and let the knocker fall. Chaumont joined her and Ada took the opportunity to encourage the lady to go to her room straight away and rest. Last year, Chaumont who had initially rented her own little house not far away, gave it up as inflation ate at her income. Ada's father and step-mother invited her to live with them in their fashionable Piccadilly home. She'd accepted and brought her own maid with her.

"I will, Miss. I promise you," Chaumont said. "I am quite exhausted from the morning's travel."

Concerned that the butler had not yet answered the door, Ada lifted the knocker again and let it fall.

Foster pulled it open, surprise widening his droopy eyes. "Miss Ada?"

"Yes. I'm a day early."

"Welcome home. *Madame* Chaumont, *bonjour*. I'm sure your arrival will be welcome."

Ada stepped into the sanctuary of her father and step-mother's home, handing over her reticule and discarding her cape and gloves. "Who's at home? My step-mother? Is Papa here?"

"No, Mister Hanniford is at his office in the City. But your mother takes her luncheon in the dining room with your sister, Her Grace, and your cousin, *Madame la Princesse*. If you'd like to join them—?"

"I would. I will." Off she went, up the stairs toward the first floor and the comfort of those she loved. "No need to announce me, Foster. Do go to your tasks, please. I'll surprise them!"

She flung open the double doors and chuckled at the three women who gaped at her in surprise. "My favorite ladies!"

Each of them rose and each, in varying stages of pregnancy, with some difficulty. Her step-mother, Olivia was a tall lady with fiery red hair and dark chocolate eyes. Her older sister, Lily, the duchess of Seton, beamed at her with crystal blue eyes so like Ada's. Her beautiful blonde cousin Marianne, *duchesse de* Remy and *princesse* d'Aumale, rushed to her, hands out to bring her into their fold.

Hugging each in turn, Ada hung back to consider each of their figures. "I see all of you are doing your duty and remaining disturbingly healthy."

Lily lifted a shoulder. "We're increasing the family as quickly as we can."

"We speak of you, dear girl," said Marianne with a flutter

of her long pale lashes, "and your need to find a man and join us in our healthy endeavors."

At that comment Ada rolled her eyes. But she kissed and hugged each one in turn.

"Do sit down, dearest," said her step-mother Liv with a chuckle, "and we can bore you with details which will make you reconsider any man's proposal of marriage."

"You'll have a difficult time selling me on the idea that all of you are unhappy." She took at chair at the table and one of the footmen appeared with a pitcher of iced water and began to assemble china and cutlery in front of her. He draped a napkin in her lap and poured for her. "Now do recount all the details I've missed."

If her relatives wished to dissuade her from marriage and procreation, they did a poor job of it. All of them naturally slender, they had gained weight. Liv looked as though she'd gained the most, but she was farthest along at six months. Lily had recently learned she was pregnant with her third child and with two sons, she and Julian wished for a daughter. Marianne was expecting her second child with her husband the sculptor, the *duc de* Remy, in November. Ada, as had often been the case for many years, felt as if she did not belong to this group. How many times had she gone to a party as she had this past week, and wished to meet a man she could love? Marry. One who talked with intelligence, listened with eagerness, danced with grace and wanted only her.

She sat, polite and eager for their news, but jealous of their good fortune. Sinking deeper into her sadness about her conflict over Victor Cole, she put a bright face on it.

"What's wrong?" asked Lily, her clear blue eyes intent on her.

"You're not yourself," said Marianne with a toss of her platinum curls.

"Didn't they treat you well at Brentwood?" her step-mother Liv asked, concern making her frown.

"No, they were courteous," she tried to brush it off and paid attention to her cutlet of veal. "It was amusing."

"Amusing? Oh, my dear, that's all?"

"Lovely people, lovely manor, really quite nice."

Liv looked skeptical. "And Ezzie? She's not with you? Did Ridgemont ask for her hand?"

Ada shook her head. "Her parents didn't arrive. Made weak excuses. It was not right. Ezzie was embarrassed."

"Of course she would be." Liv did not care for Ezzie's mother who publicly ridiculed the very English society she wished to become part of. The result was that the English critiqued Mrs. Moore as an aggressive American mother. "Dear girl. She deserves better."

"She does indeed," added Marianne. Ada's cousin lived in Paris and the Loire Valley with her husband but they visited back and forth many times a year. They were an open family, sharing news, friends and aspirations. Marianne liked Ezzie best of all Ada's American friends and former schoolmates. "Ezzie's mother needs a good dose of her own medicine. Sour pills."

"Is that why Ridgemont didn't step up?" Lily's face grew pink. Her sister had harsh words for those who didn't do right by others in manners, word or deed. As one of the first American heiresses to marry into the aristocracy, Lily had suffered many snubs. Including from her own mother-in-law. But Lily remembered the pain. "Because her parents did not arrive?"

"Perhaps. I'm not certain." Ada sagged in her chair. She could allow her family to let the blame lay at the feet of Ezzie's parents, but that would be unfair to everyone. Sighing, she recounted the whole bloody story of the weekend. Richard's betrayal of Ezzie, Sir John Edgecombe's attentiveness. "But other things happened. It was not pretty."

Lily sniffed. "Ah, I detect a tall tale here. Tell us who Richard takes up with instead." Lily had met Ridgemont on numerous occasions and did not care for him. Ada could bet Lily knew details about his recent dalliance with Dundalk's wife.

When Ada only stared back, Lily rose from her chair and came to put her arms around her shoulders and kiss her on the crown of her head. "Oh, sweetheart. He liked you, didn't he?"

Before Ada knew it, Liv had stuffed a handkerchief in her fingers and told her to "go ahead and cry, if you like. You're home now."

Both women retuned to their chairs while Ada stifled her tears.

But Marianne reached across to touch her arm and said, "Look at me. Tell us how you managed this Ridgemont."

"I was discreet. I promise you I was." Marianne and Lily could recall a few wild times when she'd not been and she had learned her lessons in bitter, frightening fashion.

"We believe you," Marianne said.

"It could have been worse," she began, hating to admit what occurred.

"Go on," Liv said.

Ada took a steadying breath. "Richard has a younger brother who arrived home from Shanghai with his two daughters and...and he was helpful to me."

Silence filled the room.

"Lord Victor Cole," Liv said and resumed her chair. She drummed her fingers on the tabletop. "I met him many years ago. His wife too. Passed away a few years ago in China of cholera, I think it was. A lovely man. Did you like him?"

"I did."

"And he...did what?" Liv asked.

She met her step-mother's level gaze and told her what a

gentleman he'd been. "Standing between me and the possibility that...well, that his brother might go beyond the bounds of propriety." She folded the handkerchief into tiny pleats. "He was wonderful. Really."

"So," a booming bass voice inquired from the doorway, "I needn't fill my rifle and shoot either man?"

"No, sir," she told her father and rushed from her chair to his open arms. "Please don't, Papa."

◈

The relief that she enjoyed that afternoon was as refreshing as swimming in a cool, clear lake. Her father, assured that no man had physically hurt her or sullied her reputation, warned her never to tolerate the presence of Richard Cole again. "He may inherit a dukedom but he needs to acquire the nobility of character to accompany the name."

He joined the ladies for the next few minutes, then disappeared to his office.

Ada gave herself over to the latest news of babies, children, estates and Remy's new exhibit of his sculptures in a gallery near Hanover Square. The opening was to be day after next in the evening. Afterward, her father and Liv would host a small supper party at the house and Ada welcomed the opportunity to throw herself into the planning of the floral centerpieces. As ever, this was her specialty, what she contributed as solely her expertise. It wasn't much. Her skills at planning landscapes of roses were much better. After all, she'd planned Liv's rose garden at her parents' new Brighton house as well as their kitchen garden. Lily had seen the bountiful results and asked Ada to design her own rose garden at Broadmore, the ducal seat of the Setons in Sussex.

The next morning, Ada rose early to select flowers at the local market. A merchant in Half Moon Street was one of her favorites. He always had the tightest young rosebuds, bushy chrysanthemums and healthy ferns too. Hurrying along, she didn't stop as she made her purchases. But as she turned for her carriage, the hair on the back of her neck stood up. Bewildered, she froze. Then glanced around. She saw no one who seemed to observe her with any singular interest and she brushed away the odd sensation as just that.

At seven, the following evening, the family gathered in the foyer. A fine assembly of all the adult members of the extended Hanniford clan. Her father, robust black-haired Killian Hanniford surveyed them like a king counting his minions. "Handsome and beyond price," he announced and had Foster open the door so that they could climb into the various carriages to take them over to the gallery.

She rode with her brother Pierce and their step-sister, Camille Bereston. Pierce, at thirty-one-years-old, was the spitting image of their father in younger, more athletic form. In his black cutaway and starched-to-a-fare-thee-well shirt, Pierce was a thrilling specimen for any young lady to savor. He sat backward facing her and Camille, exclaiming how he was quite fortunate to escort them both.

"Oh, do be honest, you terrible man," Camille tormented him as she usually did. "You hate 'the duty'." She'd always dubbed his escort services that. Tonight was no different, even though Camille with her strawberry blonde hair and nearly black eyes was a striking woman of eighteen who could glance at a man and make him swoon.

"Look, my little duck, you must learn to take a compliment when it's given to you."

Camille looked no more like a duck than a loaf of bread. In fact, Ada had often heard Liv say her daughter resembled a poppy. With that cloud of vibrant hair and come-hither eyes, the girl had the brusque charm of a *femme fatale*.

But that didn't matter. Camille and Pierce were always

calling each other silly names, taunting and testing the limits of humor...and some other emotion that Ada could not name. Ada shook her head. Mystified why two people who found each other so appealing that they sat together, walked together and often ignored others around them, they tormented each other moment by moment.

Camille picked at the bright white satin collar of her cape and said, "I chose this to look like a queen tonight. I'd like a famous French artist for my own."

"You'll find one," Ada said, blocking a remark by Pierce with a nudge of her shoe to his leg.

"And what of you, hmm?" Pierce said. "Father tells me you had a run-in with illustrious Ridgemont. Bit of an arse, isn't he?"

Recalling the laughing face of Victor Cole over a break-fast table, she shook away how she longed for him and put the proper term to this. "By popular agreement, that word is *ass*."

"Ass, it shall be," Pierce said and they managed to travel to the gallery in some semblance of congeniality.

❧

The champagne bottles were drained. Patrons praised and bought up those art works that Remy had posted available for purchase. The company was charming, discreet and within two hours the gallery grew quiet.

Pierce had disappeared minutes ago. Camille, too. If they'd gone home to Piccadilly early, that left Ada to ride with her parents. Happy to sink into the squabs and let Liv and her father exclaim over this person or that, she longed for her bed.

"This supper party will not be a late one," Liv said and squeezed Ada's hand.

"I see you're both tired," her father said. "I'll shoo them all out the door before midnight."

"Thank you. What happened to Pierce and Camille?"

"Pierce met a gentleman at the gallery whom he knew. Pierce came to me and asked if he might invite the man to dinner. I hope you don't mind we add another."

"Always room for one more," Liv said, stifling a yawn.

Within minutes, they alighted at Piccadilly and filed in the front door in a whirl of coats, and capes, gloves and hats.

"Miss Camille and Mister Hanniford are in the drawing room with their guest," Foster told Liv. "They brought a guest with them. Four of our other guests have arrived."

"I hope Cook is not fretting about the extra man, Foster?"

"No indeed, Ma'am. Mr. Hanniford already apologized for any inconvenience."

The three of them took the stairs up and strolled into the drawing room. "Well, good evening," Ada heard Liv say as she marched forward, hands out. "How wonderful to see you again. Pierce found you? Marvelous."

The man Liv addressed was a tall ginger-headed fellow with a sweet smile on his lips and a bright turquoise twinkle in his eyes. When he turned them toward Ada and it was time for her to welcome him, she killed the urge to kiss him.

"Good evening," he said as he took her hand in greeting and sounded as if they were the very best of friends. "Kind of you to welcome me."

What else can I do? "A surprise to see you here."

He cleared his throat and had the grace to look sheepish. "I have business with your brother."

"I didn't know."

"I didn't intend to take it up so soon, but I must."

"I see." *If you are leaving in a few months, then speed is imperative.* "Where are you staying?"

"I have a house in Hanover Square."

"You don't stay at Brentwood House when in London then?"

"No. I've always enjoyed my privacy." He still held her hand.

She slid it away. "How do you know Pierce?"

"Correspondence. We've written to each other for two years now. Your brother is an expert in design and operation of metropolitan gas and electricity. And I sit on the Shanghai Municipal Council that controls all such utilities in the city."

"You have much in common. How wonderful."

"I think so, yes. It allows me to contribute to the general well being of those who live in the city."

Camille joined them and pelted him with questions about life in a Chinese city. Grateful to her for the diversion, Ada carried on, though she knew not how well. He was here, and she was thrilled being near him but if he came here tonight into her home to rekindle his declarations from the ballroom, she would not have it. She hadn't changed her mind.

Could a woman ever desire a man enough to leave civilization and a host of those she adored? Some did. Could she?

Yet this exciting, desperate, nervous longing she endured for Victor scared her. While others in her family had fallen in love and faced challenges, none had expressed the reluctance she harbored. Was she childish or just skittish? Or meant to become a spinster? And all the while she asked herself those things, she admired this soft-spoken, congenial, achingly attractive man. He'd come to town to conduct his business. Had he also come to see her again? Despite her rejection of him.

The conflict set her nerves ajitter. Yet she managed to smile and comment and speak like an intelligent woman through supper. Thankfully, with ten guests and eight family plus her and Victor, the conversation was lively even though she was paired with him. He was the perfect gentleman and kept the topics light.

Had her train trip home been comfortable?

It had.

How was Madame Chaumont? She had not appeared well for much of his parents' house party.

"She's recuperating from a debilitating cough."

"She's seen a doctor?"

"Yes, he came to call yesterday. He gave her a cough syrup for the pain."

"Do you approve of the syrup?" he asked and when she hesitated, he clarified. "When we talked about remedies the other day, you seemed not to approve of most because of the opium dose."

She paused, her fork mid-air. "I do approve of this particular one. Good of you to remember my assessment of drugs."

"I remember everything you said to me." His turquoise eyes turned dark blue with the heat of his words.

Her mouth watered. *Silly*. Attention on her *blancmange*, she had to change the subject. "Did you bring Vivienne and Deirdre to London too?"

"They stayed at Brentwood. My mother is delighted to have them."

"And they to be with her, I'm certain." She ventured to ask about Ezzie. "And Miss Moore? Did she enjoy herself?"

"She did." He finished his dessert and allowed a footman to serve him coffee. "Sir James is very fond of her. I think they will continue their relationship on more intimate terms. And soon."

"Oh, that's very good news. I hadn't heard from Ezzie today and wondered how she fared."

"From what I saw of them that last day, they are close. I do believe Sir James will ask for her."

Ada put down her fork. "That is superb news."

"My brother saw that Miss Moore seemed well taken care of. He returned to his own home north of London."

"Oh, I wondered if he'd come to London." She had no desire to see him again or fight off his advances.

"You may yet see him. He has a house on Green Park not far from your sister and brother-in-law, the Setons."

That Ada had not known. The knowledge troubled her. Green Park was in easy walking distance from here. If Richard was in London, would he call for her here at her parents' home?

Victor leaned close. "I doubt he'll call. He has been properly dressed down by me as well as my mother and father. He left in a fit. But he deserved every word. He must get on with doing his duty and take care of his reputation better than he has."

She silently agreed. "Can you tell me about your business please? The items you import?"

He told her about the blue and white porcelain popular with Americans. About peonies, which he had his coolies cultivate for export and for extracting oils for perfumes. "We also export ancient Chinese art that many wish to collect. Glazed statues of animals, especially from the eighth century."

His tales sparked her imagination—and she speculated if she might help him grow flowers and choose art to sell. "It sounds like a wonderland of beauty."

At the end of dinner when Lily and Julian declared they must return to their house in Green Park, Victor took that as his signal to depart as well.

Pierce went to his side. "We'll get our coachman to come round and take you home, Cole."

"Kind of you, but no, I will hail a hack."

"No trouble at all," Killian said and told Foster to notify

the coachman he was needed. "Our man grumbles he has little to occupy him."

"In that case, thank you," he said and turned to her. "Miss Hanniford, I wonder if you will come outside for a few minutes to talk with me while I wait?"

She'd be on her own front step and it was perfectly proper, even, from the looks of it, approved by her family. Besides, she needed to talk with him and tell him not to come here again. Not for her.

"Yes. Let's," she agreed while Foster fetched Victor's evening cloak.

"Would you like a shawl, Miss Ada?" Foster would get one if she wished.

"No, thank you, Foster. I won't be long." She walked out onto the small porch.

Victor held out his hand to assist her down the steps. The wind was brisk and she shivered, but for some reason, she thought it not the breeze but that same odd feeling she'd had this morning at the flower mart.

"Can I give you my cape while we talk?" he asked her, his concern lit by the rays from the gas lamps. In the light, his hair shone like a golden halo. The man was much too handsome.

"No." She was careful to stand far enough away that she would not inhale his intriguing cologne or chance to touch him. The wind whipped up her hair and strands of it fell about her cheeks. "Did you really come to the gallery tonight to see Pierce?"

"I did plan to meet with Pierce next month. Planned it before I left Shanghai. But tonight, I went and hoped you would attend."

She lifted her chin. Did she look brave, resolute? "I don't want to see you, Victor."

He tapped his top hat securely on his head. "I should doubt that."

"Don't."

"Well, then." He stepped close to her, so near she could see the blue fire in his eyes. "I cannot stay away. I must learn why."

"You mustn't."

He raised a hand to trace a fingertip over the rise of her bottom lip. "Is there another man you prefer?"

She shivered. "No."

"There is no other woman I prefer."

She gave a sound of helpless appeal. "You shouldn't tell me that. I've no need to know."

"Are you certain?" He looked heart-broken and oh, so appealing.

He sank both hands into the wealth of her chignon, the supple leather of his gloves against her scalp a silken claim. On a groan, he drew her flush to him and put his hard hot mouth to hers. He was at once gentle, deliberate, probing and fierce. She was lost in him, all his to kiss, to persuade. She clutched his cape, pulled him ever so much nearer. He kissed her once more in a lavish claim of her mouth and too soon, too soon, he steadied her on her feet and stepped away.

She gazed at him through hazy desire. Did she love him? Hate him? Need him?

He smiled at her with such assurance that she yearned for the claim of his lips once more. She was going mad.

He laughed up at the stars. "I see you still want to kick me in the shins."

She had to grin. "I do."

"I give you the chance."

She snorted, then looked around to see who walked the streets. "I won't take it."

"Propriety?" he asked with an arch of his expressive brows.

"Society," she answered.

"I assure you I can withstand such a confrontation. My reputation is already tarnished."

"After I kick you, mine would be shattered."

"Nevertheless." He had the audacity to grin at her. "I call for you tomorrow at two in my landau. The top will be down. You will be safe. We ride in the park."

She'd never gone riding in the park with any man, but integrity demanded that she scowl at him. "I won't go to Shanghai."

He nodded once, but no emotion crossed his features. "I heard you at Brentwood."

"I won't go. You cannot seduce me."

He lifted her hand, turned it over and touched the tip of his tongue to the center of her palm. Quivering with the lure of his affection, she melted all the way to her toes. "Miss Ada Hanniford, I dare."

"Oh!" She stomped her foot—and snatched back her hand.

He traced a fingertip over her bottom lip. "Go inside. Sleep well. I will see you at two."

The ebony family coach rounded the corner, two matching grays at the lead.

She would have the last word. "You are aggressive."

He tugged on his gloves. "But principled and earnest. I am a man you could respect. Even if we both suffer from less than perfect reputations, we must discover if we suit. Now go inside. Dream of my lips on yours. As I shall."

CHAPTER 9

T he next morning, she caught her father at his breakfast. Liv, six months pregnant at age forty-one, made it a practice to sleep late and rise at her leisure. Ada's older brother Pierce was probably already out to his offices in the City.

"Ho, ho! Come sit by me." Killian folded his paper and removed his reading glasses. Black Irish Hanniford was a perfect example of his Waterford ancestors whom many said descended from shipwrecked sailors of Spanish Armada cast upon the Irish shores. With ink black hair, a few gray strands and brilliant silver eyes, he was a big man with strength he still possessed at the age of fifty. "I'm glad of the company."

The footman on duty this morning served her coffee and left them alone.

"What did you think of the exhibit last night?" he asked her, folding his hands on the table.

"Remy must be very happy."

"He sold a commission to Lord Oldthorp. It's to be a Venus in honor of his lordship's new wife."

Ada made a face. "If Venus is to be modeled on that lady, she will have a tongue long as the rumors she likes to tell."

"And forked, don't you think?" her father asked with a grunt.

"True to character," she added. "But Remy told me last night that he sold every piece he put up for purchase."

"For a man who needed to do nothing with his life except run his estate, he works harder and grows more famous by the day."

"So does Marianne," she said recalling the contentment she saw in her cousin's face. "I talked with many patrons who wished they'd done a joint exhibition and sale."

"Oil and water, don't you think? Remy now focuses only on creating men and myths in marble while Marianne paints only women and children."

"Remy sees men in crisis. Marianne sees women in tranquility. Two views of humankind. I think an exhibit like that would blend nicely."

"Hmm. And what of our unexpected guest last night?" Her father teased her with a glint in his luminous eyes. "I like Lord Victor Cole."

"Naturally." She took a sip of her coffee. "Everyone does."

"Including you."

Beginning at age twenty, her father had acquired ships, factories, and shares in others' companies. He'd run the Union blockade for one year, saved slaves off a slaver ship in the Caribbean, bought out railroad stocks of train lines going west to California and invested in European businesses. Now he ran an enormous enterprise and was worth a fortune because of his ability to read people. She was certain he understood her every thought. "I do."

"Quite a bit."

She lifted a shoulder. "Papa, I've known him only a few days."

"Is it enough?"

She exhaled. That her father could go to the core of her challenge in the blink of an eye should not surprise her. "No."

"Is that so?" He sat back, his appraisal intimate and unsettling. "How many more days do you need?"

She could play coy with him but that would be unjust—and oh so unnecessary. Besides, she needed his thoughts on another subject. "I don't know. I'll go riding with him in Hyde Park today. I can give you an estimate later, if you like."

He grimaced. "Play me along, do."

She chuckled. "I wouldn't dream of it."

He snorted. "Liv told me last night that Julian wants to invest in any new project Pierce devises. Pierce talks with Lord Victor about possibilities in Shanghai. I suspect we shall see more of Cole for business—and for pleasure."

The very mention of the Chinese city took the wind from her sails. She might as well tell her father the crux of her problem. "Even if I like him, I don't want to leave here, leave you, all of you. How could I?"

He clamped his hand over hers. "Would you really stay here with all of us abiding in the nooks and crannies of all our lives without a grand passion of your own in which to flourish?"

Sobered by his words, she slid her hand away and focused on her plate. She couldn't admit aloud to her youthful yearning for all of them. That would be a pitiful declaration from a twenty-two-year-old woman who'd enjoyed the benefits of education, travel, high society...and yes, fantastic wealth.

She felt his probing gaze upon her.

"Ada, sweetheart, it's natural to be skeptical. Anxious."

"I'm not anxious. I'm almost ill!" she blurted.

And he laughed. "My dear. Don't fret! Love gives you the ability to do many things you never thought possible. Sailing away to exotic lands physically is one of them. Traveling to horizons you never imagined with one you love is quite another delight."

"Oh, you make it sound easy."

"It can be." He tipped his head, regarding her with cool perspective. "Usually so easy, you never notice what's happened to you."

She shivered. "I want to be prudent about...love."

"Do try that. Let me know how it works."

"Oh, Papa." She hoped she didn't sound immature.

"I kid you too much, my dear. I am sorry. I find it so refreshing that you actually enjoy a man."

"Well," she said and rolled a shoulder, "I do enjoy men."

"Yes. I've seen that. Every damn one you've met, truth be told. And they've returned the favor. Except that you don't love them. You only test them."

She pressed her lips together, then nodded. "That was true."

"But we drift far from this prudence you seek in regard to men and marriage. Why do you hold back on your affections for him?"

She stared at him.

"Is it the fact he has children? You'd have his two daughters to raise. You've met them. How would you feel about that?"

"Oh, I love them. You would, too. They're charming little girls and show no signs of whatever discord lay between their parents. I have the example of Camille to prove to me that a step-child can blend in quite well with a family."

"But? What else?"

"I thought I'd fall in love with someone who had never been married. That I'd be his first bride. His first love. But I know Victor had problems in his marriage. I don't want to deal with issues years old, maybe some I can't change."

"If you love him enough, you'll have to. But then, there might not be any, either. He may have resolved for himself whatever challenges existed in the marriage. If you love him, if you find yourself enamored, if you're worried by such possibilities, you have a right to know what they are. You must ask him to explain."

That put her on guard. "Dare I do that?"

"It would be your life too, Ada. You've a right to learn what you confront."

"I know." That was what she'd told Ezzie, too. Plus, her father and Liv had dealt with her challenges from her first marriage. Whatever they were, Ada was not privy to details, but she did know it took months for Liv to address them. Ada had only four or five months before Victor planned to return to Shanghai—and she didn't like being rushed. "I promise I will ask...if I become...more attached to him."

"Good. Well!" He started to rise. "Send him to me for my blessing."

She laughed at his nonchalance. "Wait! He hasn't asked for my hand."

"He will. When he does, I'm ready."

"But—but," she sputtered, "how do you know I'll marry him? Papa, I just—"

"Couldn't take your eyes off him." He chucked her under the chin. "I like him. Liv does. From what I saw last night, others in the family do too. Who else's approval might you need?"

"My own," she whispered.

"Let him prove to you that whether you live next door or five thousand miles away, you can leave those you love and trust him with your care, body and soul." He leaned over and dropped a kiss to her cheek.

Proof. She had no idea what that might be.

꒰⁕꒱

"Mr. MacIntyre got your message early this morning, milord. He's happy to receive you. This way." The youth who'd greeted Victor led the way down a corridor toward the main office of Victor's company and his London manager.

He nodded, his teeth clenched at his difficulty to walk. Leaning heavily on his cane this morning, he winced at the pressure on his left knee. The blasted rain always gave him trouble with this old injury. No amount of meditative breathing earlier had relieved the pain.

"Good afternoon, my lord." Frederick MacIntyre welcomed him with a grin. A tall, dark-haired, good looking chap, a few years older than Victor, his manager had the sharp-eyed look of a hawk that pleased Victor as much as his excellent services. "Please, sir, do sit down. May I offer you tea, perhaps?"

"No, thank you, MacIntyre." He sank into the wooden chair with a grunt and rubbed his thigh through his woolen trousers. Recommended to him by his father's solicitor five years ago, the Scotsman came from a family of reputable accountants. He'd initiated and run the European trading operations of Cole and Company to expert efficiency and increasing profits. Furthermore, MacIntyre had done so from day one with only cursory instruction from Victor who had been rabid to leave London quickly. He was that rare employee, thorough, caring and wise.

MacIntyre focused on Victor's massage of his leg. "Whisky then?"

Five years ago, the morning following the attack, Macintyre had witnessed how incapacitated Victor had been by the blows to his legs. Alicia, in her anger at his announcement they would go to China, had attacked him with a poker. He'd seized it from her but not before she'd caused him major bruising. That she might've killed him or at the least broken his leg was a miracle. In any case, a month later—before Victor and his wife and two daughters left for Shanghai—MacIntyre had commented on his apparent recovery. Victor had not dissuaded him from his incorrect diagnosis. Last week when Victor had come here to meet with him, MacIntyre had commented on his improvement. But his man had never known what hell he'd endured to recover. The condition Victor dealt with had improved. But it had taken him three years to rid himself of the need for heroin.

"The rain can be the devil with an old wound, sir."

His Scots brogue and his kindness soothed Victor's discomfort. "I will have a jigger. Thank you." *Better that than the tincture that works only if I return to it as a slave.*

MacIntyre beckoned his assistant, then pressed coins into his palm. "Glasses and the bottle, Ian. But get us a bit of cheddar and bread from the pub next door to go with it."

The lanky red-head bobbed and turned on his heel.

"I appreciate you receiving me on short notice this morning."

"Never an imposition, sir." MacIntyre pulled up a chair. "I've already sent off the proposal to the LeGere Foundry in Grasse about the perfumes. As yet, I've nothing in return, but I didn't expect a response for a few weeks. T'is their busy time, ye know." MacIntyre was curious about the reason for Victor's appearance so soon after their recent visit and he assumed Victor wished to hear about his hope to begin supplying LeGere with the flowers for development of new perfumes.

"Excellent. Keep me abreast of negotiations." Victor had recently added flowers of China and Japan to his imports to Europe. Since the perfume trade centered in the south of France, he sought an alliance with one of the companies developing new scents. Sales of *eau de toilette* and cologne in

Europe doubled each year. The more expensive perfumes as well. He wanted a piece of that profit—and the potential growth of the industry. "If they are at all interested, those two new shipments of camellias can be diverted from Portsmouth and easily off-loaded in Bordeaux."

"And at great savings to us. I've emphasized that savings to *Monsieur* LeGere and his wife."

"They'd benefit from having this new variety of camellia," Victor added. "And if LeGere isn't interested in our flowers, we can approach Fontenaque. But I've come this morning not to discuss that but to ask you to do something else for me."

"Whatever you require, sir, t'is yours."

"When we met week before last, I expected to remain in England only until the autumn. Now, for many reasons, I may stay longer."

"That would be superb, my lord. You and I would have more time to learn each other's intentions."

"I think we are of like mind, MacIntyre. Always have been. And I am honored and very fortunate to have you."

"Thank you, sir. Just tell me what you need and it's yours."

"I know you did your usual annual review for me in December. When I received it in January, I thought it thorough and detailed."

His man drew back, concern lining his brow. "If you found anythin' lacking, milord, I'll gladly provide you with whate're you need."

"Nothing lacking in there, MacIntyre. Nothing at all." He offered his manager a broad grin. "What I need is an analysis of our current status. A review to-date, if you will."

"Of the current year?"

"Precisely," Victor said, though MacIntyre still looked alarmed and he sought to allay any of his fears. "You see my objectives have changed since we met week before last. I'm forced to think a few years ahead. I hope this analysis will not try the staff. If you need to hire another bookkeeper to help you, I can—?"

"Oh, no, sir. Not at all. This is not a burden, milord. I'm happy to help you. I promise you we'll compile all the current receipts and invoices to date for the year in order of country and get them ready for your perusal."

"How long do you think it will take you to finish?"

"We're current, my lord, with billings and collections. The accounts payable from France come in, usually when due. We have no one in arrears. But it takes us a day or so to get Rothschilds' to convert the francs to pounds. Tomorrow might be possible, but we'd have a more viable tally if ye might wait a day or two."

"Excellent. Why don't I return next Monday? Tell me if that's not enough time. I don't wish to rush you."

"You won't at all, sir. Monday will be fine."

The young assistant appeared with a wooden tray filled with two kinds of cheese and bread. He left to return with a bottle of whisky and the two glasses that MacIntyre had ordered.

"While you are here, sir, I wonder if you'd visit with me. There's much I am in the dark about. If you'd take the time to inform me about the Chinese riots of last winter. I dinna understand why they do it. So often too." MacIntyre poured two healthy draughts of spirits for them both. He handed one to Victor and sat down.

"I owe you a good education in Chinese settlement life, MacIntyre. You deserve it and need it for us to continue to grow." He lifted his glass in a silent toast to his manager and drank. "Why don't I try a bit each time we meet?"

"I'd like that." He sat back and waited.

"The riots. Hmmm. Why do they do it? It disrupts life in the settlement when many peasants who are starving have no other choice but to clammer at the gates to get in. That disruption we had last March was a bad one and cost us the month's profit." The province surrounding the Shanghai foreign settlement was agrarian and the peasants lived on rice and whatever meager vegetables they could grow in their small plots.

"Most Chinese live a life of extreme poverty. They may own an acre, maybe less, of land, inherited from previous generations of their family, but the plot is usually so small that growing enough food for a family is difficult. They do have large families. Being prolific is a sign of a good life, and an honorable one. But too many mouths to feed strains the land. The soil may be rich. But if the family lives near a body of water where the imperial government has not built a suitable dam or dyke, they could lose all in the next flood...or the next draught. Many starve. Those who live in the province near Shanghai hear tales of how life inside the settlement is different. And it is very different.

"We have paved roads, water plants and municipal sewers. We must build more. We have built solid homes and factories that do not blow away in a wind or rain storm. Not even their big winds, their *tai feng*, can bring our structures down. We have in the city other improvements those in the villages do not. Many they have not conceived of. Trams, for instance. Last December, I bought a share in one of the City Council's new businesses that will build them. You saw the receipt. The same company talks of regulating rickshaws. Schools in the city are not lacking. For decades, the Chinese compradors have run their own schools for their children to learn English and French, but the City Council will soon build schools for all Chinese living in the settlement. We'll teach languages and mathematics. Geography, too. A worker who can read and write, speak our language and calculate correctly is one we want. The city is in many ways more convenient and modern than London or Paris. Why?

Because we start from the ground up. That makes living in Shanghai settlement a dream for many Chinese. Then when they face flood or famine or drought, they naturally want food and shelter. And they stand at the gates, demanding to get in."

Victor remembered the faces of the children, pock-marked, emaciated and sullen. "We have work. But not for everyone."

"How do you decide who to take and who to turn away?"

"The ones that look healthier. The ones that seem pleas-ant. The beggars, the ones too diseased to stand a day's work, we must reject."

"And what about women and children?"

"We take a few women to train as cooks or maids. Some are taken by other Chinese who live in the quarter and employed in their homes. Some who are young and comely are taken by mandarins as prostitutes."

"Isn't that agin' the law, sir?"

"Sadly, no. The Council wants to regulate that, but many in the town refuse."

"Why?"

"Many foreigners buy the services of Chinese women. They are without their wives or have not married. A few keep them in a separate compound of their home. The Chinese mandarins all over the empire do the same."

His manager was wide-eyed. "Do they not have a rule again' such treatment of women, sir?"

Victor shook his head. "Confucian gentlemen revere many things, MacIntyre. Order, harmony, knowledge of Confucian texts and those ethics by which they should run an efficient government. As for the fairer sex, women who are wives and mothers, especially those who bear male children are honored. But the men can take more than one wife at a time and do it to ensure they have a male child to inherit. Women from lower peasant classes do not merit their attention or their protection."

"So I'm confused, sir. If few can come inside the city, why do the riots of peasants outside the gates create problems for shipping and for us?"

"Like they did last March?"

MacIntyre nodded.

"For us, where we want the tea they grow, the silks they weave and the porcelain they fire and paint, supply is vital. If they do not work, if they block the roads, if they block the ports with their junks, then commerce is disrupted and we cannot fulfill our orders. If they pillage and burn whatever they wish, often much of that is our product."

MacIntyre frowned. "And now if we add flowers, roots, bulbs to that list of goods, aren't we making matters worse for us? Getting those from the countryside, will be a bigger problem, won't it?"

"Exactly. Until we can propagate the roots and nurture bulbs on a massive scale inside the settlement, we must rely on supply from the hinterland." Victor took another drink of his scotch. "But trade in teas, fabric and porcelain raises many different issues from flowers."

"Aye. One perishable, the other not."

Victor remembered the fire in his neighbor's factory, set last year by a coolie who thought the Englishman who owned the building had dishonored the Buddha. "The bigger problem is failure to understand the other's culture. So much of who we are and what we are is so odd to Chinese that they can easily blame us for ills we have no part of."

"What do you mean?"

"For example, an English friend of mine moved a Buddhist shrine that workers had put up inside his factory. After that one of his coolies burned it down."

"That's terrible."

"Made worse by the fact that the Chinese man was put before our British magistrate and banished from Shanghai. The man's friends rioted in objection. Problems in business are the only thing. The Chinese have a mistaken idea of what our Christian ministers and priests do. They fear our mass and communion, thinking the bread and wine are poison. They fear the nuns who take in orphans, thinking the women take the children to change them into evil spirits—or worse, kill them. They fear our doctors and medicines. For those Westerners who live in the villages, their lives are often in jeopardy. Only time and education can change that."

"To go into the countryside must take great courage," MacIntyre said, mesmerized by Victor's words.

"It does. And when you navigate the rivers aboard a huge steamer belching steam and moving at the speed of ten horses, you are a god or a devil. How else to explain it, eh?"

"What did you think when you first arrived, sir?"

I thought it was heaven. "I was grateful to be there, MacIntyre. Don't misunderstand me. I love this country and I would not have left...but let me be plain. I'm certain you must know some of the reason why I sailed away five years ago."

MacIntyre met his gaze frankly. "I did, sir."

You never indicated that and for it, I am indebted to you. "I would not have left were it not imperative for my family—" *and my sanity,* "—that I go. I welcomed the challenge of building something from the start. A second son must, you know."

"I do, sir. I am the third in our family."

"Are you, indeed?" he grinned at his man of business. "I did not know. We are then kindred spirits in many ways."

"We are, sir. Wish to help you build this company as large and as profitable as you wish."

Victor took a welcome drink of the spirits and warmed to

the idea to educate his manager to maximum potential. "I may wish to grow it far beyond what we originally intended." He wished to add facts to his hope he might stay in England, but he had to reassure himself he had income sufficient to his ambitions. "Remaining here means I do not have immediate control over conditions in Shanghai. While I trust my Chinese *comprador*—extraordinary as that statement is for an Englishman to say about one's Chinese factotum, I must assess how comfortable financially we would be should the business level fluctuate with my change in venue. I trust my man in Shanghai. What worries me always are my peasant stock who work as laborers in his factory and on his docks."

"Do we pay our men well, sir? Compared to other foreigners?"

"We do, MacIntyre. I am good friends with the Chinese governor of the province, a man named Li Hung-chang. He's a well-educated man who advises the emperor and the empress dowager on Western methods and he knows quite a bit about how we operate in Shanghai. He tells me that wages of Cole and Company are among the best. Only one American pays more."

"Do we get the best men for our money then?"

"We do. And it's worth it, I'd say. Everyone wants integrity, don't they? Enough money to eat, live in peace. To be free is to hold your head up. Money can raise one up from despair."

Yet last winter the venerable governor, Li, had challenged Victor that his good wage was as much a problem as the low wage paid by a competitive foreigner.

"You provide the contrast, good sir." The Confucian mandarin who headed the province around Shanghai was in charge of a wide swath of China. But as a trusted government official he also headed his own private army. He headed in fact a mercenary force and Victor did not trust those men to keep allegiance to order or the empire, if anything ever happened to Li. "When you foreigners pay different wages, you create the tension that leads to riots."

"To pay less, Honorable Li, would test my conscience, sir."

"Persuade your friends to pay more. Then we can have peace."

Victor gave a wan smile to MacIntyre. "What my friend the governor did not add was that the other act that could release tensions among peasants and their own government was to get the emperor to decrease taxes on the people. He knows it should be done, but it's impossible. The Chinese government, bloated and inefficient, cannot reduce its income with out throwing itself into bankruptcy. The Chinese dragon limps along but five years from now, ten perhaps, when riots turn to revolution, we will have catastrophe." *Few will survive.*

"And will the West be thrown out? Us too?"

"I fear so. If we do not change our imperial ways and the Chinese government cannot change theirs, the only ones who can change it all will be the millions of peasants. I'm sorry. I've turned gloomy. We're doing well, MacIntyre. Very well and I don't mean to sound as if there is no solution. There is. It's complex, but we here in Parliament might change our portion of it." Victor drained his glass on that possibility and got to his feet. "I thank you for the refreshment, MacIntyre. Most welcome. I must go but I will return Monday."

"And you will tell me more about the Chinese peasants and your governor friend?"

"Li Hung-chang. Yes, I will. We'll make you so informed, you could go out to Shanghai yourself, if you so wished, and see for yourself."

"I'd like that, my lord."

"Would you indeed?" Victor had always thought of Shanghai as his place of exile. But others saw it as a city of opportunity. Adventure, even. A weight fell from his shoulders. Intriguing what another's perspective could do for one.

"I would. Thank you for that." MacIntyre called for his young man to fetch Victor's hat and coat.

"You may indeed, ask, MacIntyre. One thing before I go. I would ask your discretion that you not share my possible change of plans with your staff."

"You have my assurance, milord. May I hail you a hansom?"

"You may." Now it was time for his next challenge.

"What address, milord?" the cabbie asked him.

"White's. St. James's Street."

As Victor settled into the spare black cushions of the cab, he removed his top hat and ran his fingers through his hair. By God, that had gone well. He'd been so right to trust MacIntyre with his business. It had been a risk, investing all of his father's money into a new company that did not market the most profitable Eastern product of all. Opium. He did not sell it and he never would.

Pride in that difficult choice made him smile as the sun beamed down through the parting clouds.

Last week at first, he had dismissed his father's offer to launch his political career. That ambition had died in him five years ago. To resurrect it would require devotion to rebuild his friendships. But meeting Ada Hanniford had awakened in him a yearning for his former self. The man who saw possibilities where others saw despair. The man who saw progress as beneficial. The man who knew what clean water, sanitation, good roads and transportation could do for people. How or why meeting Ada galvanized his old political ambitions was a mystery to him. And though he wished to analyze that, he had little time to do it as well as assess his real prospects. Diligent not to follow his impulse blindly, he'd discussed the matter again with his father. Afterward, he'd thought long and hard about the tasks before him. He made a list of his friends in Parliament. In the party. In the Sussex borough where he would stand for office.

He wasn't convinced he should run. Wasn't ready to say he could. The current MP had held the seat for more than a decade. But he was ill with the wasting disease and ready to step down. If Victor wanted this, he'd need more than the desire. More than his father's political backing. More than the money to run the house the duke had so generously given him.

On his current income from his business, he could support a wife. However, he questioned if he could support one who was used to the finest luxury. Any bride, Ada no exception, would come with a dowry. Monthly income was helpful, but the idea that he would use it to supplement his expenses grated on him. Plus if he used whatever sum might come to him from her father, the amount might not serve well. Victor understood the ravages of inflation. Ada's dowry, any bride's dowry, could be eaten away by decline in value of the pound—and the past two years had seen a downturn in European economies. He hadn't worked with French and Germans, Spanish and Portuguese traders not to know the value of savings against the rise in the cost of living. Even with the added income his father offered him, generous as the duke's assistance was, he did not wish to use it all. He'd need his Hanover Square house repainted, new furnishings, drapes. He'd require a town carriage and a coachman as well as two or three maids, a cook, housekeeper and at least one footman to help his butler. As frugal as his Scots manager, Victor wanted to keep his financial independence and remain solvent, married or not. That required attention to every penny.

Even if his financial situation were conducive, Victor could not count on being elected. His father might control that borough, but Victor did not know the MPs from neighboring boroughs. He'd make friends...and perhaps a few enemies. Politics often meant wrestling in a barrel of monkeys. He could do it. Had the temperament for it. Wanted it. Had always wanted it. Only the disgrace of Alicia's actions had killed his hopes of serving.

Now he had to learn if Ada Hanniford might join him in the tumble of political arenas. She was bright, frank and well read, but she was that unique creature, an heiress, and an American in the bargain. Would she think British politics foreign to her? He had to learn.

Politics took a man and consumed him. If he were to be of any consequence, a politician used his name, his fortune, his wife and his family. He had to know if she'd support him, day in and out. He would never force Ada to enter a world he alone chose. One that he alone dominated. Many men did and paid prices for their audacity. He had done that once. Out of necessity. Alicia had gone with him to China because she could not remain here. He had taken her because society expected it...and because he pitied her. She had hated every moment with the 'yellow barbarians.' When she died, the only emotion he knew was relief. His living nightmare was over.

But his past raised the biggest challenge before him. It was one he could not analyze with figures in a ledger. Courting Ada meant he must come to terms with his long-held beliefs about marriage. He couldn't simply wish away the bitter memories of his years with his wife. He had to deal with the problems that he'd been part of in that union. She'd been a spendthrift. Buying any frippery that caught her eye. He'd tolerated it. She'd been impulsive, self-centered. Appearing at his club to demand of the doorman that Victor receive her. He chastised her, but to no avail. She continued to outrage society. Evidently, her father or mother could not contain her either. Yes, she'd been young. Eighteen when they married. But he'd been twenty-three. Neither of them mature enough to deal with the issues that she brought to their marriage bed. The bigger problem they'd encountered was her disregard for morals. Though he'd not understood the breadth of her mendacity, he learned all too soon—and yet not soon enough—all her devious ways. He'd forgiven one lie, two, four. He overlooked one late night, two ruined gowns. But the final revelation appalled him. Her encounters with other men at tea in other women's homes, in retiring rooms at balls, in the cloakroom in the box at the theater took his breath and his mind.

He growled, shutting his eyes to close out the worst of her offenses. He'd promised himself, two years ago after her death, to let her and all her outrages, die with her. He'd not call up all the sordidness now. Not now when he must focus on what Ada Hanniford was...not how she compared to a woman who merited no consideration at all. Alicia was dead, and thank God, gone.

He folded his hands. He needed a strategy to deal with his desire for Ada.

He sighed, acknowledged the truth of it. He must not allow himself to be carried away by his desire for her. He had to be prudent. Not persuade her, not seduce her to anything she did not want—neither Shanghai nor politics. For what value was love if not honoring the wishes of the other?

He paid the cabbie his fee, plus a bit extra. The sun shone now. A good sign.

"Good morning, my lord." The elderly doorman at

Victor's old club greeted him as if he'd never been away from London.

"Thank you, Wells." Victor appreciated the welcome, knowing full well that the gentleman he was to meet this morning must have left word with this man that they were to meet. He handed over his walking stick and gloves, then removed his hat and top coat. "Wonderful to see you looking so well. I hope your family is too."

"They are, sir. My wife is chipper."

"And by now, your son must be as tall as you." Victor wished he could remember the boy's name.

The man blinked, surprised but only momentarily by Victor's remembrance. "He is, indeed, sir. My son is in Africa this past year. The Army."

"Ah, yes, he always wanted to join."

"To see the world, yes, sir. Recently promoted, he is, to sergeant." The white-haired man beamed with pride.

"A good soldier. Dedicated to service, like his father."

"Thank you, sir. Lord Grayson waits for you in the smoking room, my lord." The man stepped aside to let him pass.

Girding for the challenge awaiting him, Victor took the winding stairs to the first floor. One key to a sound future was to always keep one's major investor appraised of one's desires. Even if Grayson need know nothing of Victor's contemplation of marriage, he would want to know that Cole and Company would change how it was managed.

CHAPTER 10

Ada had spent the morning discarding one gown after another as her choice for this ride in Hyde Park. The day was cool and sunny. At ten, clouds rushed in and rain poured down. In such a storm, she'd not be able to travel with Victor around the park. They'd have to ride in a closed carriage and taking along Chaumont would be necessary. That made her grumble.

Startling the kitchen staff, she'd walked out the kitchen door into the back garden four times. At first, she'd decided to wear a wool gown and take a parasol. Not that she'd need it. In the rain, they would not walk about. When the sun appeared, she thought to wear a pale yellow sateen with golden ribbon tucking. Her yellow silk walking shoes, too. They'd be comfortable to stroll along the paths. Couples did alight. She wondered if Victor would wish to. After all, his infirmity in his leg did much to limit him, if not so much on the dance floor.

Arrrgh. She sank onto her *chaise longue,* a hand to her brow, admonishing herself to be calm, calm. This courting business took it out of a woman. She hadn't done much of this. No man had interested her so much to go out with him and let the world presume an interest in him.

"I should be happy my days of looking for a proper beau were done. Or nearly so. *Or are they?*" She hopped up to scrutinize herself in her hand mirror. Frown lines appeared. "Not good, Ade. You're getting older, fretting. Besides, if you change your dress again, your maid will quit."

That was not likely...but she chided herself that she was too fussy. After all, who was Victor Cole? A businessman out of Shanghai. She didn't want to fall in love with him and go to the ends of the earth. Where was Shanghai? She should go down to the library and check a map.

That, however, would be after she decided on her attire.

In the end, she stuck a hand into her dressing room and told herself she would wear the fourth gown from the left side.

"Hmmm. Well." That meant she'd donned a pink spring muslin with embroidered red roses on the bodice. Her rose leathered walking boots and a pale pink parasol topped with red tassels matched and that was her attire. Period. The day had turned warmer. It was early June, so she needed no coat, only a shawl. Her ivory cashmere would do.

She knew the moment Victor arrived out front. Having checked the view down the front steps from the upstairs window at least four times, she was flying down the stairs toward Foster before the man opened the door.

Victor grinned in greeting and offered the usual polite phrases.

She was mute, out the entrance, down the steps, putting her foot up to the step when Victor handed her in. She sat forward. He faced her.

"I don't know how you do that," she said to him when she was settled.

"What's that?" Today he wore ivory cravat, ice blue satin

waistcoat and a pearl gray frock coat that complemented perfectly his turquoise eyes and thick auburn hair. His topcoat was a soft grey felt that made his complexion deliciously ruddy, his eyes irresistible. "Ada? How I do what?"

"Yes. Um. Sit backwards. Don't you become ill? I would. Have. Whenever I've had to. It was terrible."

The coachman snapped the reins and off they went.

Victor got this wicked little look in his eyes as he examined her, head to toe and back again. "I've gotten use to it."

"Courted a lot of women, have you?"

"Only one before you."

"Well, that's good." *Oh, marvel*ous. *I sound like a testy bird.*

"Like to be the only one men appreciate, do you?" He arched a brow.

"Of course."

"Why? Can't bear the competition?"

She slanted him a wary glance. "You are playing with me."

"I am." He sat back, satisfied with himself.

Hmm. Well, she'd give him something. "I've never thought about competition. I have friends or acquaintances."

"Good to know. The difference being what?"

"Friends have never challenged me for beaux. Why would they? I've never taken theirs."

"Good form," he acknowledged. "And acquaintances?"

"I never even think about them."

"What of enemies?" he asked with a somber glance.

She shrugged. "I have none."

"I wouldn't think you do."

"Since we're being honest..."

He tipped his head, his marvelous eyes alight in the sunshine. "We are."

She took her time to ask him her biggest worry. "Those things you said last night were honest?"

He grew solemn. "I'd never lie to you."

"That's what I thought."

"If I was too forward—"

Alarmed she'd fallen for his charm and he regretted it, she panicked. "Were you?"

He tightened his lips, looking decidedly uncomfortable. "I am taken by you. Far more than I knew. Far more than is indicated by the brief time we've shared."

Sadness engulfed her. "I'm sorry. I would never trap you. Or any man. That is not who I am. I don't have to..." She shifted and glanced away. "I don't make it a practice to seduce men."

"I saw that. I agree."

"You do?" She smiled, happy he saw her as she was. She crossed her hands, her fingers itching to push that one lock of his rich auburn hair up under the brim of his dashing hat. But the boyish look she liked.

"You trust me," he said with assurance.

"I do. I wonder why, given the brief time we've shared."

A hint of a smile curved his lips. "Instinct, I would wager."

She wiggled her brows. "You know me much too well. By instinct, I wager."

"You'd be correct."

"Since there is no other explanation to offer for the few days we've spent in each other's company."

"None. But we did get on. Rather well, too."

"Except for your brother," she had to remind him.

"And today we are free of him."

"Thank heavens." She bit her lower lip. "I'm sorry. I should not have said that."

"That's how you feel, so that's what you must say. Let me tell you that Richard has always been forward. Rash. Selfish."

"He should have asked for Ezzie's hand. He gave all signs he was interested in her."

"How is she?"

"I had a note from her yesterday. She's home and receiving Lord Edgecombe. So she's delighted about that."

"Does she like him?" he asked.

"She does. Better than Richard, I think."

"Good for her."

She faced him fully and grinned.

"That's better."

"What is?"

He lifted a finger to draw a circle. "You can relax. We are in public. A ride. A walk, if you care to. I don't bite."

"I'm not accustomed to this." She might as well tell him everything. "I don't have suitors take me driving."

"I'm shocked. No men have pursued you?"

"They have. Did. But I didn't enjoy it."

One corner of his mouth curved up and he folded his hands in his lap. "Ah, then. You enjoy me. Gratifying."

"Don't become too confident."

He feigned submission. "I won't. Tell me about the others."

"Is this proper?"

"I'm sitting here. You're sitting there—"

"No, I mean that you ask me such things. That we are being so forward with each other. I've never talked with a suitor...or any man for that matter, who was interested in me as if—"

"As if?"

"As if you are courting me."

He lifted a hand. "I don't wish to conceal my interest in you, Ada. That's for boys who have no courage to declare what they want."

Every nerve in her body tingled. She shifted as her breasts hardened. Her nipples peaked. Her belly swam with heat and wet desire.

His eyes turned a dark intriguing blue green. As if he knew what happened to her. "Tell me about your previous beaux, Ada. Tell me how they did not suit."

"I didn't give them encouragement. That was easy because they were nervous. Coy. Sent me flowers and sweets. Wrote me poetry."

"Well, then I certainly will send you no flowers. Nor candy."

"But poetry?" she challenged him.

"My darling, you'd hate to hear what I could do with poetry."

"Nonetheless." She waved a hand, subduing her shiver of delight that he'd called her his darling. "Do try. It's good for the mind to stretch your skills."

He leveled his eyes on her—and the need to sit closer to him ran through her like good wine. "Let's see. 'Shall I compare thee to a summer's day?' I'd try but then I'd melt away."

"Stop." She thrust up a hand. "No poetry from you, dear sir."

"I am relieved."

"Me, too!" She laughed.

"Instead, I will send you yards of silk from my warehouse. Blue to match your eyes. Combs of white jade for your hair. And pearls to be strung for your ears and your throat."

"Those are..." She could barely speak, so intimate were his words. "Very personal gifts."

He focused on her eyes, her lips, the hollow of her throat. "They are special to me and meant only for you."

"I question if I should accept them."

"Of course you should. The silk will match no one else's eyes. The jade complement no other's rich hair. The pearls will accent the purity of your skin and keep you warm until I can kiss your eyes and hair and throat."

She squeezed her thighs together. "You must not be so... so suggestive."

"Oh, Ada, I'm as restrained as one can be without running off with you this minute to the vicar."

She squirmed in the lush squabs. "Oh, you are charming, eloquent—"

"Am I? Refreshing to hear. I had it from others I was rustic in my romantic pursuits."

"They were wrong."

"My wife," he said quite simply.

She formed an O with her mouth. *What to say now?* She rallied, stiffening her spine, suppressing her desires for him, set on her purpose. "I'm glad you've brought her up."

"Want to know about her?"

"I would really like to understand if you bring any preconceived notions to any...future union from your past one."

He frowned, turned his face to the passing scenery and was silent for a minute or more.

Stuck, frightened she had offended him, she fretted. "I hate to ask—"

"You have every right to ask. When she died two years ago, I made a rule to never speak of her. Today, I must."

The sun was bright. The noise from the traffic a constant hum around them. The patter of horses and the low indescribable babble of pedestrians filled the void between them.

"I was twenty-two and she eighteen when we met. She'd just debuted. I should not have even gone to the ball where she was presented but a friend of mine wanted companionship. His mother was after him to choose a girl. I saw Alicia, pretty, petite, gay." He licked his lips and winced. "I saw the coquette and nothing beneath. Had I taken time to delve, I would have done us both a service, but I liked her looks. She liked mine. We could dance easily together. Laugh easily. She'd been educated in the normal subjects a lady was to have at her command. Household management, French, ability to play the piano. Judgment of others, she lacked. Ambition, she had in abundance. For status, finery, parties she was avid. Most of all, she determined to marry well. She was the second daughter of a viscount. Becoming Lady Victor Cole, wife of the second son of a duke, fit her idea of achievement. At first. Soon she put her sights higher. But then she was married and becoming enamored of an earl or a duke and becoming his paramour for a day or a month seemed more like a frolic than folly.

"At first I was shocked. Then angry. Belligerent. A beast demanding she reform. She loved the risks of her behavior. Adventures, she called them."

Outrage washed over Ada. "Your daughters?"

He blinked as he glared at her, the past darkening his visage. "They are mine. I see it in the color of their eyes, the shape of their faces. Thank god. They are mine. I'd not have been able to continue with the charade of marriage if they'd been some other man's. But then..."

Ada feared more.

His expression crumbled. "She came to me one night and told me she was pregnant with another man's child and that she had aborted the baby."

Ada gasped at the horror he must've felt at such a revelation.

"She was bleeding. The abortionist had done a very poor job and she was ill. Fevered. Raving mad for days. I thought we'd lose her. We nearly did. But she survived. Just as she did, her lover, a man I knew, made the mistake to speak of her condition to a friend of his. At once in a tidal wave, it seemed, all of London knew. That's when I decided to go abroad. Shanghai seemed like hell to me. I knew nothing of running a business. I'd spent my life learning the running of Parliament as that was to be my family role. Second son, you see. The government or the military. All of it gone in a flash. I could have stayed, I suppose. My parents fought with me to do so. I couldn't. I needed a new beginning."

He knit his brows. "I hope you never understand that kind of loss or shame. I hope you never witness that kind of discord."

She remained silent, expecting he had more to say.

"I thought I loved my wife. But on reflection, it was youthful infatuation. I had a perception of love that was rosier than reality." He fell quiet. His gaze upon the passersby. "Far too many marry without knowledge of the other."

"For money," she said, "or position."

"It's been that way for too long."

"But my friends come to England to find a proper match. Many, not just Ezzie, consider wedding someone they barely know because it would please their mothers or give them a title. I detect that Lord Pinkhurst and his American wife are not very happy."

"Right you are. He said as much to me at Brentwood last week."

"My brother-in-law's sister, Elanna the countess of Carbury, and her husband are very unhappy. They have been from the beginning. None of us can say what might be the cause. Useless to speculate. But they married four years ago soon after Lily and Julian. The reason she accepted him was money. Her family had little. Julian's father had not managed his estates well. Carbury, a neighbor of theirs in the country, had known Elanna all her life. He offered for her and she accepted him because she had to. She'd found no other men she preferred and so she married him.

"Nine months after they wed, she gave birth to a son. But soon afterward, she left her husband and came to London to live. It's a scandal, but she doesn't care. Carbury often comes banging on Julian's door demanding he order his sister to return home, but Julian has tried to talk sense to her and she refuses to return. Her husband accuses her of improperly receiving the Seton family solicitor. He's even ordered Julian to dismiss the man. But Julian has refused. In fact, Julian has revealed that he's taken money from the Seton estate and sequestered it from Carbury's reach. He says if she ever needs funds, she'll have something to live on."

He grimaced. "The Carburys seem well beyond discussing their differences."

She agreed. "If it's a matter of temperament, then they do not match. Carbury is forceful, belligerent. Elanna didn't seem to be. Julian declares she was a sweet young woman, but marriage soured her. She antagonizes him. He goads her. They argue in public, in the streets, of all things. From time to time, Carbury will come up from the country to their townhouse. He demands entry for one reason or another. She tries to lock him out, and he persuades the servants to let him in. Aside from their screaming arguments, they've thrown lamps at each other. He has ripped her clothes to shreds. Worst of all, she shuns their baby. A boy. Three years old, Nate was born on the same day as Lily and Julian's first son, Garrett."

To hear of another's plight had soured Victor's expression. "Let's speak of brighter things, shall we?"

"Yes, let's."

He reached across and squeezed her hand, then gave her a consoling smile.

"What would you like?" she asked, happy to be here with him in the sunshine. "The topic of which novel you currently read or the current actions in Parliament?"

"You've read this morning's news, I would gather?"

"I have. Shall we debate the current price of corn or the value of the reform measures of women's property rights?"

Amused, he narrowed his eyes on her. "Why does this interest you?"

"Because money is interesting. Don't you think? A man's? A woman's? Mine?"

"Some men are not interested in a woman's money."

"I've met few of them," she announced with a decided scowl.

"You've met me," he said with hard intention.

She folded her hands in her lap. This man was a treasure. In politics or out. "You'd support the woman's Marriage Bill?" A new one in Parliament was unusual in that it stipulated a woman may control her own money and her own stock.

"Of course. You'd want control of your own inheritance."

"I would. I think my father would too."

"Or any father."

"Or any woman who earns her own income." She thought of her step-mother, Liv who had earned a living doing interior design for clients. "If these gentlemen in Parliament want to make it possible for me to keep mine after I'm married, I'm happy to support them."

That made him beam. "Tell me why."

"Well, first of all, why shouldn't a woman control the money she earns or inherits?"

"I agree. What else?"

"If she owns stocks, she should have the ownership and dividends of those, too. Don't you think?"

"Indeed."

She stiffened in her seat. "Appalling to think that women haven't. That they've had to go begging their husbands or fathers or brothers for it."

"Dastardly." He was chuckling.

His humor was contagious. "Why are you laughing?"

"Anything else before Parliament that you'd like to discuss?"

"Yes. Actually."

"What?" he asked, almost giddy with the subject.

She tipped her head and scrutinized him. "*Why?*"

"What would you think if I considered running for office?"

"Does one...just do that?"

"Some do."

"You do?"

"I do."

She gazed on him in an entirely new light. "Fabulous."

"You approve?"

"Of course I do. You'd be useful. Constructive."

"How do you know?"

She tipped her head. "Have you not built a business thousands of miles away in only a few years? Has it not been profitable? Do you not understand foreign trade, with China certainly, but perhaps other ports as well, because you have lived abroad? Have friends and colleagues living everywhere? I see you as a marvelously useful addition to Parliament. You would refine trade. Build the Empire on solid principles."

"You make me sound unique."

"Of course, you are. A rare man."

He stilled. And if he breathed, she could not see it. But she recognized his surprise and his appreciation of her praise. "Thank you. Your commendation means much to me."

"I like a man with purpose and ambition. I've met very few."

"And I have met no one like you," he whispered.

"Too bad," she said as she considered his appealing lips, "we sit in broad daylight."

He lifted his foot and stroked the toe of his shoe along one of her ankles. "I could kiss you."

"And I would kiss you back." He was so sweet and so tempting. "Tell me how you'd go about it."

He broke into laughter and color rose on his cheeks.

She cleared her throat and scanned the tops of buildings as they passed. "I mean, how you'd run and win."

"I'd be gone each day, visiting hamlets in the borough. Knocking on doors. Talking to people about their views."

"Would you be home for supper?"

"Always," he said, "unless..."

"What?"

"You came with me."

Oh, he would want her beside him to meet people? No proper British politician she'd heard of did that. "I'd like that."

He grew wistful. "Would you, darling?"

There was that marvelous endearment again. She grinned at him. "With you. Oh, yes."

"I'd happily arrange that."

"Do."

"First, I must see if I have enough friends to win the vote."

She clasped her hands together and leaned toward him. "I've no doubts of that."

"Support me, do you?"

"If I could vote, I would. But women cannot in America or here. But they should." She eyed him. "Don't you agree?"

"I do. We'd have more cooperation."

"Fewer wars. Never good for commerce. But there is that other issue to your running for office..."

"Which is?"

"Do you truly want to do that? Instead of running your company and returning to Shanghai?" She had to know that she was not the reason he sought office. Because if he won and hated it or failed and hated his choice, and he'd changed his life to accommodate her wish not to go to China, she'd be to blame. Whatever happiness they might share would be ruined.

"I do. I always have wished to be in Parliament. Thought I'd be good at it."

"You would because you listen to others. You know how to mediate."

"Thank you. You are kind."

"And observant, too," she added. "How many friends do you have in politics?"

"*In* politics? Four. *Interested* or *influential* in them? Ah. Dozens."

"And how many must you see to garner adequate support?"

"As many as possible. Party leaders have not thought of me in years. It will take time. I know not how much until I begin."

"How long until you know if they at least favor you?"

He shrugged. "By summer's end, I should have a sound indication of support."

"That's enough?"

"It will have to be."

"Because you'll have to make plans by then to return to Shanghai?"

"Because the Member who occupies the seat now is ill. He wishes to resign for the autumn term."

"Oh." This political speculation of his would not take years and years. But merely months. "Just enough time to allow you to enjoy publication of your book, too."

"We'll hope that sells well. It may not. Too analytical, some may say."

"Why would they criticize it?"

"It outlines changes the British should make to deal with the Emperor. Problems in the ports with the clash of Chinese values with Western will hurt us all someday very badly."

She folded her hands in her lap and looked confident as the Queen. "Good advice then. A feather in your hat."

He barked laughter. "May it be so! And in the meantime," he said with more timbre in his voice, "shall I have the coachman stop so I might buy you an ice from the sweet shop? Or does an ice equate to sweets and bad poetry?"

"Bad poetry would make us run home and hide. But an ice?"

"Would cool us both."

CHAPTER 11

Three days later, Victor once more climbed the steps to his club. He'd returned from Sussex only last night late. The renovation of the house was progressing. He'd hired a team of laborers to sand down the old wooden floors and paint the inside walls. Though he'd also need gardeners to untangle the jungle that grew on the lawns, he hoped he might delay that. He hoped he might offer the opportunity to the woman who was reputed to be an expert on landscaping.

Wells beamed at him. "My lord, good morning to you."

"And to you, Wells. Have Lord Billings or Sir Arnold Meachum arrived yet?"

"In the coffee room, my lord. They arrived early and said they would order for all."

Coffee. That meant brandy, too, as the three of them had always used it to lace their morning drink. His friends were eager to renew old habits and old acquaintances. Excellent. He did not wish to tarry.

Victor made his way down the hall, up the stairs and off to the right into the coffee room. There, twenty or so gentlemen sat in enormous ebony leather chairs or at elaborately linen-draped dining tables. Here the illustrious men of title and commerce took coffee, tea, the newspapers or a morning nap.

In the far corner of the red silk papered room sat his two friends from his school days. Lord Billings, Frederick Danforth, was a year older than he, a swell fellow, jovial and hearty, who had suffered with a stutter as a child. Their other friend, Sir Arnold Meachum and Victor had befriended Freddie, taking up for him when others—like Victor's brother Richard and his friends—had bullied the boy.

"My God, you look like you've grown ten inches taller!" Freddie jumped to his feet to pump Victor's hand, then hugged the stuffing out of him.

Meachum opened wide his arms to embrace Victor and pound him on the back. "Put on a few pounds. Life in Shanghai must be very good. I shall have to invest."

"To hell with you, man. You already have put in enough." Years ago, Arnie had put in one hundred pounds to help Victor start his company. Freddie twice that. Both had received nice annual profits on their money.

"But if I'd like to look like you," Arnie teased, "I should pass you another hundred."

"If he gives you more money, Cole," Freddie said feigning innocence, "can you find a Chinese cure to grow his hair back?"

Victor frowned at his very bald friend. "Yes. On his toes."

"Long enough to braid?" Arnie chuckled when the others groaned.

"Afraid not." Victor grimaced.

They motioned for Victor to join them at the table. It was already laden with coffee service, scones, muffins and marmalade.

"I see the kitchen has not changed its menu." Victor

smiled at a footman who silently draped a serviette over his lap, then poured for him.

"That's because they're forbidden to read any new recipes," Arnie offered.

"Can't read." Freddie mashed his lips together.

"But you two still come here." Victor knew they did because they had a legacy here. Both their fathers were members, as was his own.

"I like the scones," Arnie said.

Freddie snorted. "You can tell, can't you, by the size of his waistcoat?"

His friend had indeed put on more weight around his middle. Victor put hand to his chest. "My clothes fit more snuggly since I've arrived in England."

"Potatoes and bread," Arnie said, as he spread orange marmalade over a crusty scone.

"Puddings and pies," Freddie added. "Means you have to dance a lot to keep fit for the ladies."

"Are you?" Victor asked Arnie and raised his cup. "Dancing to keep fit for the ladies?"

"Not I. But this fellow?" Arnie poked his friend in the ribs. "Tell him, my lad, who it is."

Freddie's cheeks flushed. "I do prefer one lady in particular. Dancing is not my best activity. You both know that. It never was."

"Sadly," said Arnie faking a pout, "the lady in question loves to dance."

"Then you must," Victor said into the jest now. "We could refresh his memory, couldn't we, Arn?"

"Indeed. Just like we used to."

Freddie held up a palm. "I will pass. Thank you, gentlemen. The memory of your days as my dancing masters is too painful to recall, let alone revisit."

"Oh, come now." Victor chided him. "We could ask Wells

to give us one of the meeting rooms upstairs. Push the furniture aside and—"

"No."

Victor barked in laughter. "But—"

"I like Lady Jessica Baldwin and I choose to court her without your assistance."

Victor stared at Arnie. "Has he been this stubborn all these years and I've forgotten?"

"He has. And you did."

Victor laughed, happy to be home with his oldest friends enjoying a tease. He'd missed the familiarity of men with whom he'd grown up and gone to school and learned in general how to be a man. In his circle, he should have stayed here in London with them, taken his place here and prospered. Instead, he'd gone another way. Far away.

"I say—" Arnie nudged him. "Have you gone dark on us, Cole?"

"Not at all. In fact, I'm delighted to be here with you."

"Long overdue," said Arnie in a solemn tone.

"We'll value what we've regained, eh?" Freddie picked up his coffee cup and toasted Victor and Arnie with it.

"I intend to."

"How long do you intend to stay?" Freddie asked. "Your brother told us just until October or so. True?"

Before Victor left Brentwood, Richard had bid him goodbye and told him he was headed for his own estate north of London. "Oh? You saw Ridgemont recently?"

"He came in yesterday. Irritable with Wells. Uncalled for." Freddie had never liked Richard, not as a child or adult. Not surprising. Richard could be an uncaring cad toward men or women.

"You can't see from your chair," Arnie said beneath his breath and leaned forward, "but he's just come in the far door."

Freddie sat, hands folded, assessing Victor's brother with disparaging eyes. "Well, do rise. Here he comes."

"Good morning, gentlemen, brother." Richard looked in good form, if a bit bleary-eyed. "An early meeting of the clan, is it?"

"Seeing Tildon, are you, Ridgemont?" Victor always addressed his brother by his formal name in public and ignored his jibe at the three of them. Tildon was not only Richard's best friend, but also his drinking companion. Over the decades, the two of them had caused more problems for the sheriffs of various shires than escaped prisoners.

"Hmm, yes. We're planning our week. Going to the high tea at the Wares' today, are we? Meachum? Surely you are attending, aren't you, Billings? Will the countess of Ware expect you for Jessica? I wonder."

Freddie, no longer cowed by Richard at age thirty-one, stood two inches taller and four stone heavier than the man he faced and stared straight in the eye.

Victor silently praised his friend.

"I do go, Ridgemont. Meachum comes too. Victor as well."

"Have an invitation, do you, Victor?"

Freddie said, "He's coming with me."

Victor saw no reason to add that he had received an invitation to tea from the earl and countess of Ware this morning. He was eager to attend to widen his social mark but also because he hoped Ada might be there.

Richard gave a critical glance at Victor. "Splendid. Into the swing of the season, then. Good for you, dear boy."

Victor bristled. He wanted to box his ears for acting like such an ass.

"So, Billings, I suspect you are there to talk with Lady Jessica? I go to sit next to a certain American girl. What of you, Victor?"

Victor inhaled, more tired than irritated at Richard's priggish behavior. Ada might converse with Richard...or she might find herself quite occupied elsewhere. "Good to see you this morning, Ridgemont. Thought you'd gone north."

Richard stared at him with cold regard. "I've business in the City. Mama told me you do, too."

The edge to his voice told Victor that their mother had shared some of the changes in their father's will. Richard preferred the family money be regarded as his own, even when it was still their father's. But the fact that their father would grant Victor a house and the prestige of the Brighton borough added insult to injury. Richard might not like politics, but he liked control of anything he thought should be only his. "I did."

"Concluded well, was it?"

"Indeed. And not a subject for this moment."

Richard thinned his lips. "Later, of course."

"Good day to you," Victor pre-empted any further discussion.

Richard inclined his head, none too politely, and off he went.

Victor resumed his chair. "He gets worse."

"He's old enough to become a bore," Arnie complained. "What happened to his relationship with Esmerelda Moore? The scandal sheets had it he was to propose at your parents' party?"

"He was. Then he didn't."

"Why not?" Freddie said, his eyes still on the egress of Victor's brother from their presence. "What happened?"

He found another woman he preferred. "He got cold feet."

Arnie smacked his lips. "My mother told me last night at dinner that she heard Miss Moore is to wed Edgecombe."

So. Edgecombe must have asked the question yesterday. "Superb. I'm happy for her. Him, too."

"Good man, that Edgecombe." Freddie trained his attention on Victor.

"Ezzie is a lovely young woman," Victor said. "They'll be happy."

"Ezzie, is it?" Freddie asked at Victor's familiarity.

"Yes. I met her when I was home and have come to know her as simply Ezzie."

Freddie looked at Arnie, then blinked at Victor. "Because...?"

"She is very good friends with—"

"Ada Hanniford," all three men said at the same time.

"Do you both know her?"

"Who doesn't?" said Arnie with a laugh and reached to pour a draught of brandy in each coffee cup. "Miss Hanniford was at Brentwood with Ezzie, wasn't she?"

"She was." He tried for a simple declaration but he knew his friends were on to him.

"That's where Ridgemont saw her," Freddie said with a sly look to the doorway, "And where Ridgemont decided he wants Miss Hanniford."

He cannot have her. "That may be a difficult task for him."

"Oh?" Arnie was all nonchalance as he reached for a muffin.

"Why, pray tell?" Freddie leaned forward.

Victor saw no way out but to declare the truth. "She does not care for him."

"I knew she had sense," Arnie said.

"Who does she like better?" Freddie asked with a jolly twinkle in his brown eyes.

Me.

"Well, well." Freddie arched a brow and sat back. "That is good news."

"It's nothing to discuss."

"No? Not yet?" Arnie asked.

"I'd say it is," Freddie said.

"Please, let's not," Victor pronounced.

"Fine." Arnie nodded. "I bet she'll attend the Wares' tea, don't you, Freddie?"

"Oh, yes. Then we'll know."

Victor rolled his eyes. His friends joking made him feel like a silly swain, instead of a jaded thirty-one year-old widower with two children. "You should keep your attention on Lady Jessica, Freddie."

"I will."

"But we have to help you along with a chance for happiness," Arnie said.

Both had been set against him marrying Alicia. They'd argued against it. Insisted he needed a different sort of woman. One who was more educated, personable. Someone to match a politician, they'd both told him.

"She's lovely. Interesting."

"Someone who will willingly go to the ends of the earth with you?"

Victor knit his brows. Alicia had screamed and cried and wailed against sailing so far from England. Even though she had no choice, even though she had given *him* no choice to save their reputations—to save their *faces* as the Chinese said —he had made her go. His two friends had commiserated with him and drunk with him to near oblivion. Now here he was with the same problem with a different woman and for a different reason. "I have called on her only once."

Arnie shot a glance at Freddie. "Ah. He called on her. Once. Fred, this is Cole's mating song you're hearing."

"Stop that." Victor laughed.

His friends leveled serious eyes on him.

Very well. "I may not be returning to Shanghai," he announced.

"You'd let that fine business die?" Arnie asked. "Why? I don't— Oh. I think I do understand."

Freddie chuckled. "Well now. That's bloody marvelous."

"I see the possibility to remain here if I can possibly reclaim my former reputation."

"As if there is doubt of that." Arnie drank from his cup.

"There is." Victor had to persuade not only men in his political party, but merchants, traders, land owners, government workers.

"So you'll run the business from here?" Arnie examined him closely.

"I can. It won't be quite the same but with my manager's help, I might continue to turn a good penny."

"And then you'd marry again," Freddie said as if it were fact.

Victor might want Ada, but did he want the chains of matrimony? A ripple of his old disgust with his wife's perfidy swept up a taste of bile. "I'm not— No."

"Hmmm." Freddie chewed on his muffin and swallowed. "What's that old line, Arn, about 'methinks the man doth protest too much?'"

"Well, Freddie, you've got something there. There is the fact that Ada Hanniford would make a fine politician's wife."

Victor scanned the expressions of both men, surprised and pleased that their perception of the American girl matched his political aspirations. "Do you think so?"

"Why not?" Arnie said as if it were *fait accompli*.

Freddie took a drink of his coffee and put down his cup. "Why couldn't you rekindle your old ambition for a seat in Parliament? Your father's borough seat was what you were to have long before the Debacle."

His friends' old term for the catastrophe Alicia had wrought made Victor wince.

"Will you take it?" Arnie pursued the matter. "Does your father want you to?"

Word had gone out evidently that the MP for Brighton was to vacate due to health. "He does and I look into it."

"Well, then. I approve," Freddie gave him one of his ear-to-ear grins.

"A celebration is in order." Arnie lifted the brandy decanter. "A prodigal son returns. A charming wife for the man home from his exile. And a new position."

"You both make it sound easy."

"We know it won't be." Arnie observed with narrowed eyes. "You'll have to convince the old dragons of the *ton* that you're a serious man who can control his destiny."

And a wife, should I chose to take one. "Before I persuade society, I need to start with a few good men." Arnie's father was a fixture in the party, serving for more than sixteen years. Victor must speak with him and sound out his views on his candidacy. "I need your father's opinion. With his approval, I can find backing from others."

"He always liked you, Cole. I do too. And I'm to take his seat, come the next election."

"Dear me," said Freddie, catching the eye of the servant for their table. "I say we need a good bottle of champagne."

❦

Lily leaned forward to glance out the coach window as it approached the Earl of Ware's home. "I'm eager to see Jessica."

Ada was eager to see Victor. But up the broad alabaster steps of the Wares' elegant Mayfair house, a few men awaited entry to the tea party. None of them was Lord Victor Cole. Disappointed, she sank into the blue velvet squabs. She'd not seen him for three days. After their ride in the park, she'd expected him to call each day. He hadn't. Nor had he sent word. Was he suddenly uninterested? Or was she gullible?

That made her bristle.

"Ada?"

She focused on her sister. "I'm sorry."

"Gathering wool?"

She put on a brave face.

Lily grinned. "I understand. You have not seen Lord Victor since the other night, is that correct?"

Ada winced. "And I'm surprised."

"Was he that charming?" Lily's blue eyes twinkled in curiosity.

"He was."

"Ahh," she crooned. "Has Papa noticed?"

Ada gave an exasperated sigh. "He has."

"You cannot get much past Killian Hanniford." Lily squeezed her hand. "I'm sure Lord Victor has an explanation. He does not seem like one who'd elicit the affections of a lady and run."

"That's what I thought."

"I'd tell you that the best romances are ones that are slow and sweet. But then, I'd not be telling you what I know to be true."

Lily and her husband Julian had met and married within weeks. And even though the wedding was forced to forestall a scandal, they'd loved each other from the start. Their marriage was sound and their lives together serene. Many had not expected their marriage to last let alone prosper. When Lily had arrived in London five years ago with their father and their cousin, Marianne Roland, she'd entered English society as that rare and much maligned creature, an American heiress. She'd formed a few friendships with young English ladies. One of them who had accepted her immediately was Lady Jessica Baldwin, the only daughter of the earl and countess of Ware. Lily had confided earlier this morning that she feared her friend's choice of husband was creating problems in the Ware family. Today's tea was to prove the pudding. Could the earl and his wife accept Lord Billings, a lowly baron, as their son-in-law?

"Be patient, Ada. He's newly arrived home and I'm sure, has matters to settle. His daughters, his house here in town. Especially his business."

"And more." Ada bit her lip.

"Oh?" Lily's crystal blue gaze ran over her.

Ada demurred. "I shouldn't discuss his private matters."

"You are the judge," Lily said with acceptance in her voice. "Shall we enjoy this afternoon?"

The Seton town coach idled before the Wares'.

"Yes. Has it been a long time since you've seen Jessica?"

"More than two weeks." Lily patted her black hair and smoothed her gloves. "We had Marianne and Remy in London and Jessica's mother has been ill."

"Oh, I'm sorry to hear that. She's recovered now, I imagine? Else, why hold this party?"

"She told Jessica she was better. But if you ask me, her mother was only playing cat and mouse with her." Lily sighed. "She told her to decide on a beau."

"But you said she had. That she would accept none other than this Lord Billings." Ada had not met the man, but if Lily liked him, he must be a good choice for her friend.

"Her mother used her so-called illness as a delaying tactic to usher in the man she really wished Jessica would consider."

"But that's terrible to do to your own daughter."

"It is. But the Countess of Ware has fine ideas for her chick."

"Oh, dear." Ada disliked these meddling mothers. "Who?"

"She'd like a duke for her girl. Been pushing her to marry up for all the years I've known her."

"Dear me. Not Ridgemont?" Ada had told Lily about his behavior in the country. Lily had dismissed him as a cur.

"Oh, yes. *Him*. Among others."

The footman opened the door and handed them out.

Jessica was Lily's age. Twenty-four. Old, some said, for a society girl to still be husband hunting. Many even thought Ada was approaching the pre-conceived age of retirement from the marriage mart. "How many dukes are there left in the realm?"

"Two? Three? One is sixty. Another...I've no idea! Certainly not enough for every young thing who'd like one."

Ada wanted to laugh. But then she thought of Ridgemont who should have asked for Ezzie. And anger flowed through her all over again.

Lily had met and married the heir to the duke of Seton four years ago. As that oddity, an American heiress, Lily was educated, eloquent, irreverent and lovely. Uninterested in marrying just any English aristocrat, Lily had made it plain to their father that she'd only take a husband whom she loved. That she found one within months of arrival was a pleasant surprise to all of them. Lily and her husband Julian were very happy, with two small sons, and another child coming in five months.

"Shall we survey the battlefield?" Ada challenged as they climbed the steps.

"We'll rally round our friend and look for your man of the hour." They approached the Wares' butler and Lily was being discreet not to mention proper names.

Inside the main salon, Lily and she found the countess and Jessica near the doors.

The countess did look rather pale. Her daughter, whom Ada had met many times over the years, appeared jittery. Having paid their respects to their hostesses, they glided along and greeted others whom they knew. Jessica said she would join Lily and her in a few minutes.

"I think we shall get acquainted with a few guests, don't you?" Lily said with a quick glance toward the garden doors.

In a group in the corner stood four men. There was Edgecombe, Ezzie's gentleman and beside him stood tall, debonair, ginger-haired Lord Victor Cole. Ada could look no further when his turquoise eyes caught hers. His gaze lingered on her lips, exciting her as she'd not been since last she saw him days and days ago.

Lily went toward them. "Good afternoon, Lord Edgecombe. It's good to see you here."

"Your Grace." He bowed low over Lily's hand.

"And Lord Victor," Lily continued. "How good to see you again."

"Your Grace. I am delighted." He inclined his head, then asked if he might introduce his friends. "Sir Arnold Meachum. Lord Billings." The jolly looking bald man was Meachum. The tall, dark-haired fellow with a jovial smile was Billings.

"Lord Billings, Sir Arnold, my sister, Miss Hanniford."

"A pleasant surprise," Ada said to all.

With her heart beating like a drum, she tried to concentrate on the conversations. But the magnetic pull of Victor's intent regard was irresistible. She could find nothing to say. Nothing to add. Nothing...

Billings and Meachum told Lily of their interest in her dispensaries on Julian's estates. Lily organized and stocked medical cottages at all of Julian's estates. She'd even built one on his land in Ireland. "Everyone deserves proper care and medicine, sir."

"I wonder if you'd advise me on creating one for my own estate?" Billings asked.

Lady Jessica joined the group. "Has Lord Billings decided

to bend your ear about a dispensary for his people, Your Grace?"

"He has and I'm honored to help."

"Her Grace," said Jessica with pride, "has every herb and powder you might need, Billings. I think she could pull a tooth or deliver a baby, if she were required."

"Let's not exaggerate, my friend," Lily warned.

"And I need no instructions of dentistry or midwifery," added Billings.

Victor leaned close to Ada. "Will you come talk with me?"

Her knees went to water. If he hadn't taken her arm, she might have evaporated. Irritated at her fascination with him, she sought refuge in chatter. "Lily will talk his ears off about serums and herbs. What's fake and what's helpful."

She led the way to two chairs in one corner. As she sank to her chair, a footman approached with a tray for the card table between them. He poured tea and left them.

"I'm pleased to see you," she said admiring the cut of his emerald satin waistcoat and ivory cravat. How had she forgotten the high arch of his cheekbones or the clean line of his nose? The way his hair swept over the crown of his head...

"And I to see that you wear my gift."

She touched a finger to the white jade comb that held tight her elaborate chignon. It had arrived the morning after their ride in the park and she'd hidden it away to treasure it. "It is magnificent."

"Matched only by your own lustre."

Her cheeks turned hot with a blush. "You must not be too eloquent."

"I don't know how to be other."

"Of course you do," she challenged him. "You could just say, you wear it well."

"I knew you'd wear it well." He took up his tea and drank. "I have more to send you."

What she wanted from him, she dare not name. That would be so...intimate So...indecent.

"Silks," he whispered. "Pearls."

"You mustn't." She shook her head. "It's not allowed. Not until...unless..." *We are engaged.* She bit her lip. "Not permitted."

He moved nearer, his cologne of bergamot and lemon enchanting her. "I missed you."

Her pounding heart thumped to a stop. She could admire his eyes forever and never tire. "That you must not say."

"If I cannot do this and cannot say that, what would you have me do?"

Her gaze fell to his marvelous mouth.

"Oh, my darling, I definitely cannot do that."

She burned to have him say or do whatever he wished. But she took a large drink of her tea and gulped it down.

He set his jaw and surveyed the room. "I say, it is rather warm in here. Yes? Shall we stroll in the garden? I understand the countess has prize roses one must see to believe."

A warmth gush of desire swamped her. Prudence demanded she be wise. "We'll stay to the path."

"In sight of all." He shot to his feet and put out his hand.

She grasped it as if it were a lifeline.

"My dear Miss Hanniford," he said as they rounded the doors and passed two other strollers, "how wonderful you look in that ice blue gown."

"My lord, how marvelous you look in that green waistcoat."

He tucked her arm through his. "Forgive me for not writing these past few days."

"Where have you been?" *Dear god.* She sounded like a fishwife.

"In Brighton."

"Brighton?" Had he been on holiday while she pined for him like a schoolgirl?

"That would be my constituency."

Ohhh! "I love Brighton. My father has his country house there."

"I know. I met with him two days ago."

What had they discussed? Her?

"It was business. Politics, really. He was among friends. His. Mine." He paused by a tall topiary. "We discussed my chances."

"And?" She clasped her hands. "Would they want you?"

The boyish delight that lit his handsome face made him years younger. "I do believe they might."

"That's wonderful." She wanted to hug him.

He narrowed his gaze on her mouth. "I wish I could hold you."

She spun to one side. "Don't do that. Not here."

"Darling, there *is* nowhere else."

Her eyes fluttered closed. The mere memory of his arms around her intoxicated her. "You must be more discreet."

"Sweetheart, I'm as discreet as a man can be when I wish only to carry you away."

She put a hand flat to the satin of his waistcoat and prayed for control. "You try me."

"As you do me." He was chuckling and covered her hand with his own. His heartbeat was as strong a drumbeat as hers. "I thought to invite you and your sister to luncheon with me. At my home here in town. Next Wednesday."

The invitation thrilled her, but to wait until Wednesday seemed an eternity. "Yes, that would be nice."

"Nice." He barked in laughter. "There will be more."

"More?" Confusion about his intentions rattled her.

"More kisses. More caresses. But I must be certain."

"Of me?"

He arched a long red brow. "Of you, I am totally certain. I must be positive I can do right by you."

"Oh, I am not a demanding—"

"I never thought you were. But I must hold up my head in society. More than that I must respect myself, Ada. If I take a wife, I want to support her, keep her, make her happy, my own. I cannot—no, I will not do that unless I have first established myself as I see fit. I did not...before. I had to make compromises. It ate at me that I did less than I should have, that I tolerated failures of my own and because of that, those of my wife, too. I will not do that again. Not again, Ada."

What he had suffered in his marriage was truly horrid. He had told her what he wished and she would not ask for more. "I will certainly honor your need to attend to your affairs as you see fit."

"Thank you. Give me time, my darling."

Swallowing tears, she nodded. "You have it."

"Come back inside," he said, his rough voice an apology and a balm.

They joined Lily who stood talking with Jessica and Billings.

"I wonder if you would like to join us at the theater tomorrow night, Lord Victor? My husband and I do like to attend and we'd like you to join us in our box. Lady Jessica, her parents and Lord Billings have accepted my invitation. Ada, too, will join us. Next week my husband and I retire to our country house for the summer months and this is my last chance to enjoy the theater before I am otherwise occupied for many months. What do you say, sir? Will you come?"

"I'd be honored, Your Grace."

Once Victor appeared in the Seton's box tomorrow night many would assume they were matched. The prospect delighted her, but she questioned if she could count on that. Lily seemed to have no problems with the impression his appearance with them might make. He had none. She couldn't either...except for one nagging question. Would all that Victor did now lead to the result he wished? Would he garner enough support to be appointed to the vacant seat in Parliament? Or would he have to return to Shanghai? And if he failed here and he had to go, could she whole-heartedly support him and go with him?

Suddenly there was a hush in the room.

All turned, one by one, as if they were on precision wheels, toward the salon entrance. There stood a petite but elegant brunette, impeccably coiffed, exquisitely attired in ruby red satin of the latest fashion. Her hazel eyes scanned the guests like a fox sighting prey. She smiled, a rueful curve to her rouged lips. With a look of disdain for all, she made a line for Lady Jessica.

"Elanna," Lily breathed.

Someone behind them whispered, "She never comes out."

This was Lily's sister-in-law, the Countess of Carbury, a woman Ada had met many times at her sister's homes, always in private, never with any others in attendance. Always unescorted except by a mute and dowdy maid. Known to many as the reclusive hellion who'd met, married and deserted her husband, Elanna was a feared feminine creature who could attract ridicule and envy in one searing moment. She cared not for their approval. Cared not for their rules. She was the daughter of a duke without fortune but who'd been forced to marry a man decades older. A man whom she loathed from the first day she'd wed. And even the birth of a child, her son and husband's heir, had not allayed her need to live far way from him. She'd abandoned her husband and child years ago to live in the Carbury townhouse and rarely appeared at social gatherings where the *ton* could gape and marvel and then shun her. Yet today she had come.

Ada understood why. Jessica had been Elanna's childhood

friend. And it was she who had introduced Lily to Jessica. She was here to wish Jessica well...or so Ada hoped. Elanna could be snappish and abrasive. Not the kind of guest one wished for on any occasion.

"Dear Jessica. Lily. Ada." Elanna kissed them each in the French manner.

"I'm happy you've come," Jessica said, holding Elanna's hands.

"Thank you. I doubt your mother is." She gave Jessica a true smile, then appraised Lord Billings and Victor.

Jessica moved forward. "Allow me to introduce my friends."

Elanna brought out her best behavior for that, appearing congenial and not at all predatory. For their part, Billings and Victor took her acquaintance with polite nods.

Billings and Jessica excused themselves to talk with other guests.

The niceties done, Lily lowered her voice. "Elanna, it's good of you to come support our friend."

"My dear, you know I always want to see proper marriages done." She turned an intense gaze on Victor. "We've not met before, my lord. But wouldn't you agree?"

Ada would wager Elanna knew about Victor's past, who he was, his wife, his career abroad. Even if one aristocrat had never met another, they read scandal sheets, they gossiped, they lived amid the wreckage.

Victor put both hands behind his back. With a hard look of indifference to any implication she might raise, he tipped his head to one side. "I do indeed, Lady Carbury."

A commotion at the door had all turning to view two men who raised their voices at the family butler.

Ridgemont and another man laughed at the servant.

Victor's mouth thinned.

Ada caught her breath. That prickly feeling she had whenever she was near Richard set her teeth on edge. A thought flashed through her mind that this was the same discomfort she'd felt lately whenever she'd gone out to the flower mart or the shops.

Victor inched closer to Ada as his brother greeted the countess and the earl. Richard's tall thin friend Tildon lurked at his side.

"He is drunk." Elanna gave a very unladylike snort. "Ware will have none of that."

"I say, a wonderful group." Richard greeted them. "Your Grace. Lady Carbury. And Miss Hanniford. The family's jewels out in force, eh?"

Victor stepped toward his brother. "You are being rude."

"Not by half, Victor, dear boy."

Victor's eyes flashed. "Now you must leave."

"Oh, no."

"Tildon?" Victor took in his brother's leering, inebriated friend. "You too."

"Now just a minute, Victor," Richard began.

But had no time to say more as Victor seized his arm. "Come with me."

"Making a scene, dear boy. Tsk, tsk."

Victor was frog-marching him toward the foyer.

"I want to talk to Lady Carbury. Out rarely. You know she has only that clerk of Seton's, what's his name? Phillip? Phillip Leland to her bed. Man has no money—"

"That's enough, Richard."

"No title. Only Seton's salary and yet he has this very nice piece in his bed."

"Stop!" Victor seethed.

"What? We cannot tell the truth now?"

Victor pushed him through the doors as the throng of guests stood agog.

Ada stepped forward.

"No." Lily grabbed her arm.

Elanna seemed in a trance as she gazed toward the door.

When Ada looked, Elanna had tears on her cheeks.

"I must leave," she murmured to no one. She put her glass down and strode to the Countess of Ware and the earl to bid them a hasty *adieu*.

"Oh, no." Lily choked back a sob. "She goes out so rarely. Now she'll retreat again."

"Let's go home." Ada took her sister's hand and led her away.

CHAPTER 12

Victor donned his top hat as he left his cab. Theater patrons in their formal attire milled about the entry and among them, he searched for the Setons and Ada. The catastrophe of yesterday's scene with Richard had eroded much of his euphoria since returning from Brighton. But he tugged at his gloves, determined not to let that affect his evening near Ada.

"The Setons' box?" he asked an usher and was shown the way up the stairs to the grand circle. The man opened the private door for him and he was happy to see that Julian, Lily and Ada had already arrived.

"Good evening," he bid them all and bowed to Lily, then smiled at Ada.

Julian offered polite greetings, and in an aside said, "I thank you for yesterday."

"I wish I might've done more, Your Grace."

"In those circumstances, quick action is best. Discretion with the perpetrator is not necessary. We can talk more. Later. For now, know I am grateful."

"Lord Victor, how good of you to come." Lily went up on

her toes to kiss his cheek. The extraordinary greeting mellowed him.

Ada stepped forward, grasped his hand and held tightly to him. "How are you?"

"Recovered as best as can be." He noted the faint blue around her eyes and wondered if she'd slept last night. He hadn't. "And you, I hope, have had time to forgive me my behavior yesterday."

She put a gloved hand to her throat. "Oh, dear, no. You have nothing to regret. You saved us."

"Not one lady." All through the night, he had ridiculed himself that he'd not been able to remove Richard from the premises before he did such hideous damage to the Countess of Carbury.

"Come sit. We will enjoy this and forget yesterday."

The countess and earl of Ware arrived with Jessica and Lord Billings just as the curtain rose.

The play—thank god, a comedy—gave him a few blithe moments. But he fretted, replaying the scene of last night when Richard pounded on his front door and demanded entry.

Victor's portly butler who knew Richard by sight had let him in, but had scurried upstairs behind him as Richard ran from one room to another to find him.

Victor shot to his feet just as Richard burst in the library door. "What the hell do you think you're doing?"

Richard lunged forward. His clothes were wrinkled. He wore no frockcoat. His hands shook. His eyes did not focus. They were dilated, red-rimmed. *Was he taking opium?* "Warning you!"

"Of what?" The fact that Victor was taller than his older brother by at least three inches had agitated Richard since they were at Eton. He glared down at him as they stood toe-to-toe. "That you'll never act like an idiot again?"

Richard spread his thin lips in a sneer. "That you'll not marry her, dear boy. She deserves better than you. Cuckold. Outcast the you are."

"And you? Philanderer. Adulterer. Drunk. Do you think she deserves you?"

"Why not? Her sister caught a duke, why don't I eat this little plum myself?"

Victor suppressed the urge to gag. "You could not shine her shoes."

"Dear boy. I'd do other things to her that would make her shine mine."

"Get out. Never return. Never!"

How he'd left, Victor did not remember. Through his red rage, he saw only that he must somehow marry Ada very soon. To rush them both into marriage was not ideal, there was so much yet to settle. His assurances for political support. Even the analysis of his company's current finances. But he questioned his brother's mental state. His acuity. If he was an addict, he'd not be the only one. Many in Britain took the poppy. Victor had seen what it did to the poor Chinese who smoked it and the rich Chinese who thought they could control their consumption. All failed. He knew first hand. He'd spent years weaning himself of the desire for it. The physical, aching, repulsive need.

"Will you come?" Ada pressed her hand to his sleeve.

"I'm sorry." The play had ended and the others were standing, the gentlemen going to the cloakroom at the rear of the box to acquire the ladies' coats. "What did you ask?"

She gave him an understanding smile. "You will accept my sister's invitation to join the rest of us at the house for a small supper?"

"I will. Thank you."

The Wares, Jessica and Lord Billings took the earl's coach to the Setons' Green Park home. Victor joined the Setons and

Ada in the duke's town carriage. Seated next to Julian, facing the ladies, he allowed himself to consider what it might be like to be welcomed into this family. They were educated, jovial, liked books and theater, commerce—and yes, Killian, had assured him the other day, that they even enjoyed politics.

"Not that any of us is involved. Americans as we Hannifords are, we cannot vote here," he'd said when they met in Brighton with other men of business. "But we are as ready as any to debate the issues. Especially Ada."

"As I have noted, sir."

"Glad you find that appealing," Hanniford had said.

More than appealing, he thought as he gazed at the beautiful lady who sat opposite. *She becomes vital to my well-being.*

While the ladies repaired to the withdrawing room, Julian invited the men to join him in his library. The smell of old paper and leather bindings, the wealth of books upon the shelves assailed Victor with a measure of peace he'd sought all day. He took his glass of wine and strolled to the huge windows overlooking the park. A double set of doors led out to a wide veranda.

"We can go out if you like," Julian offered him and the other men.

Pierce arrived with apologies. "Hope I have not missed anything. Sorry to be late. Dinner at the Langham. Took forever to conclude my business."

The men adjourned to the veranda and spoke of the mild weather, welcome for June. A few people walked in the park. Two men in dark suits stood talking in the shadows of a large oak. The Wares discussed how they would soon retire to their country estate.

"Haven't been here in years, Seton." The Earl of Ware gazed out upon the vast lawns of the old park. "Always did like this view."

"My grandfather would complain that people used to throw stones at the windows to get him to come out to talk. He built this veranda, but many use the steps anyway and come right up to the library doors."

"Cheeky," Ware said. "How do you deal?"

"As with anything else, one hopes the incidents are few." Julian grew circumspect. "Which brings me to my subject. I want to thank all of you for your forbearance yesterday with the scene in your home, sir and madam." He made a small acknowledgment of the Wares. "I remain indebted to you, Lord Victor, for your assistance with my sister, even though I know that was a difficult task for you to confront your brother."

Victor noted how Pierce froze. In the moonlight, his stark features tightened over his bones. As if all blood drained from him. The reason for that puzzled Victor.

Julian exhaled. "My sister has had a difficult life since her marriage. She wed her husband under duress. I always wished I'd had the opportunity to dissuade her from marrying, but I was not in position to do that. My father, you see, was devoted to his financial well-being more than to Elanna's happiness. She rebelled in the only way she could. She turned on him, my mother and at first, me as well. I regret that. In many ways, she does too. But her choices to leave her husband and live here in town, away from her child too, have meant that she suffers in ways she never anticipated. Ostracism can be cruel. It's made her worse, erratic, sad, sometimes wild. She wishes she could change the past. She's tried to re-enter society. But it is difficult. Many cannot forgive or forget."

Pierce examined the ceiling, a nerve ticking in his jaw.

The earl contemplated his wine.

Victor downed his. He had the scars to prove society could be beastly.

"The condemnation of others," Julian went on with sorrow, "including the altercation yesterday, were never goals of my once quite charming young sister. I will be so bold as to ask for your tolerance of her. But I will ask for your compassion for her, too."

"My brother," Victor needed to say, "is totally at fault here. He grows more..." *Contemptible.* "Irresponsible. Unmanageable."

Lily was at the door, sprightly and beckoning them in. "Aren't all of you chilly out here? Do come in. Supper is ready."

Victor was thrilled to be done with this topic. Ada came to his side with a broad smile and looped her arm through his.

They filed out of the library into the wide white marbled foyer, headed for the dining room across the hall.

A carriage pulled up outside, the horse whinnying amid a clatter of wheels and shouts. Unusual sounds for this neighborhood where the *ton* did not draw attention to themselves with crass behavior.

But voices out on the street carried in.

The party stopped, all of them, to stare at each other.

Someone banged on the door. "Open up! I beg you."

Julian stepped forward.

"I'll get it, Your Grace!" Julian's butler rushed ahead to grab the knob. He flung it wide.

In stumbled a young man. Tall, lean, with a shock of disheveled gold hair, he had remarkable large eyes, wide with terror.

"Your Grace!" the stranger gulped. His chest heaving, he gasped for air. "Help me."

Julian caught him up and virtually dragged him to the night watchman's chair. "Leland? What's wrong?"

Leland? That was the name of the man Richard yelled about yesterday. According to Richard, this was the Countess of Carbury's *lover*?

Tears welled up in the man's eyes. "Oh, Julian! Jesus. Come help us."

The duke leaned over the man who was obviously his friend. "What? Why? What's—?"

"Christ, Julian." Leland gulped. "Carbury's dead!"

"What?" Julian jerked upright, incredulous.

Someone cried out.

Beside Victor, Ada gasped.

He curled an arm around her waist and pressed her tightly to his side.

"Dead," Leland got out.

"How?" Julian clutched the lapels of his coat.

Leland dragged air into his lungs. "Carbury. He came tonight. To the house. Had a gun and de-demanded to see Elanna."

"No!" Julian groaned. Shrank away in horror.

"I— She—"

"You were there? *At this hour?*"

Ada's nails dug into Victor's sleeve.

Leland blinked at Julian. "I—. Yes. *Yes.*"

"Tell me how, Leland? Where?"

Leland cast about, as if looking for his sanity. "He barged in. Waived his pistol. Charged up the stairs. Elanna went out. He yelled at her and—"

"He what? Went out *where?*"

"The stairs. She said—" Leland went silent. Blinked as if he were a blind man.

Victor registered that Leland's story sounded disjointed. But then was that not normal for a man so distraught?

Julian hauled him to his feet. "Where is she?"

"He hit her!"

Julian exploded. "He *shot* her? Is she alive?"

"Yes! Yes! Alive."

"And...and what?" Julian shook him.

"He fell. On the stairs."

Julian stared at him, mouth open.

"I checked. He's...he's not breathing." Leland grimaced.

Lily was crying. Pierce, his eyes bulging, grabbed his sister close.

Ada ran to them, arms around them both.

Leland staggered back to the chair. Head in his hands, he sobbed. "I might've pushed him. I can't remember....But he's dead."

CHAPTER 13

Julian, Pierce, Freddie, Victor and Phillip Leland climbed down from the Seton town coach minutes later. Lord Ware had volunteered to remain at the Seton house to provide a cool head for the ladies while the men went to Elanna.

They took the front steps up to the front door.

Julian banged the knocker time and time again. "Let me talk to her first."

Pierce was white as a ghost. "I'll check Carbury."

Leland stood limp against the door frame. "He's gone."

The four others mutely regarded him.

Victor had encountered a similar death in Shanghai last year when the wife of a German *tai-pan* had died accidentally. Preserving the scene of the crime was helpful in the inquest. And there would be one here, whether Leland had pushed Carbury or the man had fallen accidentally. "Don't touch anything. Don't move the body. We need to call the constable as soon as possible."

A distraught and anxious butler answered the door.

"Maxwell," Julian said to the little man. "Let us in. Where's Lady Carbury?"

"Parlor." He pointed a shaking finger toward the far door. "Back parlor, yes, yes, Your Grace. She's...she's not well. Not well."

Julian swept past him. But within two steps he balked.

Victor and Pierce were right beside him, Freddie behind. There before them splayed on the rose and white marble tiles was the body of a man, contorted, legs at odd angles, his head bloodied, his mouth open in grotesque death.

Victor squeezed shut his eyes. No doubt here. This man was dead. From his position and his injuries, he'd fallen down the circular steps. Marble, all of them. No runner covering them. Nothing to break his descent. Or soften the blows.

Without his gaze glued to Carbury, Julian said, "Someone check the servants. See who's here now. Then, too."

"I'll do it." Freddie nodded to the butler. "Show me the way below stairs, will you?"

"Yes, sir."

Off they went.

Pierce was bending over the body. "Broken legs. Gashed his head. Broke a few teeth." And beneath his breath he murmured, "Bastard."

Victor surveyed the scene. A white lace handkerchief lay on the edge of the top most step. And something else, small, white and glistening. A few of them. *Pearls?*

"He was a tyrant," Pierce spat. "A bully. She hated him. From the first minute they were engaged."

Victor licked his lips. *Still. Not a way for anyone to die.*

Leland had found his way to a chair by the door to the porter's closet. "He beat her."

"*What?*" Pierce glared at him.

"You didn't know," Leland bit off. "No one did. She never told anyone but me. He would tie her up. Thrash her."

Pierce cursed. "Why the hell didn't she divorce him?"

"How?" Leland asked, his nostrils flaring in contempt. "A woman can't get a decree. Not for that. Not for anything."

But a man could acquire one for a wife's adultery. 'Criminal conversation' required a trial and legal decree. But the newspapers got hold of the story before any decree came down. Victor's pulse quickened and he gazed around the hall. He could not erase the vision of his wife telling him he could not leave her. Could not divorce her. "You wouldn't want your precious family name sullied. Your parents would hate you."

Victor tore himself from the past. The ugly, unchangeable past.

A missing piece of this puzzle niggled at him.

"Where's the gun, Leland?"

The man's large green eyes registered the question. But he shrugged.

"Did he have it when he ran up the staircase?" Victor pressured him.

"I...can't remember."

Can't or won't? "Of course you can. Better to recall it now before the investigators get here. They will ask you."

Leland's attention traveled up the stairs. "Yes, he had it. He ran in. Maxwell opened the door and he flew in. He was a madman. Wild about some rumor. Yesterday at some tea party. Crazy that some man had accused her of having an affair with me."

What? No. Christ, no. Richard's accusations caused this?

Victor put out a hand to steady himself, but caught himself from touching anything. "So...where...where's the pistol, Leland?"

"Up there." He lifted a hand toward the top.

"And what's that on the top step?"

"Where?"

Victor had no tolerance for whatever subterfuge this man

was attempting. He glowered at him and it forced the required effect.

"Her handkerchief. And...looks like her necklace."

"Why are they on the stairs?"

"He tore them from her."

"Before or after he hit her?"

"Hit her?" Leland's mind drifted away. "I—I don't know."

Don't know or can't remember? Victor inhaled. "You have to."

"Yes." He slumped in the chair, defeated.

"At what point did you push him?"

Weary, Leland hung his head.

Terrified for this man, outraged for the dead man and his wife and their years of mutual torment, Victor fought valiantly to contain his anger. "For your own defense, you must remember exactly what happened here."

Pierce scowled at Leland, then Victor. Leland did not catch his glance, but Victor did. Pierce tipped his head in question.

And Victor nodded, then shook his head in disbelief.

Julian emerged from the back room. Defeat hung around him like a shroud. "No delaying this any longer. We need to summon the police."

Victor volunteered. He had to do something constructive before he went mad as a hatter. Richard was to blame for this. Richard, the catalyst to so many calamities. The shame and outrage of what his brother had become enraged him. And if he saw him anytime soon, he'd have to kill the urge to throttle him.

❦

"I don't want any more of this." Lily pushed away the hot cocoa and pressed her hands to her cheeks. "I wonder why they're taking so long."

After the four men had left for Elanna's, Lily dried her tears and decided to sit on the veranda. The night was warm, a soft breeze whispering through the trees in Green Park. As they sipped hot cocoa, Jessica and her mother and father discreetly remained inside. Because of Lily's condition, Ada was devoted to keeping her sister as calm as possible.

"Julian will deal with everything." Ada had no idea what police procedures were for a death like Carbury's.

"Elanna is so difficult." Lily sighed heavily, staring out at the shadows cast by clouds and the moonlight through the branches. "She always has been from the day she knew she had to marry Carbury."

Listening to her sister recount the sad tale of the transformation of her sister-in-law, Ada heard the story of Elanna's life in more detail than she ever had.

But Lily, who knew her better than Ada, had sympathy for the young woman. Ada had been in Elanna's company occasionally over the past few years, but she'd never had a conversation with her that allowed her an insight to her character. Each time, however, Ada was impressed by Lily's tolerance for a young woman whom Ada saw as self-centered and who had caused as many of her own problems as her husband. Perhaps that was not fair to Elanna. Ada had witnessed three of Carbury's outbursts when he searched for his wife. In those instances, he'd been belligerent, threatening physical violence to his wife, Ada's father, and her brother Pierce.

"I'm going up to bed." She bent to put a hand to Ada's. "Stay. I know you like the fragrances of the garden."

"Try to sleep. It's good for you."

Lily tried to smile, then strode away.

Ada strolled down the steps to the small rose garden that bordered the house from the public walk. The best buds had bloomed last week and only a few flowers remained. London with its smoke and fog was not kind to flowers. In the countryside, where a person breathed more easily, flowers did too. The azaleas and rhododendrons flourished at her father's and step-mother's home along the seaside cliffs outside Brighton.

A prickling sensation made her stop. Odd. She felt that in the theater tonight, too. She shivered. Perhaps she'd go in and—

A shadow emerged from behind the nearest tree.

She cupped her elbows. Surprise had her stepping backward.

"Good evening," he said in a saccharine tone. "I thought your sister would never leave."

"What are you doing here?"

Another man stepped from the gloom. "Convenient, eh, to come down here for us?"

The two of them were quite mad. Drunk, too. Or...or by the looks of their eyes, intoxicated by some other means.

"Good night." She spun toward the house.

The first one caught her around the waist. "I think it soon will be!"

CHAPTER 14

"Your Grace," Victor addressed Julian who sat with his sister in the small first floor parlor. "Lord Billings and I will return to the house."

Two Bobbies and an inspector from the Metropolitan Police had arrived minutes ago and they were in the hall, examining Carbury's body.

By the policemen's orders, Julian was to keep his sister away while they worked and questioned Leland. "Take Pierce with you."

Lily's and Ada's brother stood by the door, his arms crossed, his gaze upon the paralyzed form of Elanna. "I'll stay here."

Julian waved a weary hand at them.

Victor questioned the wisdom of that. But he would not argue. Whatever Pierce's rationale—and his motives seemed less than practical—Victor sensed Pierce could not be dissuaded.

As the Seton coachman drove them back to Green Park, he and Freddie sat exhausted. Before the police had arrived, they had gone over events with Leland twice but he answered differently each time. Victor worried that his interview with the police inspector would not go well.

The only sound in the streets was the horses' hooves upon the cobbles as Freddie took a deep breath and asked, "Shall I utter the question or will you?"

"Hell, yes. I have more than one. You?"

Freddie blew out a gust of air. "Did Carbury fall?"

"Where was Elanna when her husband barged in?" Victor still did not believe Leland's claim he was upstairs with her. The way Leland described the initial encounter with Elanna's husband struck a wrong chord.

"Where was Leland?"

Victor gazed out the window and noted how clear the night air was. Unusual, that. "Did Carbury strike her? I saw no marks on her."

"But her pearls are scattered down the stairs. A handkerchief, too. I assume they're hers. How did that happen?"

"And did Carbury fall? Or was he pushed?"

"And if so—"

Victor had to say the words. "By Leland or by Elanna?"

The clatter of a horse's hooves upon the stones rent the night air.

"Someone's in a hurry," Freddie noted.

"Wonder what—"

A man shouted at their coachman and the carriage careened to a halt.

"What the hell?" Victor craned his neck.

"Highwaymen?" Freddie burst out, a tone of jest mixed with incredulity. "In London?"

"Milord! Milord!" The rider came to the window and shouted at them.

"*Who is that?*"

"I'm groom from His Grace's stable! Roll down the glass, milord!"

Victor and Freddie frowned at each other.

"What's wrong?" Victor asked.

"Sir, come to the house. I'm to fetch you. Hurry. Her Grace sent me. We need you!"

"What's the matter?"

"Miss Ada is gone!"

Victor practically jumped out of his seat. "*What?*"

"Vanished."

"How?"

"Dunno, milord. Just come!"

Victor's head swam. How could Ada be gone? And where? At this hour of the night, only one possibility could be true. Someone had abducted her? But how and why?

Ransom?

The coach rounded the street corner and he yanked open the door before the horses came to a full stop.

He pounded on the Seton's front door. The butler flung it open and led them to the salon where Lily awaited them. The earl of Ware, his wife and daughter Jessica stood near the fire, defeat etched in their expressions.

"I went up to bed." Lily wrung her hands, dried tears marred her cheeks. "Ada decided to remain on the veranda. She loves the silence of the night air and the fragrance of roses, you know."

In a robe and slippers, her dark hair down around her shoulders, Lily stared at Victor and Freddie. He doubted she truly saw them. The gaslights in the sconces flickered, putting her harrowed face into sharp and unflattering focus. Her eyes were red from crying and she paced, then paused and resumed it all again. "I should not have left her there. But no one..." Her mouth quivered. "No one's ever been so bold as to come up and take one of us."

Victor put a hand to his forehead. "How was she dressed?"

"Still in her gown."

"A shawl?"

"No." Lily clamped a hand to her mouth. "The night was warm."

Not now, it isn't.

"Victor," Freddie said in a quiet voice, "we need to notify the police."

The earl grunted. "The police can be such an interference."

Victor spun toward him. Many a crime went unreported while an aristocrat tried to ameliorate whatever problem—or crime—had occurred. "But they have the best means to track the culprits."

Lily groped for a chair and sat. "This nasty business with Carbury, now Ada gone. Julian will die trying to right it."

"Your Grace, forgive me." The earl cleared his throat. "I hope my displeasure with calling the police will not deter you from doing that. Your sister is gone. Some fool has obviously absconded with her. They can find her. Much as I hate to admit, they are capable."

Good that the earl came round.

Victor would employ heaven and earth and the very devil himself to find her.

"Who had the chance to abduct her?"

Victor blinked. Freddie was asking him the very question he asked himself.

The first answer that dawned on him nearly toppled him. He steadied himself, reaching for the support of a chair. Damn cane, he'd left it home tonight because the weather was decent.

"She told me she thought someone was following her." Lily put a hand to her throat. "I didn't think much of it, but... but perhaps I should have."

That shook him to his core—and he went to kneel before Lily. "When? Where?"

"After she returned from your parents' house party, she had an odd feeling that she couldn't explain. The first time she experienced the sensation was when she'd gone to the flower mart. Our ladies' companion, Comtesse de Chaumont, has been ill and so Ada took a maid with her. She said she'd experienced the odd feeling a few times. When you took her riding."

Victor's stomach lurched. Richard had come to London after the house party, not to his own home as he'd told everyone he intended. Could he be so hideous as to follow Ada? Stalk her? He had proximity, curse him. His London house faced Green Park. Two houses away. Steps away from Seton House.

He got to his feet. "Did she ever see anyone? Man? Woman?"

Lily shook her head and wiped at new tears.

"My lord?" Victor faced the earl. "May I ask you to summon the police?"

"I'd be at your service, Lord Victor."

"Freddie, come with me, will you?" He leaned over Lily and took her hand. "I'm down to Ridgemont's house."

She pulled back, appalled. "Oh, you don't possibly think—?"

"I pray not. But God forgive me for saying this, I think his actions yesterday at the earl's and countess's tea party inspired rumors that led Carbury tonight to assault his wife. His threats to me there yesterday lead me to question if he might be so...erratic as to do something rash."

"If he did this—"

He squeezed her hand.

She trembled in her horror. "Papa will kill him. And Pierce—"

He swung toward the earl, his wife and daughter. "Give me ten minutes. I should know by then...but if I don't return, if I need Freddie to help me, you'll take care of the duchess and her family."

He didn't wait for an answer, but fled the salon and the house, Freddie on his heels.

"Where is he?" Victor demanded of the bleary-eyed butler who'd answered his furious pounding.

"My lord?" The servant stared up at him, harried and confused.

"My brother?" Victor scanned the foyer, the central stairs. The mansion was dark, deserted. "Is he here?"

"No, no, no, sir. Not." The butler secured the sash of his robe around his middle.

"Where is he then?"

"Out." The little man drew into himself, intimidated by the menace in Victor's voice. "He went out with his friend."

"Tildon?"

"Yes, sir. Lord Tildon."

Freddie ran up the stairs to the next floor. He thrust open a few doors. "All dark. Not here, Victor."

"When?" *What was the butler's name? Hell if Victor could remember.* "When was he here? Samuels? Samuels, is it?"

"Yes, sir. Yes, Samuels."

"When did my brother leave the house?"

The man thought a second. "An hour ago? More?"

"Drunk? Sober?" *Befuddled by opium?*

"Oh, sir. I couldn't say, sir."

"What did they say when they left?"

The butler scratched his head. "The first time?"

That stymied him. "They left *twice*?"

"They did. Yes, sir. Came back for the carriage. Or Lord Ridgemont did."

The carriage? "Not Tildon, too?"

"No, sir."

Victor prayed for forbearance. "Tell me what they did. What Ridgemont did, Samuels. A lady's life may depend on it."

"Oh, sir. I'd hate to think that Lord Ridgemont did any harm to a lady."

"I know you would, Samuels." Victor considered the man with sympathy. Whatever had happened, whatever Ridgemont did, this man was not complicit. Only doing his service to his master. "Tell me where they went, Samuels. What they said."

"The first time they said they were going for a walk."

"In the park?" Victor could've jumped out of his skin with fury.

"Yes, sir."

"And when they returned and ordered the carriage, did they say anything?"

"Yes, sir. Lord Ridgemont told me I could go to bed. He and Tildon were going to the manor."

Richard's estate north of London. "At this hour of the night?"

"That's so, sir."

"And they'd have you awaken Ridgemont's coachman to ready the carriage?"

"Told me to tell him to hurry, too."

"Did they both come in the house after their walk in the park?"

The butler shook his head. "No, sir."

"Did my brother explain that?"

"Tildon was ill. Wasn't coming inside. He would wait for the carriage by the mews."

"Thank you, Samuels. You've been very helpful. I will not forget your service to me."

Out on the street, Freddie caught up to him and grabbed his arm. "We'll need two horses from Seton's stables."

"The carriage...." *No matter Ada's condition, she'd need the confines of a coach.* "And two pistols."

CHAPTER 15

Richard's estate north of London was on a main road four miles from Hertford Castle. His holdings were modest but at one time had been profitable, even during periods when crop failures had decimated other nobles' lands and tenants. Richard had been a good steward of his lands until the past eight years when he neglected reinvestment of money into farm equipment and storage facilities. His inattention to his work and his salacious endeavors with ladies who were not his to claim had cost him dearly.

Victor led Freddie up the byways toward Hertford at a gallop. He knew the road well, having visited his brother at his manor house frequently when a young man before his marriage to Alicia. In the dead of night, they traveled quickly. Passing only a night watchman or a drunk finding his way home, they made the house in good time. The Seton carriage, covering the miles more slowly, would arrive at most an hour later than they.

They approached the main gate and Victor slowed to a walk. When he raised his hand for Freddie to do the same, his friend nodded.

The elaborate iron gate stood open. In their haste, Richard and Tildon had forgotten to close it.

Victor fished out his pocket watch. Two-ten. All of them tucked in.

He grit his teeth. He prayed to God both his brother and Tildon were asleep, incapacitated and not tormenting Ada.

He growled, cursing himself that he might be too late. That the two men might have already done their worst to her.

Victor stopped beneath a huge oak tree, hoping the shadows would hide him and his friend. "We'll go round the back to the kitchen entrance. We'll more likely awaken a footman than the butler. If I'm right, Richard would still make his footmen sleep on the floor in the kitchen." *Bastard.*

"No light from the second floor," Freddie noted.

None anywhere shining through the windows. Victor's heart took flight. Maybe he did have a chance to save her...

As they'd helped the Seton grooms and stable boys saddle their horses, Victor had described the floor plan of the house. The first floor, a few steps up from the foyer, had only public rooms, salons, dining room and breakfast room. "Straight up the curved staircase to the right is the master suite. Richard's."

Victor shook with outrage as he and Freddie circled the front lawn, keeping to the shadows. At the rear of the house, he led Freddie toward a copse where they looped the reins over branches and proceeded on foot, pistols at the ready.

They crossed the lawn, swift as eagles, the grasses soft and silent beneath their feet. He tried the door. And when it gave, he grinned at Freddie.

His friend crooked a brow—and waved him forward with his pistol.

They ran up the servants' stairs, the way familiar to Victor who'd played hide and seek here with his brother. *A different form of it tonight.*

When they got to the second floor, he gingerly slid open the green baize door. There, before him, was the hall. Dark. Quiet. Moonlight streaming through the far Palladian half moon windows. But no rays of light visible beneath the frames of this bedroom or that. Nor even of Richard's.

He caught his breath. Their prior plan was to search out the secondary bedrooms first. If they did not find Ada there, then they were to invade Richard's suite.

Freddie advanced on the bedroom next to Richard's. In a whoosh, he thrust open the door. Silent as a cat, Victor trod past him into the sitting room. Snoring in the bed, flat on his back, arms out, Tildon lay in his shirt and trousers.

The two left the way they'd gone in.

Victor indicated the other bedroom across the hall. But he had an inkling Ada was not there but in Richard's bed.

At that door, Victor paused. His guts churning, he thrust it open to draw back at the odors of sweat, alcohol and vomit. And spread upon the *chaise longue* beneath the wide window was Richard Cole, the Marquess of Ridgemont. His waistcoat and shirt unbuttoned, his braces down, he lay in a stupor. His fingers dangled to the floor. But he had once grasped the bottle of whisky, now turned on its side, its contents an ugly brown pool upon the plush Axminster carpet.

Freddie nudged him, his head tipping toward the far door to the bedroom.

There she was. Curled on her side, she lay upon the satin coverlet in the medieval poster bed that was the prized antique in the house. She faced the window. And in the moon's glow, she was pale. The red gown that she'd worn to the theater was crumpled, a wreck. She still wore her shoes and stockings. *So Richard hadn't done his worst, thank God.* In her hand, she clutched a handkerchief and beneath her on the floor was a rare blue and white Ming bowl. Victor recognized the porcelain as one he'd exported and sent to Richard one year for his birthday. She'd gotten sick in it.

Loathe to move her, Victor stepped nearer. "Ada, darling."

Her lashes fluttered open but her eyes did not focus.

What in hell had he given her?

Freddie tore a knitted blanket from the end of the bed and handed it to him. "Hurry. I'll watch him."

Victor gave him his pistol, then wrapped the throw around her shoulders as best he could.

But she awakened, shrank from him and pushed at his chest. "No. No, don't touch me!"

"Sweetheart, look at me." He cupped her chin. "It's Victor."

Her eyes rolled back, then she lurched forward, gagged and pushed him away.

He let her lean over the damn bowl.

She retched a few times but her stomach was empty. She wiped her mouth and sank back.

"I've got to carry you. Let me."

She whimpered. "Victor?"

"Yes, my love." He gathered her in his arms, her body dead weight, her head lolling. But he found his balance. Tonight, he vowed, he would leave here without the need of his cane. Ada's life depended on it. And his indignation alone might propel him to the moon and back.

And so he strode with her through his brother's bedroom, past the man splayed upon the chaise.

"Let me down," she begged. Clamping the handkerchief to her mouth, she gulped but did not wretch.

The sounds were enough to rouse Richard.

But nothing aided him to get to his feet and stay there. Or to reach Victor when he finally did stand straight. Instead, he held his ground as he reeled. "What in hell d'you think you're d'ing? Y' can't take her. She's mine. Ruined her for you."

Freddie however had more eloquent things to say with his pistol. He poked him and Richard unceremoniously fell back to the chaise.

"Hell, Billings! Think you can fire that?" Richard struggled up.

"If you want to learn," Freddie sneered, "I can oblige you." He motioned for Richard to return to the chaise.

Richard cursed at him.

"Walk on," Freddie urged Victor.

Ada inhaled deeply, then dropped her head against his shoulder. Her nails dug into his clothes. "Victor."

He made it to the central stairs and leaning his hip against the massive black walnut banister, used it to support his weight as he took one step down. And another.

He sensed Freddie behind him.

Richard followed. "Can't get far."

Freddie chuckled.

"Where the hell is Tildon?" his brother yelled. "Tildon!"

But no one answered.

"She's not for you," Richard sneered, trying to provoke him.

Tonight he'd already hit his limit though. Victor kept on taking one sure step and then another.

"I had her," he called down.

Freddie snorted. "Doubt that, dear boy."

Victor would one day laugh at Freddie's use of the term that Richard so often employed in his quest to sound superior.

A clatter came from the far end of the hall. An older fellow stumbled into the foyer, tying his robe, mumbling. The old butler.

Victor knew the man. Sweet, harmless, hard-working.

Wouldn't be able to do a damn thing to prohibit him and Freddie from taking Ada away.

"Very well! Take her!" Richard howled. "No matter, Victor. I'll let it out that I had her. A sweet meat, she was too."

He stopped, anger molten in his veins. *Yes, this man—his brother—would do that. Never stopping at anything to win his way.*

No matter. Victor would make it right for her. He would.

"I'll fix it so you can't have her."

Victor had told himself as they rode here—had chanted silently his Buddhist mantra—that he would not succumb to his brother's taunts. He caught Ada closer and put one foot out.

"I had Alicia, Victor."

Red rage blinded him. He paused to center himself. But he fought back, concentrated on a white ball of purpose. White peace that he had trained long ago to sooth his nerves, rolled up his backbone and neck, over his crown to his forehead and down his nose and chin to his heart and his stomach to replace his *chi.* He praised his good fortune that he could save his serenity—and not charge up the stairs. If he maintained no control over himself, he could have killed his brother then and there. Would have. Then he would have paid prices for this catastrophe that only Richard should pay. And pay in full he would.

He stepped down and away from the past.

"She was a nasty piece, your wife." Richard tittered like a child. "So eager. So agreeable to every little act."

The revelation was one that in another day and time, might have been his undoing. Might have been the death sentence of Richard. And his own. But the crimes Alicia committed against him were old. Desiccated. Dust in the wind. So insignificant that he no longer felt their vicious stab.

"I'll tell the town that too!" Richard yelled, desperate now. "You bastard. You can't deprive me of what I want."

"Watch me." His words reverberated in the cavernous foyer. Then he paused while his brother's butler scurried to swing wide the front door for him.

He emerged into the night air, free of the past, holding the promise of his future in his embrace.

CHAPTER 16

Freddie strode into the parlor of his cousin's gate house, newspapers under one arm and a few letters in his hand. "I've brought more clothes for Ada from the main house. I gave them to the maid to put in Ada's bedroom."

Unable to travel far that night with Ada so ill, Freddie had suggested they seek asylum at his cousin's home a few miles south of Hertford. Lady Fallon was young, a widow with two children, living quietly on her deceased husband's small estate. Freddie had emphasized that they could not journey far and should not return to London to Victor's house or his own. Richard, he'd pointed out, was fool enough to search them out in their homes and that would result in more chaos. Plus the three of them, especially Ada, needed time to recover and rest.

Victor, who'd been writing letters all morning to his parents and his business manager in the City, shot up from the desk. He needed news from London. The death of Carbury was one matter over which he had no power. But

Ada's abduction and his rescue had consequences, immediate and long term. He had to manage them all.

The three of them had been here two days while Ada recovered from what appeared to be a toxic reaction to some drug that Richard had used to incapacitate her. Aware Ada's family would need word of her, he'd sent messengers that first morning to Ada's father Killian and her step-mother Liv, as well as Lily, Julian and Pierce. He'd assured them all that she was secluded with him, safe, but very ill and could not travel. When rumor got out of Ada's abduction and his rescue, he knew what their extended stay here would mean. Scandal. For her. Him, too. But fearing for her health as he did, he could not care about tomorrow's challenges when he needed to get her well first.

Freddie pressed the mail into Victor's hands. "A courier delivered this for you this morning."

He tore open the letter from Hanniford Manor. "Her father wants details of what Richard did. Tildon too."

Freddie took a seat by the doors to the garden and snorted. "Hanniford has means of revenge you and I never imagined."

"True." Whatever Killian Hanniford would do to Richard would be too little retribution. But her father did not focus on his revenge in his letter as much as the other issue Victor had written to him about. And Victor rejoiced at his response. "I told him I sent to the Commons for a license. He gives me his blessing. Says he knew the first night he met me that Ada and I were to be married. Thank heavens he'll not object. It makes this easier. If indeed Ada will have me...."

Freddie sat back in his chair. "I doubt she'd refuse you."

Victor looked toward the garden. The peonies in Lady Fallon's parterre bloomed in luxurious pink profusion. Oddly, he wondered if the plants were ones that had come from his imports. No matter. He must carry Ada out there, if she was strong enough. She'd love the fragrances.

He glanced back at Freddie. "You know, I would not have been able to do this without you. I shall be forever grateful."

His friend crossed one leg over the other and grinned at him. "I must proclaim my own gratitude. You've solved my own problem for me."

"How is that?"

"I've my own missive this morning." He patted his frock-coat and paper crinkled in his inside pocket. "From the earl of Ware, no less."

"Oh? And?"

"It seems all the troubles of the past few days have pulled the curtain from the man's eyes. First hand, he saw the disaster that resulted from Elanna's and Carbury's union and appreciates the love he saw you act upon. Furthermore, he applauds me for aiding you."

"Which means—?"

"If I would like to address him on the matter of marriage to his daughter, he'd be happy to receive me."

Victor caught his hand and shook it. "Congratulations. One challenge solved."

"Without our even planning."

"Good results from a horrid night. Now to solve the other issues." He glanced toward the hall—and knew he must talk with Ada soon about marrying him.

"You cannot imagine Ada will refuse you."

"Oh, Freddie, I doubt she has a choice. And that's what worries me. She's not a woman to do what society tells her."

"Perhaps not. I don't know her as well as you. But I think she will see reason."

"Reason!" Victor scoffed and ran a hand through his hair. "Not the best *reason* to marry, is it?"

"The other is. She loves you."

Victor stared into Freddie's brown eyes. "I hope that might come." *But what can I do if she associates me with the actions of my brother?*

"I'd not worry on that score if I were you. Simply pose the circumstances and ask the question."

Victor buttoned his waistcoat. "Today's the day to do it."

"Come in!"

Ada smiled at Victor who from his apprehensive expression, needed a good welcome.

"The housemaid told me you were up and feeling better."

This morning, she felt more clear-headed than yesterday. And the day before that when Victor had taken her from his brother, she did not remember with any clarity at all. Only a terrible headache and nausea. "Indeed, I am. Almost ready to read the daily newspapers."

His face fell.

"Well, then. Perhaps not, am I right?" She crossed her arms. The news was not a fine idea.

He crossed the room to her *chaise longue*. He was alone. After all, with what he'd done to save her, undress her and bathe her, a maid was an unnecessary accessory to her claim of any virtue. "I'd rather you waited another day before you attempted to read them. You do look so much better this morning, sweetheart."

She took his hand and pulled him down to sit beside her. "And I have you to thank for that. I was rather a mess."

"Get well." He threaded his fingers through the tendrils of her hair along her cheek. This was the first time he'd seen her with her hair down around her shoulders. And in the pale pink dressing gown that Lady Fallon had given her, she appeared before him in very inappropriate attire. "That's all that matters."

"Tell me what news of home. I know you spoke of all you'd written yesterday, but frankly I don't recall. You can, I'm sure, inform me of it all with some impunity."

"All your family send their best wishes for your recovery."

"Papa? I hope he was not harsh with you." She searched his turquoise eyes.

"Not at all. He was grateful."

"As he should be. Were you detailed with him or—"

"I summarized and promised the rest when we are together."

"Soon?" She was eager to learn when she'd go home and face the consequences of this hideous event.

"We'll see how you feel tonight. If you'd like to return tomorrow, Lady Fallon has offered us her traveling coach."

She closed her eyes, trying to recall something about a coach. "Whose did we use to come here?"

"Your brother-in-law's. We had to be quick about it. I sent it back after we arrived here."

"You were very organized that night."

"Ha! Well, glad you think so, my dear. It felt like chaos."

"I'm certain it did. And to come here was smart, too."

He smiled sadly. "All Freddie's idea. And the rest of this is his cousin's."

She picked at the knitted throw over her lap. "She has been terribly generous. I will thank her forever for all she's done."

"As will I." He squeezed her hand.

"And Freddie." She had to add Victor's friend. "I must hear the story of your rescue again. I did listen yesterday but I'm afraid I've forgotten the details."

"Oh, my dear, you needn't—"

"Yes. I do." She set her jaw. "I must know it all."

"It will do you no good."

"There, you are quite wrong, Victor Cole."

"Darling—"

"No!" She threw back the coverlet, turned away from him and put her feet to the floor. The action, so swift, made her head spin. She cupped her forehead and sat back. "Sorry."

He rose, went to the far table, poured a glass of water from the pitcher and returned to hand it to her.

She eyed him, angry he'd try to protect her from the full story of what she'd endured. "I deserve to know. Keep it from me and I will demand Freddie tell me."

He nodded, frowning.

She flexed her shoulders, uneasy with the topic that was vital to her future social standing and her personal self-worth. "From what I can detect, Richard did not rape me."

That brought a flush of anger to Victor's cheeks. He took his time to respond. "I did not think so. When Freddie and I arrived, you were on the bed with your shoes and stockings on."

"And when you undressed me? Here? I do remember that, so there is no need for you to dissemble and call it other. If I blush to say it, you must forgive me. Training, you know. But facts are facts. We must go on. Tell me."

"When I removed your underclothes, I saw no evidence he had violated you."

"No blood?"

He inhaled sharply. "None."

"Nothing else?" When Victor stared at her, she indulged her anger and her prerogative. "Come now. I know what happens with animals. And I am no fragile flower. Nothing else from him on my clothing?"

"I do believe that by the time they arrived at his manor house in Hertford, he and Tildon had drunk so much and perhaps ingested so much heroin that they could not engage in any physical exertion."

She gave him a flat look. "Oh, nicely put, Lord Victor. No wonder you wish to become a politician. I would vote for you."

He took both her hands. "Listen to me, please, Ada. There is much we must discuss."

Tears burned her eyes and she snatched her hands away. "I can wait."

"We can't."

She drew back. "You must show me those newspapers."

"Later."

"You are stubborn."

He tossed her a wicked look. "Meet your match."

She grumbled and traced the patterns in coverlet. "Go away. I'm tired."

He inhaled. Then whirled to pick her up in his arms.

"Where are you taking me? Put me down. You'll hurt yourself without your cane."

"I didn't the other night. That was practice. Open that damn door."

They stood before her bedroom door. Suppressing a chuckle, she fumed and glared but yanked it open.

Out he walked through the small hall to the other side of the little house and into a parlor. There he headed for double doors to a garden.

"Open this one, too."

"You are impossible."

"True. Very true," he said as he marched to a garden bench and sat before the small sculptured garden. The summer breeze lifted her hair and enchanted her with the fragrances of peonies and grasses, the glories of the earth. He nestled her into his lap—and he held her there.

"Now. I've pondered how to do this. I thought bad poetry might help."

She rolled her eyes and shook her head. If this was what she thought it was, then bad poetry might be the worst thing to do.

He cleared his throat and took on the persona of an actor upon the boards. "Because of you, I will be true, to vows I'll make in earnest."

"Oh, that *is* poor." She giggled.

He smirked at her. "But if you'll love me evermore and marry, we can furnish—"

She burst out laughing. Then twirled her finger in the air. "Do continue."

"A house for two—"

"Or four—"

"Or more!"

"And then," she said, "we'll never perish."

He fixed her with feigned dismay. "And I thought I was bad."

She curled her hands around his neck and ran her fingers up into his marvelous thick hair. "I like your curls," she said and grabbed a handful of them. "You smell marvelous too. Bergamot?"

"Lemon. Lime."

She pressed the tip of her nose to his. His proposal was delicious and she savored every word. "I think the other night I recognized you by your cologne. I'm so sorry this is what we must face now. I've done this to you and now you must endure it."

He grabbed her hand and brought it to his lips to kiss. "Darling, you are not responsible for what Richard did."

"No, I know. What I meant was that if I hadn't encouraged you then he wouldn't have taken me and you wouldn't have had to save me from him."

He kissed her knuckles. "Did you not want to 'encourage me'?"

She brushed her mouth over his. "Oh, I did."

He gave her a lopsided grin. "That's what I thought. I wanted to encourage you too. I saw you with my daughters that first day and thought the one he intended to marry was you. Not Ezzie. I wanted to save you from him then. But I wanted to do more than save you, I wanted you for myself. I want to marry you, darling. This is sooner than I would have liked to ask. I wanted so much settled about my future before I dare ask for you. I never want to force you to do something. Not to go abroad with me if you really don't want it. But now, we cannot wait. I have a special license. And your father approves of the match."

Her heart pounded. She stared at his handsome face, his concern for her written in every debonair feature.

"Will you marry me?"

She hugged him fiercely close, her face nestled in the crook of his shoulder. And then she began to cry.

He stiffened. "If this is not what you wish, then you must tell me. I know it's not ideal."

She pulled back to stare up at him. Did he not realize what was missing from his proposal?

He fished a handkerchief from his pocket and dabbed at her tears. "If you don't want me, if you'd rather go home to America, then—"

"No." He thought she didn't want him? Oh, she did. She wanted him. Every bit of him. His humor and laughter. His sorrow and pain. His ambition and his success. Even his failures. She wanted all he was, all they could become together. She loved him. But he had no words of love for her. Duty. Honor. Those were his concerns. She was proud of him, this man who had saved her from real ruin. She would be proud to be his wife...but her heart was breaking for what he did not grant her. "I won't return to New York. That's not my home. Not anymore. And I won't run away."

"You are brave, Ada Hanniford."

To marry a man who does not love me? To marry because the world demands it? "Not at all."

"Will you marry me?" He sounded desperate. "I will never be a duke. I will never be a millionaire. I will never be prime minister. But I will give you a good life, Ada. I know not yet whether that will be here or in Shanghai. But I'll be the finest husband to you, my darling. Loyal, wise as I can be, honest, affectionate. Say you will have me, please."

"If you promise always to recite bad poetry." She sniffed and surrendered to the necessity of it all. "And to kiss me as you once did at your parents' home."

He planted a quick hard kiss on her lips. "Ada, darling, marry me next week and I will kiss you every day so much better than that."

She laughed. Then went still. "Show me."

He nestled her close, his fingers sinking into her hair. In the thin muslin dressing gown and nightgown, her breasts flattened against his chest and her nipples hardened in the warmth. Tingles of desire flooded her veins and she sighed as he took her lips with his own. He was soft, his mouth a sweet caress, his body taut. But his kiss was a claim greater than the others they had shared and she welcomed his possession. Rejoiced in it. And he broke away, breathless, searching her gaze for her reaction.

"Sweetheart," he called her, and she yearned for the sound of it and the taste of him again. Her hands fisting in his hair, she kissed him back and he bent over her to take her in a bold and sensuous kiss. He nipped her lower lip and she held his face and laughed. He rained kisses down her throat across her shoulders and down between her breasts. She arched, her head thrown back and he took her invitation, cupped a breast and through the delicate cotton, he savored her nipple with the hot wet draw of his mouth. She moaned, wanting more.

But he drew up, his turquoise eyes glazed with a passion she felt in every inch of her body. "We'll save the rest for the night we're wed. We'll be proper."

She rolled her eyes at him.

He laughed, his cheeks red, his hair on end from her rough embraces. But he stood, returned to her room and summarily deposited her in her bed. By the door, he bid her *adieu*. "Get well quickly. You've a gown to choose, a trousseau."

"On such short notice, those will be difficult to acquire, dear sir." She was teasing him, of course. Her own modiste in Half Moon Street would devote herself night and day to work her fingers to the bone to claim she finished a wedding dress for the American heiress, Ada Hanniford.

He threw her a tolerant look. "I want you to have everything you want. Always."

"You. I want only you, my darling man."

He seemed to weave, deciding whether to stay or go. "You test me, my dear."

"Never. I am yours. I have been from that first day."

"And I yours, only yours." He left her with a wicked grin promising more erotic delights they would share.

That helped to salve the wound of his failure to declare his love for her. His passion for her restored her confidence. If she could not have his love, if he could not surrender his soul to another woman, if he waited to conclude his political future or abandon her here for China, before he left her, she'd take all his desire for her. She'd revel in it. She'd have his lust for her—and hope one day he could declare he'd always loved her. Never another.

CHAPTER 17

Ada descended the staircase in her father's London house and forced a smile at her family assembled there. Her father—a man whom many feared for his business acumen and his ability to make millions—stood at the forefront on the bottom step regarding her with pride. The others—her step-mother Liv, her sister Lily and her husband Julian, her brother Pierce stood behind him, were a phalanx against the bitter winds of fortune.

Killian Hanniford had forgiven her much over the twenty-two years of her bold and carefree life. This marriage, while he knew it necessary to quell whatever scandal she understood brewed beyond the front door, was the most outrageous of all. But then it was also the means to end the rumors that blackened her reputation.

"Tarnished my name?" Killian had been shocked after Victor had brought her home two days ago and she'd expressed her sadness that what had occurred had damaged the Hanniford family perhaps irretrievably. He'd scoffed. "Ada, my girl, the toffs will say whatever they wish. I go on.

You will too and with a good man. The blame for this is squarely on the shoulders of Ridgemont."

He'd taken her in his arms and kissed her forehead. "He'll pay, my darling daughter. You will not."

He admired her now as she came to stand before him in her silk and satin finery. White, too. Her modiste, as Ada expected, was a wizard to have sewn the pearl encrusted gown in such a rush. "You're beautiful, my lovely Ada. The world will come to see you as you truly are. Sweet, kind, popular and right-minded. The new Lady Victor Cole is to enjoy this day. I decree it."

She laughed at his contagious self-confidence and reached up to kiss his cheek. "I obey, kind sir."

"Let's go. You've an anxious groom at the church."

Victor could not wait to leave. His bride—*his wife*—appeared to be heartily enjoying herself but he did yearn to hurry her away. Here in her home on Piccadilly with her family and a few friends, she shone like the jewel she was. In the ivory gown adorned with pearls, her heavy cinnamon hair caught up in an elaborate chignon, her crystal blue eyes shimmering with joy, she glowed. His first sight of her as she entered St. George's Chapel yards from his townhome had nearly felled him. This gorgeous creature was his.

He smiled as she laughed with her friend Esmerelda Moore and that lady's beau, Lord Edgecombe. Ada had helped to make that match a secure one and the gratitude appeared in both Ezzie's and Edgecombe's regard of her.

"She's a charming creature." Pierce appeared suddenly at his side, a flute of champagne in his hand. "From childhood, mischievous. An imp. Headstrong, but then what woman is interesting without that spark, eh? I trust you to take good care of her. You have so far and we are grateful."

"I'm honored, Pierce, that she accepted me."

Neither one mentioned that she had to. Three days and nights alone with him, accompanied only by another man, albeit Victor's friend Billings, meant she had to marry him. He would work diligently to ensure her decision never became a sorrow for her. But with all the furor of her abduction mixed with the death of Carbury, the *ton* was probably full of speculation. To hurry the ceremony, he and she had insisted the ceremony be a small affair. This wedding breakfast included only another sixteen guests who were their unwavering friends.

The past few days, what with a wedding to plan, his house to put in sparkling shape, his parents to notify, he'd pushed any word of scandal to the back of his mind. He'd not read one newspaper. Nor did he have time. Marrying quickly meant that he needed to have that meeting with his man MacIntyre in the City. If his finances for this half year showed less profit than his totals for last year, he'd go to this new union less secure than he wished. No help for it though, he would marry Ada were he a pauper. She, on the other hand, might not adjust well to the step down, but he doubted money meant so much to her. Still, he had to know. When MacIntyre had assured him that Cole and Company had grown in the first five months by four percent over last year, he breathed easily at the positive sign.

Day before yesterday for two hours he'd spent with the inspector from the Metropolitan Police. The man and his sergeant had called upon him and immediately inquired why he'd left town the night Carbury died. Victor's explanation seemed to satisfy the man. But restating for him the details of his actions the night Carbury died was a sorrowful exercise. Concluding the interview, the inspector told him the coroner had autopsied the earl's body and concluded he'd died of a broken neck. The fall down the stairs had also resulted in a broken jaw and two broken legs. The jury that did the inquest had declared Carbury's death an accident.

But the inspector by his own admission suspected that might not be the case. "What do you think, my lord?"

"I cannot tell you more, Inspector. As I told you, my fiancée was missing from her home and I hastened to find her."

That sparked more interest in the policeman who asked for more details of Ada's abduction.

When Victor explained he wished no inquiry into the matter, the man balked. "That is a serious crime, my lord. Your brother may be a lord, but we can pursue the matter."

"I assure you neither my fiancée nor I wish further attention to this. You may interview the lady if you like. But we'd appreciate that you do not. My future wife has suffered enough. Surely you understand society will deal appropriately with my brother."

"Is that enough for you, my lord?"

"It will be."

He'd asked Freddie to telegraph his mother the first morning they were at Lady Fallon's. In summary, he'd told her what Richard had done, how he had rescued Ada from him and that he would soon wed her.

His mother had responded by cable her horror over Richard, but her joy at news of his marriage. Once he and Ada had decided on today as the wedding date, he'd cabled her again. She had promptly packed up, his daughters and Wu-lai included, and boarded a train from Bath to London. He'd visited her and them yesterday at Brentwood House in Upper Brook Street. His girls babbled on, happy to remain with their grandmama while he took his wedding trip. They were agog that he was to marry their favorite Miss Hanniford. That she'd become their mama overjoyed them. That they would, contrary to social customs, attend the marriage and the breakfast, put them over the moon. His mother was equally as delighted for him.

"You deserve happiness, Victor." She'd dabbed at tears in her eyes as she'd told him. "You've had little and much to rise above. Now this with Richard is a hideous blow. Your father wants me to tell you that he will deal harshly with Richard."

"If Chancery did not protect him because of his rank, he would be arrested for abducting a woman. Drugging her. You must know, Mama, I think I would have killed him if he'd hurt Ada."

"I would not have blamed you. But you would have paid a hideous price for his crimes. I'm glad you kept your head." She sniffed and met his gaze boldly. "I do not know how or why we failed to temper him. But we did not. Perhaps because his own mother died while he was so young. But that puts the blame on her and it should be on us."

He took both her hands then and refuted that with all his might. "He is responsible for his own actions, Mama. He is a grown man and he made poor, very poor decisions. He cannot cast the blame on you and you must not take it. That is not fair."

The secret that Richard had thrust on him as he carried Ada from the house would be one he'd bury along with the ashes of his first marriage. He was well rid of his brother.

To see his mother now enjoying herself talking with Killian, Julian and Lily made him thankful he'd fallen in love with a woman who had such a supportive family.

His two daughters, however, took the hands of his bride and walked her toward him. Ada wiggled her brows as she approached him.

"Papa," said Vivienne, giggling, her turquoise eyes dancing, "you must leave now. Take Miss Hanniford away."

"She's 'Mama' now, Viv," Deirdre proclaimed. "Isn't she, Papa?"

He grasped his wife's elegant fingers and stroked her wedding ring with his thumb. "She is indeed Lady Victor Cole, your new mother."

"The girls asked me where we're going," Ada said, her voice soft and her eyes full of fond regard for him. "But I told them I have no idea."

"It's a secret." He led his wife to his side and looped her arm through his. From this day forward, he wished to never let her go. He wanted her so badly, he'd have to tear his heart out if all failed and his hopes to remain in England were dashed. "If everyone knows then they can intrude...and they mustn't."

Ada leaned close, her small smile angelic, her blue gaze molten with desire. "Please. I've seen everyone. Might we leave?"

"It still smells of fresh paint. I'm sorry about that." He lifted the sash of one of the bedroom windows. The gentle breeze of the June afternoon billowed the sheer white curtains and made her smile.

She took a stroll around the master bedroom, her fingers stroking the azure brocade bed hangings and the white silk upholstered chairs. The way she caressed them made his body swell with need of her touch.

She spun toward him. "Did you choose all this yourself?"

"I did." He folded his arms, refraining from grabbing her and throwing her to the mattress. Steadying himself, he admired the way she moved, graceful as flowers that turned their faces to the sun. "The fabric is mine. From my warehouse in the East India Docks."

"May I visit?"

He arched a brow. "The warehouse?"

"Yes."

"I suppose so... I've never had a woman to the floor."

"Now you will. I'm no stranger to factories. We often went with our father to the Baltimore wharves. We'd play among the crates. He owns a clothing factory there, too, and we'd go to sew with the seamstresses."

"I never knew," he said astonished and proud she'd go. But he wanted less talk, fewer clothes, her maid...

"Papa said we must know how to sew on buttons. Have you any clothes with buttons missing?"

He barked in laughter. "No."

"Good. I want to go."

"Go where?" The only place he wanted to go was to bed with her, quite stark naked.

"Your warehouse."

"Oh, right. I'm delighted you'd ask."

"Are you?" She flounced upon the edge of the four poster bed. "Why?"

Well, he had to be honest with her. And wouldn't wish to side-step the issue. "I've never known a woman to want to go."

"You do now." She folded her hands in her lap. "Come here."

He pointed a thumb over his shoulder. "I should call your maid."

"No. You shouldn't." She widened her eyes in demand and crooked her finger. "Come here."

He swallowed back madness and took his time stepping to her.

"You're quite remarkable, you realize." She was unbuttoning his morning cutaway and pushing it from his shoulders. At once she went to work on his suspenders, undoing the buttons of his white satin waistcoat and stripping it away. Her warm hands working on him made him stiffen with erotic needs.

His lashes fluttered and he stared at the ceiling for forbearance. "How's that?"

She undid his cufflinks and laid them aside. Then she reached up to unhook his stick pin from his cravat and drop it to the end table. "To arrange the wedding so quickly."

He locked his eyes on hers. *I had to have you.*

She cupped his cheek, all too briefly, then resumed her work on his cravat. "How did you manage that?"

"I'd sent for the license when we were at Lady Fallon's. The same day, I wrote to the archdeacon at St. George's to secure the date."

She slid away his cravat, the slip of silk a sensuous sigh against his skin. Then she rose to her feet to stand against him and run the tip of her nose from the bottom of his ear along the line of his throat to his collarbone.

He slipped his arms around her, her wedding gown satin beneath his fingers, and she soft willing woman in his arms. "You are seducing me."

"Am I?"

He tipped up her chin. He was giddy with delight. "Do you think there's a need?"

"No," she said, her voice suddenly a husky tone lower. "I just want to please you."

"You always have."

"Is that so?" She leaned back and his hand came up to cup her nape and hold her there. She was a delicious scamp and he was such a fortunate man to have her. "How so?"

"I loved the sound of your laughter. It was the first thing I knew of you."

She circled her arms around him and nestled her head

against his shoulder. Her legs were long, tangled close to his. How had he never noticed that before? "What else?"

"The newspapers made me laugh."

She snorted. "I haven't read any lately. But I venture to say, they wouldn't make you laugh today."

He stroked her back. All those buttons were going to be the death of him. "The flowers intrigued me."

"Mmm." She kissed the hollow of his throat. "It's what we have in common."

He breathed heavily, his heart beating loudly in his ears. "I love the way you smell."

She pulled away, her eyes blue flames. "And I you, my darling husband. And I you."

He gulped. "I'm going to have to take this dress off you."

"Why?" she asked quite frankly though her voice was a purr. "I rather like it."

"Ada—"

"Why don't I just remove my petticoats and my step-ins, hmm? The corset is a terrible bother. But if I get out of it, you can take off my stockings and my garters."

"To leave it on is not proper, my darling."

"We're man and wife. We don't have to be proper."

He kissed her quick and hard. "Because I want you, all of you, not half of you. I want this first time to be complete. For you. For me. Nothing will resemble a tumble. Nothing."

Her eyes said she appreciated that. And so she presented her back. "Then undo me."

His clumsy fingers worked on the tiny satin-covered buttons that lined her spine and he grumbled.

"But you must do the same," she said, hands on her hips.

"The same what?" he asked totally confused.

"Naked. I want you naked. All of you, not half of you. I want you completely mine for this time and always. Nothing to resemble a tumble. Nothing."

His arms bound her tightly to him, her back against him, his cock hard as stone against her derriere. His hands slid up to cup her breasts. The gown draped low over her shoulders and her corset was now the beast that kept him from her. He pushed the gown down further and attacked the laces. They were bound tight and in his inexperience with such ribbons, he was fumbling in his haste.

The thing half undone, gaping from her body, she groaned and pulled it away. Then she somehow shimmied out of it. The contraption followed her petticoats and bloomers to the floor.

She turned and oh, dear god, she was lovely. Bare, her skin glistening like alabaster in the gaslight, she was naked save for her garter belt and sheer white stockings. He'd seen her as God had made her the night he'd taken her from Richard. Frantic, crazed, he refused to let one of Lady Fallon's maids minister to her. Tears burning him, his mind ablaze, he took her garments from her to assure himself and her that his brother had not touched her. Not abused her. Not in any way. Her nakedness had been more proof of her survival than a lure to his libido.

This afternoon, as his wife, she was quite a different vision. A charm against the cruelties that life could bring. A beauty in contrast to the world's ugliness. She stood here, a tender smile curving her luscious lips. Smart, sassy Ada.

He glanced down and looked his fill. Her breasts were high and generous with pink nipples like large rose petals. Her waist was small. The garter belt gave way as she unhooked it and the sight of her red curls almost made him come.

But she swallowed loudly and tugged his shirt from his trousers. Yanking at his sleeves, she made a frustrated sound.

They'd be frustrated for hours if he didn't help her. He

pulled her close to him and kissed her. God, she was heaven. Supple, warm and whimpering.

Enough! He kicked aside her clothes and lifted her in his arms to place her surely in the middle of his bed. *Their bed.* A new bed he'd purchased. Unused. For them to make a new union.

He crawled on top of her and she opened her thighs and let him fall between.

"Take your pants off," she moaned and slid her hands beneath the grey-pin-striped wool. There, beneath his small clothes, she found him and cupped him.

He lost his breath.

She licked her lips and wrapped her fingers around his cock. "Oh, my. How big you are."

He ground his teeth, her firm claim a spur to decadent hours, nights, days, years with her.

She slid her hand away and burrowed back into the bedding. Her hands above her head, she stared at him with a lazy needy smile. "Now, Victor. Hurry."

❦

"Hurry?" He pushed up on his elbows and surveyed her. "Not tonight. Not ever."

She fought the urge to squirm in bashful reaction, but he'd seen her before. Seen her twice quite stripped to her skin. But she wanted to see how he liked her. And from his half-lidded look, he seemed quite taken with her. Mesmerized, she might even say.

"You are the most beautiful creature."

She squeezed her bare thighs against his hips. Encased in the supple wool of his trousers, his legs seemed firm and very hot. "I need to see that you are beautiful too. Take your clothes off, will you please?"

He dropped a hard kiss to her lips and groaned as he left her.

But he was rather fast, and for that, she was grateful, even if she wished he might afford her minutes to admire his perfection. His shoulders she'd always known were wide. His arms, strong. She'd felt them around her and he had carried her from one room to another, despite his lameness in one leg. But the expanse of his chest, the taut pull of skin over his ribs, that she'd not anticipated and by heavens, he was a marvelous specimen.

"What?" he asked her, his hands to the waistband of his trousers.

She twirled a finger at him. "You are exquisite yourself, sir."

He blushed.

Oh, she was enjoying this. "How did you get that way?"

"I lift crates in my storerooms. And I do exercises with my employees."

"What kind?"

"Movement upon the floor or against the wall."

"Unusual."

"They are. Some involve chants and that improves one's ability to hold the pose."

She licked her lips. "Superb. You must show me how. But for now? Your trousers, sir, must come off."

He flicked open the clasp on the waistband and pushed down his pants and his underclothes.

She swallowed hard and rubbed her naked thighs together. His hips were lean. His abdomen muscular. His thatch of hair a darker auburn than that on his head. And he was, she could say with certainty, a very impressive man.

She caught his gaze.

"I love you, Ada Cole."

Tears sprang from her eyes. She caught back a sob and

suddenly he was above her, hauling her close, cradling her against his hot skin and sculpted body.

"Look at me." He turned her face toward him. "My sweetheart, did you think I didn't?"

She gasped and threw her arms around his neck. "I didn't know. I wasn't sure. I—I hoped."

"Know. Be sure. Let me show you." He bent over her, spreading kisses along her chin and down her throat, blessing the hollow of her shoulder and the valley between her breasts. His legs between hers, she felt the weight of his manhood and the evidence of his virility. She arched her neck, wanting all of him inside her, around her, possessing her. And then he cupped one breast and took her in his mouth. She undulated, his homage wet and wicked. But then he shifted and took her other breast, this time licking her nipple until she cried out in admiration for his talents.

He gave a little chuckle and nipped her.

"Fiend," she laughed.

But he slid lower, nuzzling her belly and smiling against her feminine hair. His hot breath fanned her skin. She gulped, thinking he'd go even lower, but he caught her up behind her knees and lifted her legs to wrap around his own.

She sighed, deliciously content, but for only a moment as she knew a wild surge of need for something...something more.

Against her core, she felt the probe of his flesh.

"Look at me. We will do this and we'll go slowly. You'll look at me through it all. We'll do this until you feel only rapture. But you must look at me."

She nodded. "I trust you. How could I not?"

His features went stark, severe, and he moved forward so that he moved ever so slowly inside her.

"Oh, god." He said, his head going down against her breastbone, perspiration on his temples.

"What?" Was she not formed the way woman should be? He couldn't go on?

"You are so ready for me." He gazed at her, but his eyes lost focus as he took her lips like a man dying. "You're wet and so warm."

"That's good?"

He inserted his penis another inch. "Very good. And more. Very...good."

She marveled at the girth of him inside her.

At once, he stopped. "And this?"

She feared he'd paused because there was indeed a drastic problem with her. "What?"

"This proves you are all mine forever more."

Richard had not raped her. She reached up and kissed her husband. "I love you."

He smiled at her, all beneficence and erotic delight, and then he broke the last barrier to complete union. "I know. Let me show you how that love grows, my darling."

And for the hours of that afternoon, he took her twice. After dinner, the meal shortened by their haste to have each other again, they hurried upstairs and enjoyed each other once more. They slept, to awaken and caress in the night, too exhausted to make love again.

But as the sun pierced the drapes, she rolled to him and asked for more. If he loved her like that with such unbridled ardor each time they coupled, how could she ever spend an hour without him?

CHAPTER 18

For their wedding trip, he took her to Paris. Ada had been often, her father renting a house in Rue Haussmann. But Victor had not been in eight years. With her, the City was new and glorious, alight with elegant gas works upon broad boulevards. And though he took a suite in the Hotel Splendide across from Opera Garnier and though he had purchased tickets to plays and the *Folies-Bergère* and intended to show off his lovely bride in the City, they rarely went anywhere. She had even cancelled an appointment Victor had made for her with the designer, Jacques Doucet. If the two of them did venture out, they did not remain for very long. The call of their rooms and the grand bed was a siren's song too resonant to ignore.

On their last day in Paris, Ada rose from their bed, deliciously bare, and pulled on the Japanese silk kimono he'd given her the first morning after their wedding. The ivory silk shot with gold sparkled against her complexion, the red and pink chrysanthemums on bronzed leaves highlighting her blushes and her glistening golden brown hair.

She spied the newspaper he held rolled in his hands,

feigning innocence to her real question. "The maid has already brought up breakfast?"

As with other hotels in Paris, visitors could hire servants by the day, week or month. Victor had hired a maid for Ada, a valet for himself. And the hotel staff affiliated with the kitchen and cafe brought food service promptly.

"Would you care for coffee or hot chocolate?" He loved teasing her, when she cared not to drink so much as to know what he had inserted into the morning news. Each day for the past seven, he'd placed a small but precious token of his love for her inside the printed pages. The kimono had been one of the larger pieces to hide. The two jade fu dogs, meant to guard their future home from sadness, had been the worst. The others—the cinnabar hair comb, the double strand of opera length pearls and a cutting of the turquoise and green Chinese wallpaper that would line their Brighton dining room —had been easy to conceal.

She pulled her waist-length hair up and out from under the standing collar of the kimono, threw him a sly and lazy smile, then strolled toward him. Rubbing her hot and supple body to his own, she made his head swim with desire as she said, "Whatever you have in there, it seems small today. A good thing. The train porters at Gare du Nord will develop back injuries loading those fu dogs."

He wanted to stay in Paris forever. But England called. He had business to attend to. The house in Brighton to settle. His daughters to fetch from London. And the rising tide of scandal that was soon to engulf them...or destroy their future had to be faced. With it, and his possible failure to convince the influential men in Brighton of his worthiness as an MP, came the question of whether she might return to China with him.

Of all this, he'd told Ada nothing of the rumors, the letters his mother sent or of the innuendos in the London scandal sheets. What he gave Ada each morning was the current issue of *Le Temps* which he had checked first for hints of problems at home. The morning newspaper fed her need for politics and international news.

Therefore, he was greedy attempting to extend the ecstasies of their wedding as long as possible. He curved his arms around her, all serenity he wished for her in his embrace. "What makes you think I have anything in here, but the day's headlines?"

She rubbed the tip of her nose along the column of his throat. Her hands undid the sash of his dressing gown and he swelled, his blood roaring to be lost in her. "Because you've been so generous, I doubt you'll stop. When we're home, I expect you to behave and stop spending money on me."

"Not ever." When he spoke, he heard the sand and fog of his own voice filled with nigh unto feral need to be inside her again. Her musky fragrance mingling with the scent of himself as he made love to her last night robbed him of much logic and so without forethought he said, "Open this. See if you like it. If not, we can change it to whatever you wish."

Her eyes faceting in the thousand shades of morning sky, she took it from him. Carefully, she unrolled the paper to take in her hand the cut glass vial he'd ordered from his friend in the Rue de la Paix. "Perfume?"

"I told them they must try. On such short notice, I could not get a new formula from my perfumer in Grasse, but I asked a friend of mine here to work some magic. Lift the stopper."

She did so and inhaled, her eyes closed. "Lime and lavender with...peony?"

"I thought the peony had come through. Should it be more predominant? What do you think?"

"I like it as it is and I'll wear it today. Where will we go?"

"I thought we'd take a picnic to the Luxembourg gardens. You will be the loveliest flower among all the others."

"And tonight, we'll go dance at the Moulin de la Galette." She had suggested it time and time again here in Paris. The ball in Montmartre, she told him, was an informal, sometimes raucous event where Parisians of all classes met to drink and dance. "You and I will be at home with others who dance for the fun of it and no one attempts to be perfect."

❦

The ball at the Moulin de la Galette offered everything Ada adored. Spontaneity, a small band, good beer for sale and people of all ages and from all walks of life. She'd first come here years ago when her cousin Marianne and her future husband, the famous sculptor the duc de Remy, escorted her and her friends. Then the ball was a novel event, but now it was famous. Parisians came in greater numbers. No one dressed formally. A lady was never to wear jewelry. Nor was a man to bring a wallet full of cash. The revelers danced until midnight and occasionally, if they could persuade the musicians to linger, until one. Then because many who lived in Montmartre awakened early to go to work, the partiers went home respectfully quiet.

"I'm afraid we're overdressed," Victor confided as he took her arm and they jockeyed for a table near the garden wall.

"No one will notice." She balanced her full glass of beer as a dancer bumped into her. Hoping to heaven this night might bring back the gaiety she'd seen on her husband's face those first few days. "They're not here to assess how much money you earn."

"I never would have thought you'd like this sort of thing." They took two chairs.

Grinning at him, she raised her glass. "That's what comes of marrying a woman you've known less than a month."

He looked as if she'd truly insulted him. "Are you sorry?"

"Victor Cole." She pulled back, her heart in her throat. How could he possibly ask that? "What have I not done to convince you that I adore you?"

"I apologize. I'm not pleased to return home."

She took a drink of her beer, assessing him. She was not a nincompoop and she had long since girded herself for whatever chaos they might meet upon their arrival in London. But she'd pushed it from her mind for this little while because her honeymoon was a once in lifetime event. She wanted a crystal clear memory of it. And she wanted Victor happy. "Will you share why?"

"I hope we can survive the uproar."

There he stopped. His usually lively turquoise eyes fixed blankly on hers.

His past challenge to kill the scandals brought by his first wife rose up like a dragon breathing fire. But she would not allow either of them to be consumed. She reached over to grasp his hand. "We will."

"You can't know."

"Together, we will deal well with this."

He smiled, but the effort cost him much.

"Come dance," she said. "Tonight is ours. Tomorrow is soon enough to face what ever else comes."

❦

The six-hour train ride from Paris to Ostend was tolerable, but the four-hour steamship trip across the Channel was rough. Sick to her stomach, Ada was grateful to disembark at the London wharf.

"We'll be home in bed in minutes," Victor promised as he hailed a hansom.

They fell into their bed exhausted.

Rain washed the streets the next morning, but she was sunny.

"Shall we go to your mother's and get the girls?" She asked at breakfast, aware he had no newspaper in his hand this morning.

His smile, as it had been the past two days, was a weak imitation of the ones she'd come to admire. "Their rooms are not finished."

"They won't care," she assured him. "They want to be with their father."

"And their new mother." He reached over to kiss her on the forehead, then reached for his coffee.

She fixed her gaze on him.

He devoted himself to his egg and toast, but finally lifted his gaze to hers. This time he wore the mischievous smile she'd come to love. "What are you staring at?"

She fluttered her lashes, innocence far from her intent. "Do I take this absence of newspaper to mean the honeymoon is over?" *Or is there something in the news you wish to hide from me?*

"Ah, well." He wiped the corners of his mouth with his serviette. Her stab of fear dissolved when he grinned. "Now that you mention it...."

She sighed, raised her face to the ceiling. It was then he grasped her hand and tugged her toward the door and the stairs.

"We'll go down."

"To the servants' quarters?"

"Out to the yard."

He led her down and toward the rear of the house. They passed the butler standing near his wine cellar and conversing with the new housekeeper. Both were very curious, but Victor only smiled. "Lady Cole wishes to see the yard."

He opened the little door and out they walked onto the slate stones. A drizzle fell upon them but the day was warm.

She didn't mind, especially when she saw the glassed-in cupola. "A miniature conservatory!"

She strode around the tiny little house. The structure he'd had built was an inch or two taller than she, and perhaps four feet wide. Inside a few wooden planks awaited pots and plants.

He waited outside, his arms folded, looking all too pleased with himself. And when she emerged and kissed his cheek, he said, "It's all we can fit in the space, but I thought you'd enjoy it."

"I certainly will. We need a kitchen garden more than flowers. But we shall see. I'll start as soon as we hire a cook and learn what she'd like to hand."

They walked arm and arm upstairs to finish their breakfast.

"I have an appointment this morning, my dear," he said when he finished his coffee. And still no newspaper was in sight.

"Do go." She would never keep him from his work. "I'll go to your mother's to get the girls, shall I?"

"If you don't mind doing that alone?"

"Not at all. I'll go this morning. Powell, Mrs Reynolds and I will discuss our needs for servants." The butler and new housekeeper seemed to be getting on quite well and Ada wanted to set up the household as quickly as possible. She wanted Vivienne and Deirdre happy in their home with their father, Wu-lai too must be feeling adrift in a new strange land. If she herself seemed at sea it was because Victor was not sharing his concerns. That she would not have. Secrets always made trouble. She'd not ruin her marriage before it'd begun by being a submissive woman who allowed her husband to make all choices, good, bad and indifferent.

If her marriage was to be a success or failure, she would actively participate in its rise or fall.

So her first order of business this morning when she went out was to order her hackney driver to stop at a news kiosk. She'd buy every newspaper available. Some things a man could not keep from a woman. One of them was gossip.

Victor left the house minutes after finishing his meal. Worried he had not fooled his young wife one bit showing her his newest gift, he put on his top hat and yanked on his gloves. He climbed into the hack his butler Powell had hailed for him and chewed on his lip.

Earlier he'd had a shock when he'd opened his mail of the past week. Reading three letters, he'd nearly run from the house in his dressing gown. One other letter addressed to Ada he did not open. But he pocketed it. He was being dastardly and unethical to keep her father's note from her, but he had to save her from a few terrors as long as he could.

He'd fired off notes to his three correspondents and a fourth to his mother. From each man he requested meetings. From his mother, secrecy about Richard's recent crazed behavior.

His first stop this morning was to have been his mother's in Upper Brook Street. Although he certainly wished to combine that with bringing his daughters home, he did not want to delve into Richard's recent public tirades with Ada in the room. He'd let Ada go to get his girls, but he'd first see Lord Grayson. As his major investor, Grayson held the key to his livelihood. And from the man's letter to him which he'd written yesterday, Victor knew he owed Grayson a hearing immediately.

Two hours later, he sat in MacIntyre's office alone. Grayson had been adamant: End the scurrilous rumors or he would pull all his funds from Cole and Company.

Hollowed out by Grayson's ultimatum, he allowed MacIntyre to take him to the local pub. There, the two of them ordered up an early lunch of sausages and mash and tankards of ale. He wanted to reassure his manager of their future but had not the heart for any chicanery. It was his man who had fine words for him. "Even if Grayson pulls his capital, sir, I know we can attract more."

"I know not who that would be," he said.

"I've a few ideas, sir."

And so, Victor had hailed another hack and taken it to Fleet Street. The owner of the disreputable scandal sheet that pilloried him was "not in," said the ink-stained pressman.

"I'll wait," he told the man and took the only chair in the chilly, grim and airless room.

When the publisher did arrive, Victor got no satisfaction from him. He hated that he'd tried to use logic on the man.

His last appointment was at his club. Most delicate of all was this meeting with men he'd known and revered all his life. They were party leaders, long-standing members of Parliament, men with whom he would love to work.

❦

Ada waited dinner for him. The girls were at table too, wishing to greet their father in their new home. But he did not arrive for dinner. Nor did he arrive before Ada sent them off to bed with Wu-lai in charge. She understood his reluctance to discuss the news reports she'd read in reputable papers.

For the virulence of the fabrications she'd read in the scandal sheets, she was bursting with outrage and sorrow. She'd also read a letter from her father, dated two days ago, delivered to her by Powell today after teatime.

All day she reaffirmed to herself the truth of her circumstances: she loved Victor and whatever ill befell them because of those stories, she would face them with him—and solve them. So she waited in the front salon, listening for the clomp of horses' hooves or the crack of a cabbie's whip. Tired, anxiety eating at her sympathy for his distress, she went upstairs to undress. Waiting in their sitting room, she'd tried to read and failed. Wearing a hole in the carpet from her pacing seemed the only solution to her fears.

When she finally heard footsteps on the stairs, she glanced at the clock. Twelve past midnight.

She braced for a confrontation. Was he drunk? Where had he been? Not that she mistrusted him, but she was owed an explanation. She waited, hands clasped, her teeth clenched...but he passed the room by.

Fury filled her that he would so disrespect her. That he would dismiss her and her interest.

She yanked open the door in time to see him disappear into another bedroom two down. She cut the distance between them in seconds.

"I waited for you," she opened by announcing the obvious as she stood on the threshold.

His beautiful eyes were hooded as he took her in. He was sober. That was one good sign. "Go to bed, Ada."

She marched to the bell pull.

"Do not summon my valet. I can do this." He pealed off his frock coat and unbuttoned his waistcoat, then dropped them to the *chaise longue*. Sinking into the overstuffed chair, he bent to remove his shoes.

"Tell me everything." She wanted to know where he'd

been, who he'd seen, why. She had a right to know. After all, the scandals that lived on everyone's lips were about her. Mostly her. He suffered as a hero, an unwitting accomplice in a tragic tale.

His brows knit. And then he went back to attending to his shoes. "Not tonight."

"Yes. Tonight. Now."

He shook his head, weary.

She sank to her knees before him. "I have a right to know."

He examined her as if he did not know her.

"Victor, I bought papers. I know what they say. You cannot hide this from me."

"I don't intend to."

"Then...then come to bed. Why are you here? You belong with me."

He hauled her close, his fingers digging into the soft flesh of her upper arms, her knees sliding on the silk of her night-gown across the rough carpet. "Go to bed. Stay there. Do not come here because I cannot have you. Not tonight. Not... perhaps ever."

"What?" Her head spun with his rejection.

"Listen to me. I have had a hellish day. I must make sense of it. And I must deal with all the loss—" He gulped and his eyes burned red with sorrow.

Loss? Because of Richard? "No! You must not say that. You have us. Your family. Me."

"Go to bed, Ada." He untangled himself from her and padded away in his stocking feet.

She struggled to stand. "I know what Richard's done. I read it all everywhere. Dear god. No one can escape reading it!"

His brother had declared that she had enticed him, promising him an affair, a few evenings alone. That he'd taken her to his estate and that his brother had intervened, drugged her and carried her off. Then subdued and confused as she was by chloroform and laudanum, Victor had violated her. When she came to her senses, she blackmailed him into marrying him. But Richard would see his brother vindicated and the vicious little American taken to task. Richard declared that his younger brother did not need to honor a marriage made under duress. He would help his brother get the union annulled.

His shoulders sagged. "Then you see what must be done."

"Yes! We'll fight him with the truth!"

"We can but it will bring us nothing."

"Don't be absurd!" She flung out the words but hated how he recoiled at the insult.

"I'm not," he said and in his anger, it was as if he grew in breadth and stature. "This—this fiasco brings us to an impasse."

"I—I do not understand. What impasse?"

In two swift strides, he was before her. Looming, a mighty Samson wounded by love, he clasped her to him. "All is lost here, Ada. The possibility of a political career for me is dead. My reputation once more falls to pieces."

"Explain that to me."

"My major investor in Cole and Company threatens to withdraw. My business, profitable as it is, will then be half as rich as yesterday. I might be able to go on. But we would live on substantially less. And I had hoped to leave your dowry intact for any of our daughters to inherit. Now I am blocked even in that."

She wanted to object and soothe him but with a wild shake of his head he warned her from speaking.

"The final blow is that members of my party will not have me. Even with my father's blessing, I am too much a scoundrel in the public's view to hold any office."

This hollowed her out. Her urge to fight all odds and to argue with him died in her throat.

"I had a wife who wanted more than I could give her. More status, more money, more attention. She went looking for what she could not get from me. And in her search, she found her own erotic perversions and her ruin. I had to leave England, Ada, to save my own face. To be able to walk among my peers and hold my head up, I had to find a new life and earn a new respect. When she died, I did not grieve. I felt relief. Freedom. I vowed never to marry again. Never to want to please another spouse. Never to be required to care for her."

That made her step backward. What was he saying?

"I must return to Shanghai. There is no future for me here. And you have never wished to go abroad. Nor will I force you. I had hoped to make us both happy here, you with your family around you and me with the career I so desperately wanted. But that is not to be. So I will prepare to return to China and I will take my daughters with me."

"And me?"

"I leave you here with my name, my houses, my servants, my parents and with your own family. I would never persuade you to live in any way you do not want to."

"But you love me."

Regret lived in his expression. "I do."

"But—"

"I will go and you will stay. Because love is not enough to change the world."

Then he left her where she stood. At the door, he swung it wide and stepped aside for her to leave him.

CHAPTER 19

Numb, Ada retired to their suite and sat before the fire all through the night. Tears did not come. Logic either. To be so summarily dismissed was a loss too deep for movement or expression. Soon after dawn, her new maid, a young woman aged twenty-two, knocked. Ada dismissed her and said she'd ring when and if she wished her presence. Wu-lai appeared at her door soon after. Ada told her to take the girls to the square. The day seemed sunny and she had no idea if Victor planned activities for them. But she would. After noon, she reached for the bell pull and requested a bath and her walking suit.

"Breakfast downstairs in an hour. Tell Powell I wish a carriage soon after."

Her father and step-mother had adjourned to their Brighton country home after her wedding. But her sister Lily and her brother-in-law Julian remained in London in mourning dealing with the aftershocks of the earl of Carbury's death. Ada's first visit would be to Lily. She sent round a note that she would call at two.

At Seton House, the mood was subdued. The butler,

glum. Lily somber in dove gray, her pregnancy slowing her gait. She greeted Ada heartily though, then whisked her into the salon. They commiserated, each with the other's problems, and Lily was utterly dumbfounded by Ada's.

"Oh, my dear." She hugged her and sat her down. "You haven't cried. I can tell."

"Tears can't cure this."

"You'll find what does."

I will certainly try. "I'm here to ask a favor." She measured out her words, fearful if she gave in to emotion, she'd shatter like glass.

"Anything."

"I know that Julian devotes himself to his sister in her crisis, but if he might call upon me at his convenience, I must speak with him."

At Lily's agreement, she rose and left.

Her next call was to the countess and earl of Ware and their daughter, her friend, Lady Jessica. Their expressions of support touched her heart and when she asked their help, they readily agreed. They would appear at her home for tea three days hence. Ada assured them she would personally invite Lord Billings—Freddie, as Victor was fond of calling him.

That afternoon, she penned another note to Victor's other friend she'd heard him speak of. Sir Arnold Meachum—Arnie—was invited to tea as well.

At tea time, she called in Vivienne and Deirdre. The three of them enjoyed what she often had as a child—time to converse. Though Ada's mother had died when she was five, she had memories of snippets of their conversations about flowers. Not knowing what these two girls recalled of their mother or of what delights they might have shared with her,

Ada wished to make their lives richer, if she could. With Victor's intent to take them back to China with him, Ada had a little time to enjoy them. And she would.

Stuffed with cucumber sandwiches and cream and strawberries, Ada requested no dinner and retired to her rooms. She heard her husband climb the stairs at twenty past eight and retire to his new bedroom down the hall. She fell asleep in the chaise, a book unread in her hands.

The following afternoon, she called upon her new mother-in-law in Upper Brook Street and took the girls with her.

"I'm honored you have called upon me, Ada." The woman had dark circles under her eyes. The sign of her sleeplessness could mean many things. Ada had to know precisely what that might be.

She sat in the drawing room surrounded by portraits of past dukes and duchesses of Brentwood, the splendor of the Regency decor soothing her dismay. With Vivienne and Deirdre present, they could not speak frankly. But then, Ada counted on the duchess to respond to her presence with an openness that did not require words as much as the visible signs of her acceptance of Ada.

"I trust you can and will help me understand my current circumstances, Your Grace."

"I will. I wish to see you both happy...and together in Brighton and elsewhere. My husband wishes the same."

"Thank you. I came for that assurance and I will ask that you and your husband tell that to all you know."

"I plan it. A dinner party next week. My husband is too ill to travel but I have invited my two daughters and their husbands."

Ada had met Victor's two younger sisters and their husbands at their wedding. "I look forward to getting to know them better. Will others attend?"

"Twenty-two more. I will not allow this to—" She halted

with a sidelong glance at the girls who chatted between themselves.

"I am grateful." Ada offered her the smile that should have been an embrace. But she lowered her voice to ask, "Have you any idea if Victor accepts?"

The woman drew to her full height. "He knows that he must."

That night, Ada sat down to her dinner table and gave the nod to Powell that he might serve her. She was finishing her soup, when Victor appeared.

"Good evening," he bid her, his gaze assessing if she might accept his company. "Do you mind if I join you?"

She inclined her head and allowed the course to be removed. Then she waited until the butler and the footman had left them alone. "No."

He took his chair far from her down the long polished mahogany table. Two candelabra marked the length and obscured his face.

She snorted. Even the table arrangements consorted to conceal him from her.

Powell reappeared and though Ada did not watch him, she detected his movements were furtive. Smart man wished to be nowhere near them.

"I understand," said her husband after Powell had hastily exited, "you've paid a few calls."

She rose, moved the two silver pieces to one side, then regained her chair. She examined her husband in his evening finery. Much too appealing to her senses, he seemed much too congenial as well. "I am not one to sit and wait for events to turn my way."

He set his jaw. "I know."

She attacked her fish course.

"I'm pleased you went to see Mama. Glad you took the girls, too. They need that kind relationship with their grandmother. They had little companionship from their mother."

Ada inhaled. Put down her fork and knife. "Yet you will take them from their new mama?"

"Ada, I want to be fair to you."

She shot to her feet. Not ready to talk with him, she only wanted to argue...and that would gain her only rancor. "This is a case where fair is foul."

The following afternoon, Ada saw her brother-in-law Julian to the foyer when Victor appeared on the doorstep. He'd been out since early morning and was just now arriving home.

"Your Grace," he welcomed the duke warmly, but his curious gaze shot from his wife to his new brother-in-law. "I regret I have missed you."

Julian donned his top hat, his coach idling before the house. "I called upon Ada. We settled much. Do come see me if you wish to talk, Cole. We are family and you and I have not had much time together. Especially since we share that night of tragedy."

"Perhaps tomorrow?" Victor asked.

"Let us say, two o'clock?"

"Two it is."

Satisfied at that exchange, Ada spun on her heel and retired to her rooms.

The next morning, she took her breakfast at half five. She was very early, but she preferred to dine alone. When she arrived in the breakfast room, the place for Victor was set. He had not eaten which meant, if she wished solitude, she'd have to pray for it, then eat quickly. The morning papers had not yet arrived so that lack sped her along.

But as she took her last sip of coffee, her husband appeared. In a dark brown herringbone suit shot with turquoise thread, his auburn hair gleaming and a creamy shirt under bronze satin waistcoat, Victor was every bit the man of business.

He bid her good morning and handed her a newspaper.

She arched a brow, said her thanks and took it.

No longer concealing the news from her, he took his chair at the round table and waited as Powell poured his coffee.

Though she felt his gaze upon her, she resisted the urge to look up from her reading. After all, one does appreciate it when one's tea party is published in the papers as a proper social event.

"I read there that you are having guests here this afternoon."

"I am. I'm rather pleased." She let her eyes lock on his. Damn him for his good humor.

"I know what you're doing."

Now for that, she could offer him up a smile. "Good."

"Am I invited?"

She slowly rose, rolled the paper in her fingers and schooled herself to regard him with only mischief. "No."

<hr />

Two evenings later when Ada climbed into his mother's borrowed Brentwood town coach, Victor was right behind her to return home to Hanover Square. To look at her was to witness how she had regained much of her confidence that he had stolen from her the other night. He'd wounded her severely, rejecting her, removing himself from her bed. Observing her tonight as she talked with his sisters and the other ladies, he noted how she sparkled. No hint of their marital discord showed on her face. She even looped her arm through his at one point in the drawing room and laughed up at him as if she still slept in his arms each night. Would to God he could allow himself to take her.

Her scent, her stride, every gesture of her elegant hands tormented him. Tonight, she was particularly delectable. She wore a vermilion satin gown that set off her bright eyes and dark honeyed hair, and to complement it, she used his wedding gifts of pearls and the cinnabar hair comb. She could charm a toad and had done so tonight with two of his party leaders. Victor ached to have her in his arms and show her how he did adore her. But if he did, if he weakened, he'd curse himself. Especially if he got her with child, then he'd have to force her eventually to go to China with him. And to ensure she did not lose the baby or suffer from the thousand and one diseases on ships crossing the seas of the world, he would have to remain here in England until well after she was safely delivered. He would never harm her. Not by demanding she accompany him to China nor by accepting any compromise she might offer and see her die or the baby along the way.

Over the past week, she'd been busy. It was not lost on him that all her efforts were sound logical ones. Ones that had turned in her favor. To ask her brother-in-law the duke of Seton to speak on his behalf socially was the easiest task she'd performed. He himself would never have been so brazen. Freddie and Arnie's good words were a given. She'd given urgency to their utterance. Then too, the Wares had announced their intentions to support him and for that, he was indebted to them. But again, he would not have asked. In America, he presumed, one suffered no loss of face to ask for help. Nor did one flinch from the task.

Stepping into the foyer at home, Ada shed her cape into Powell's care and sailed up the stairs. Taking the steps two at a clip, Victor followed and caught her elbow just as she would've entered her suite.

"May I please talk with you?"

Regal, cool, she nodded but stood her ground.

"Not here." He was urgent, insistent.

"Why? The servants know what happens here."

He ground his teeth and thrust open the door to their sitting room. He swung her inside. In the dark, the heavy drapes shrouding out the street gas lights, the sitting room was lit by only a small lamp. "I know what's wrong here. And it's not so easily remedied by teas and dinner parties."

"Noted." She stepped away from him but he got in front of her and drew her near. In the dim light, her complexion warmed, her eyes devoured him with hunger.

She blinked. Too soon, their glances broke and so did the enchantment. She tried to leave his embrace.

But he stopped her. "I thank you, Ada. But this cannot help. Even if I can persuade them to grant me the seat, I've lost half my business."

"And you cannot gain it back another way? Without your prior investor? I don't believe it."

"You've seen your father and your brother not only survive but prosper. I understand how you can think that business is a matter of looking for the money from someone else."

She arched her brows at him. "Then perhaps you've not met the right people."

"I have! I do! But this nasty business with Richard has scared off not just my political friends but potential investors who now do not trust my judgment."

"Then prove to them your judgment is sound."

He dropped his hands at his sides. "Of course. Why didn't I think of that."

She snorted. "I'm leaving for Brighton tomorrow."

"Why?"

"I prefer it to London in the summer. The sea, the sky, the sand. They call to me. I like fish, too, you see. And I like it fresh from a good monger." She pressed a hand flat to his chest in prayer or benediction he knew not which. "Do take good care of yourself."

"You're leaving me?" He wanted to laugh, to scream.

She stared at him, nonplussed, allowing the irony to sink in, he supposed.

"I'm going to our new home there. I sent word down yesterday. I must staff it, finish the furnishings. All of it." She walked around him.

He stood with his mouth hanging open like a damned hooked trout.

"Oh, I'm taking the girls, too. Wu-lai. Powell stays here. I told him to hire a new cook, but we may not need her for long since you will soon leave for Shanghai." And there, for all her bravado, was the precise word on which she lost all her hauteur. The mask of her indifference was just that. Her longing for him was a heartache so palpable he felt his own sore heart squeeze tight.

He had her in his arms in a thrice. He cupped her face, kissed her lips, her cheeks, her eyelids, her mouth. Dear god. Her mouth was bliss. She wanted him in spite of his failure and his callousness, and he needed her. Needed to taste her earlobe and to nuzzle the hollow of her throat, needed to kiss his way across the top of her bosom. He needed to feel the chiffon of her breasts in his hands, her nipples on his tongue. But the multitude of clothes meant he could not get to her breasts and he groaned. She murmured her own frustration, grasped his hand and led him to their bed. There, she sat, undid his buttons and his flies, then bared his stomach to kiss his hip bones and drive him to madness. On a cry, she lifted her petticoats, shimmied out of her drawers and shifted back upon the mattress. Then she led him down.

He sank inside her and gulped back a cry of triumph. He sought her mouth again. "I love you," he told her.

"I know," she whispered and with a hand upon his bare backside, pressed him farther into her.

CHAPTER 20

The next afternoon, Ada climbed into the Setons' traveling coach. Lily and Julian had been generous to allow her to borrow it. Though they had wished to retire to their own country estate weeks ago, Carbury's sudden death and the problems afterward mitigated against that. They would not use it soon, Elanna's hysteria a challenge to her doctors. So was her continuing rejection of her three-year-old son, Nathaniel.

"Please use the coach, Ada." Julian had told her when he had called upon her the other day. "I cannot leave Elanna as she is. And Nate cries all day, wanting his father. Lily tries her best to comfort him, but he seems inconsolable. Let me do this for you. Make your life easier as we deal with our challenges here."

She could have taken the train from Victoria Station in London to Brighton. But that would have been unwieldy as she had quite a few trunks, clothing for herself, Vivienne, Deirdre and Wu-lai. The journey, short though it was, required comfort for her, her two step-daughters and nurse.

Ada would send back the coachman and footman tomorrow after a hearty meal.

Curious about the house Victor's parents had gifted them, she delighted at the prospect of decorating her own home. She'd learned much from listening to her sister Lily manage her many Seton properties. Visiting often with her cousin Marianne who was a French princess and a duchess, had exposed Ada to the dynamic of complementing the delicate medieval with the boldness of her husband Remy's contemporary sculptures. Now Ada had the means, courtesy of her father's generous personal allowance, to make a house a home with her own taste predominating. Of course, her best adviser would be her step-mother, Liv, who still took clients who wished their homes appointed by her.

As to the quality of the house, she had asked Victor this morning at breakfast to describe it.

Last night after they had made love, he had kissed her cheek, gathered his clothes and left her.

This morning, he had appeared none too rested. His eyes bleary, nonetheless, he was conversational. "I believe you will like it immensely. It's old. More than one hundred years. Built at the same time as Marlborough House and on the Steine. Though Robert Adam never worked on it, the structure has many of those features. I give you *carte blanche* to do as you wish."

"Thank you. I have a note for your Mr. MacIntrye."

"Oh?"

"Yards of silk I'd like for the salon or dining room. Draperies or upholstery. Not certain which at the moment. But I thought we'd show off your imports."

"A lovely idea," he said, and the curve of his mouth implied his pleasure. "Please write and let me know about all you do, will you?"

"Of course." She wanted him aware of how she'd manage the house. "It's your home as well as ours."

He paused over his breakfast plate at that to check her features. What he saw there must have satisfied him, because he returned his attention to his eggs. "I imagine you will be happy to see your father and step-mother."

She beamed at the idea for there was much to discuss with those she loved. "Liv is soon to deliver her next child and I'm to remind her, says my father in his note this morning, that she must sit down not run about town. I'll be pleased to introduce Vivienne and Deirdre to their new little uncle."

Liv and her father had a young son, born only eighteen months ago. Though his name was William James, they dubbed him Liam.

"Odd to have a brother who is young enough to be your own son."

"True. But it won't be a mystery. We'll all draw charts so everyone understands who belongs to whom and how."

Victor paused again. "Yes. And who should not belong."

In the *Daily News*, Ada had read a piece that the marquess of Ridgemont was to appear before his bankers in the City. The duke of Brentwood, Richard's and Victor's father, had changed the security on one of Richard's loans, calling in the principal. She had wondered if Richard had the means to pay it off, but she had not asked Victor. Quite frankly, she wished to know nothing about the man.

Victor stood then, threw down his serviette and bussed her on the cheek. "Enjoy yourself."

Powell told her hours later, that Victor had said his good-byes to his daughters earlier and then had departed for his offices. Ada was glad of that, she wanted no more kisses from him until she had completed her plans.

· · ·

Hours later, the Seton coach entered the curved gravel drive of her new home. Gazing upon the exterior of the white stucco Palladian with cast iron *porte cochère*, she had the premonition that she would indeed enjoy herself tremendously. The girls jumped down and ran onto the front portico. A breeze off the shore bore the smell of the salty sea air that refreshed her. And she took the footman's hand to help her alight. At first sight, she loved the looks of it. The house, she noted with a grin, needed new paint outside and the grounds needed one more essential—a good gardener.

She sent round a note to her parents that she had arrived, but that she would not call until three days hence. She needed to assess what the duke had ordered be done to repair the house —and she immediately appreciated its cleanliness, the new plumbing and electricity. Her next thought was to servants. The butler named Goodings and the only maid named Patsy appeared attentive and useful. She told them what she expected each day and asked them to remain for at least two more months. She would then decide if she would retain their services year round. What they had to work with was next on her list. She had to do a preliminary analysis of the essentials —china, silver, linens, the kitchen equipment, storage and wine cellars.

To ensure that Vivienne and Deirdre were well occupied, she placed ads in the *Brighton Gazette* for a French tutor and a piano teacher. The next afternoon she took them to the Lanes where shopkeepers sold everything a child might love from easels (for the artist in Viv) to books about zebras (for Deirdre who loved animals). Afterward, they strolled the promenade along the beach, ate ices and later, she took them to the aquarium to marvel at the fish. For herself, she ordered watering cans, picks, hoes and seeds to plant once she'd strangled the weeds in the old kitchen garden. Satisfied with her progress, she wondered how long it would take for Mr. MacIntyre to fill her order of silk. She would hire Liv's favorite upholsterer to finish the main salon's furniture as soon as the material arrived. This house, she was determined, would speak to who Victor Cole was. Past, present and future, Cole Manor—as she now called the rambling beauty— would be a place Victor could love. And if he wished, a home where he could be loved.

When she and the girls climbed into a public hack to journey a few miles west of Brighton to her parents' home, Ada had a list of questions in her reticule that seemed long as her arm.

Her father and step-mother came out on the drive to meet the carriage. Killian Hanniford at age fifty was a tall, strapping man with a full head of iron grey hair and a hug that told her he was as strong and able as many men half his age. Olivia Hanniford, a beauty with hair the color of autumn leaves, was forty-one, married now for less than three years but pregnant with her second child by Ada's father. Behind them stood Camille Bereston, Liv's oldest child and daughter by her first husband. Camille held in her arms a chubby, grumpy baby boy who had inherited the large silver eyes of his father and his once bold black hair. Introductions and a few tears all around and they were soon in the house that Killian had built and Liv had decorated.

"Oh, it's wonderful to be here," she told them as she sank into the sofa and heard the sound of the surf against the sands.

Camille had taken the children and Wu-lai away to the nursery. Her father stood by the French doors to the terrace which looked out over the cliffs above the sea. He focused on her with the intensity of a man who had arrived a poor Irish immigrant to the Baltimore docks and built a fortune in ships, factories and investments within a few decades. Lily had married with an enormous dowry for her husband Julian. Marianne's was equally as large. Ada's exactly the same. Pierce, their brother, made his own fortune, in shipping but also in newer investments in French copper and pipe manufacturing. He had at one time talked with Victor about the Shanghai city council's plans for electricity for the foreign settlement.

She knew what they wished to discuss, but her heart was not in describing her marital discord. Because she was here alone, she concluded that these very intelligent people had a good idea what her problems were.

"I'm happy to tell you about the wedding trip. Paris is... delicious. But the newspapers have robbed me of much of the fun I had there. I'm here to enjoy your good company and your help."

"What do you need, sweetheart?" her father asked, his brow quite wrinkled.

"Your friends."

His mouth spread in a wicked grin. "How and when would you like them?"

"Here to reacquaint me with them say...perhaps...two weeks from now?"

Liv laughed, a hand upon the rise of her belly. "I can do that."

"How soon now——?" Ada asked.

"The doctor estimates the first of September."

"Another big baby then?"

Liv cast a rueful eye at her husband. "What else might we have in this family?"

"I don't want to burden you with my needs. That's why I'm hoping you could have a dinner party to announce my arrival in the town. A newspaper piece. Something showy."

"I imagine," Killian said, "we should invite the town council."

"Yes, the mayor and town council. The church leaders of St. Anne's, St, Paul's and All Saints. The men who run old Prince Regent's Royal Pavilion for the city. Who have I left out?"

Killian chuckled. "The lady who runs the lending library in the Lanes?"

"Exactly. We should have her too."

Liv said, "Poor woman. She hands out leaflets for the women's vote. Many a customer she'd lost because of it, too."

Ada acknowledged that with a nod. "All the more reason to have her. She'll add more lustre to our stance that women should have the right."

"Victor endorses that?" Killian was surprised.

"And the new marriage bill in Parliament. He believes a woman can handle her own money." She winked at her father.

"Ahhh," he crooned, his Irish lilt strong in his voice. "And who could deny a woman such a thing, eh?"

"Not you. Not Victor, either." She was happy to leave this topic for now and go to one less weighty. "There are a few other things I'll need and I hope you can help me, Liv."

"Name it, my dear."

"I wonder if I might borrow your cook for a week or so. Perhaps a scullery maid, too. A few pots and pans. The new house has a meager supply of everything and if I'm to host weekly teas, I must quickly get up to snuff."

Liv crossed her arms, an approving grin upon her face. "Weekly teas. Why I do like the idea."

"Little teatime conversations," Ada said with mischief in mind, "to acquaint the townsfolk with their potential new MP."

"And his charming wife," added her step-mother.

"His strongest supporter," said her father.

. . .

By the third week in August, when many Londoners flocked down to Brighton on the train for a swim in the sea, Ada had already hostessed two of her afternoon tea parties for local dignitaries. Rather she should have called them Lemonade Parties because that had become the preferred beverage of her guests in the hot and sticky weather. This morning, she prepared for her third.

She thought she was ready. She had a new cook, a new scullery maid, two footman, china, silver service for tea, table linens, a bright Chinoiserie sapphire blue and yellow decor for her luxurious salon—and a bad case of nerves.

She was to receive today the mayor of Brighton, the three wealthy and influential members of the board of directors of the Cantwell Orphanage, the owner of the Albion Hotel, the haughty leader of the local Temperance Union—and her own husband.

Victor had cabled early this morning that he would be down from Victoria Station on the eight o'clock train.

She glanced at her bedroom clock.

"'Arriving ten-thirty,'" he'd written.

It was now eleven oh-five.

"How is that, milady?" Her new ladies' maid gave a last tug on her corset stays.

"Wonderful. I'll have my red silk dressing gown, if you please, and you may go. I'll ring when I'm ready for you to do my hair." She could wait a much longer time to don her gown.

She'd ordered a new one for today, a pink and white striped muslin that made her feel young, carefree and more healthy than she'd been in days. But if she was correct, this new dress would not fit her for long. She was with child. And whether she'd become pregnant on her wedding trip or the day before she left London, she knew full well that news of a child was not in her favor. She would not force herself into his life with such news. Yet she'd worried how to tell him. Go to London? Write a letter? Cable?

Ridiculous.

What would she say? "Weather fine here. All's well. Girls happy. House in good form. Me, carrying your child. Write soon!"

But he was coming here. And if he looked closely at her, he'd see she seemed a little green around the edges.

Ohhh. She hated the idea. Went for her tea tray and sipped the tepid stuff. Baa! She even hated that. But coffee sent her running for a basin. And she'd had to stay in bed in the mornings to drink it too. Which irritated her back.

She sighed. Why couldn't she just go out and dig in her garden? She put her forehead to the pane. The tangled mess she'd found out there was now weeded, plowed and furrowed. She and the girls had planted a few tomatoes, some lettuce and a row of cilantro and parsley. Each morning and late afternoon, Viv and Deirdre watered the plot. Sprouts had shown their little green heads yesterday and the two of them giggled in welcome to their work.

A clatter in the hall met her ears. Squeals of delight meant the girls were ready for their walk into town with Wu-lai.

And then suddenly the far door of her sitting room to the hall was open and there stood her husband.

Oh, my. He was grand.

With a straw bowler in his hand, a navy coat, white shirt and dove grey trousers, he was the very model of an Englishman visiting the seashore.

"Ada," he seemed to breathe more than say. And he was across the room, hesitant to approach her or touch her, but his eyes caressing every inch of her and returning to lock on her own eyes. "You look wonderful."

He'd gone blind, clearly.

She closed one eye and looked at him with skepticism.

He threw his hat sailing away toward a chair and scooped her into his arms.

A palm to his chest, she had to ward him off. He couldn't just rush in here and with one embrace, wipe out the fact that he had not bothered to come see her in nearly two months.

"You won't let me kiss you." That was more statement than question. Yet his mouth was temptingly near and she was lured. Definitely lured.

She pushed away, headed for a chair because either her condition or his nearness made her head spin. "Good to see you."

He snorted. "Very well, I suppose I deserve that."

She looked up at him, standing as he was in the center of her bedroom of what might one day be—if he was repentant —their bedroom.

"Okay. You are angry with me."

"Angry? No. Why would I be? Do you deign to put pen to paper once a week? I read more in the London papers about you than you tell me yourself. Why would I possibly be angry, Lord Cole?"

"I deserve that," he said, his tone repentant even if he did not say the words. "I've come to attend one of your famous tea parties."

She narrowed her eyes at him. "Who said you had an invitation?"

He laughed, but it was short-lived and nervous. "Please stop."

"Why? Will you apologize? And how long do you intend to stay? I'll have Goodings make up a room for you."

He took that in with a souring expression. "May I sit, please?"

She extended a hand toward the far Chippendale chair, then pulled her dressing gown close about her.

He took it. His gaze went round the room, the yellow Chinese wallpaper filled with dragons and butterflies bringing surprise and humility to his face.

The decor of her bedroom was a cheerful resurrection of some of the best artistry he'd seen in Shanghai. The dragons breathing benevolent fire as the butterflies of pink and yellow danced about the larger ugly creatures were a whimsical allegory. He'd forgotten the details of the story of how the dragons had saved the butterflies, but it was a Chinese fable that told how the strong often saved the weak and the weak one day showed their greater strength to save the strong from themselves.

Just as Ada had saved him.

They belonged together and he'd suffered pangs of despair without her. Visions of her came to him at night when he was alone and fraught with doubts. He hungered for her company, her bright hair and dancing eyes, her humor, defiance and her spark. At times, he could even taste her on his tongue. Just to think of her made him swell with need. Even to contemplate satisfying himself left him hollow. He never tried. But he'd had to do without her because until two days ago, he'd had no definite means to reclaim his dignity and their reputations, let alone reclaim her as his wife.

"I have read daily of your triumphs here. You've been busy."

She acknowledged that with a slow nod.

He licked his lips. "The vicar of All Saints wrote to me last week, praising your tea party and your beauty."

"Kind of him. Do men of the cloth notice women's looks?"

"A man would need to be blind not to see yours."

She pointed a finger at him. "A silver tongue."

"And true."

She inhaled, shaking off the compliment. "Are you here for the day or—?"

He could take the train back tonight, but he didn't want to. "I'd hoped that you let me stay."

"Oh?" She arched a brow. "Why not return to London or better yet to Paris?"

He felt the chill from four feet away. "I went on business."

"So I understand from the papers. With my brother, no less. Did you have fun?"

"No! Not without you."

"Can you imagine what I had to say here? That you were off, away—" She flung out a hand and tears dotted her lashes.

He squeezed his eyes shut a moment. This was horrid. He'd known it would be. But nothing for it but to go on. "I know I've caused you so much heartache. But I had to work night and day to figure out how to survive. How to earn enough money to keep you and the girls."

"*Must* we be rich?"

He clenched his hands. "No. But we must have dignity. I must have it. I was raised with it, born to it. One cannot leave off needing it. You must see that."

She dropped her gaze to her hands. "I do."

"Oh, Ada, forgive me for all this."

"There is no need for it. We both were sullied by Richard's actions. Never apologize for another's actions. Certainly, not his."

"Very well."

She glanced at the clock on her mantel. "Tell me your news, will you? I've much to do before the guests arrive."

He had such high hopes this morning that she'd welcome him, hear him out, give him a chance to show her that he could succeed, could change their lives and their marriage for the better. "Perhaps I'm too late."

"I need to be the judge of that, Victor. Tell me what you wish, for God's sakes." She clutched her stomach and she appeared a little bug-eyed.

He startled. "Are you well?"

"This conflict makes me...uneasy."

"I hope to end that."

She sank backward in her chair and studied him.

"I do have very good news. Pierce and I have met often these past few weeks and we've come to a business agreement."

She merely tipped her head in query.

He cleared his throat. "He and I had corresponded while I was in Shanghai about investment opportunities for him in the Settlement. I'm a member of the Municipal Council and we hold the ability to award contracts for gas, water and now electricity suppliers."

"Pierce," she said with a glance toward the window, "owns shares in that French syndicate which manufactures steel tubes."

He smiled at her, all his hopes to have her back a living creature inside him. "He and I went to Paris to meet with them. They begin a process to manufacture rods for electrical works. We have formed a *Société Anonyme* to raise money to perfect the process to make electrical cords large enough for entire cities to have services."

"And the money you used to invest in this was from Cole and Company?" Pleasure dawned on her lovely face.

"My yearly profits this year and next go to it, yes. But what I bring more importantly are my friendships with those on the Municipal Council and my knowledge of Chinese literati and their politics."

She shot to her feet, her movement so quick she swayed.

He caught her.

"You're leaving me?" she breathed, her face upturned to him, agony in every line.

"No."

"Returning to China?"

"No." He circled his arms around her and held her tenderly. His hands in her silken hair, he pressed her head to his heart. "I'm staying here, my love. That is my role. I'm here. Pierce goes to Shanghai. Only Pierce with letters of introduction from me. I'm going to stay here because it seems with those friends you've made for me, I am to be appointed to the vacant seat for Brighton."

She broke apart in his embrace then, all sobs and a fountain of tears. But he picked her up and took her to the *chaise longue* where he fished out his handkerchief, wiped her tears and held her for long minutes to reacquaint himself with the joys of having his wife in his possession.

As the hall clock struck nine that night, he mounted the steps behind his wife. They'd had a most successful and enjoyable teatime. He'd conversed with a few residents of Brighton whom he'd met years ago when he'd come here with this family to the seaside for summer retreats. He'd also met new acquaintances whom Ada had cultivated. But the party had gone on far too long and afterward, dinner with his children had extended far into the evening. His wife looked piqued. So much so, that he worried about her health.

"I must tell you, I like what you've accomplished with the house. The salon is a riot of color. The Chippendale complements the Chinese decor." He took her arm to help her climb the stairs.

"I'm pleased that you are."

At the door to her suite, he brought them to a halt. He

would not assume he was invited to share her bed. He'd hurt her by his extended absence, though he vowed to spend his life making it up to her.

She cupped his cheek. "Would you like to join me?"

"If you'll have me, I'd welcome the fine company."

"And I, yours. But you must know first that I may not be such fine company."

"If you mean to say I must not presume too much, then I can join you in bed and only hold you."

"You may have to."

He tried not to let the disappointment show.

She traced a fingertip over the fullness of his lower lip. "Often in the mornings, I am not well, Victor."

He ran his hand up into her hair and sent her pins scattering. He'd always loved her hair, the rainbow of golds and bronze. He loved every bit of her and to think she was unwell and he'd not been here to help her. "My darling, I knew it. What is it? Have you seen a doctor? You must tell me all. I need to know. We'll get the best advice, the best—"

She laid back in his arms and let her eyes encompass him. "I have the best advice. The best there is."

"What is it then?"

"We must wait about seven months to know."

"But months? Why? I—" The reality hit him like a blow to the stomach. He stared into her twinkling eyes. What a simpleton he was. "Ada, sweetheart, a baby?"

"Are you happy?"

"Happy?" He swept her up into his arms. "Open this door."

She obeyed and he whirled her inside. He took her to their bed and sat her down, then he knelt before her. "You were not going to tell me, were you?"

She bit her lower lip. "Not if you continued to live away from me. Not if you were returning to China and not taking me with you." Sobs wracked her and he took her shaking body in his arms.

"I was a fool to say such things, Ada."

She pushed him away, tears streaming down her cheeks. "I would have gone with you. When I said I wouldn't go, I was selfish. And then I grew to love you so that I needed you for breakfast and for Viv and Deirdre and for tea parties, too."

Hot tears sprang to his own eyes. He swallowed hard but smiled through them, determined to cheer her. "And... perhaps bad poetry?"

She cried then on his shoulder, his sweet wife who loved him beyond the terrors of scandal and the emptiness of loss. Who loved him so much she'd prepared the way for his success in her own inimitable way.

He settled them to the bed, he propped against the headboard, she curled in his arms as he stroked her back. "I've composed a new poem for this occasion," he said after many minutes. "Are you ready to hear it?"

She peered at him through lowered lids. "Rave on."

"Come with me and be my love, And we shall all the measures prove, That life is short, And love is sweet, And never will I again remove, Myself."

She grimaced but kissed him as if she'd starved for him these many weeks. "I love you, Lord Cole, but as a politician, you must become more facile with words."

"I swear I'll find a thousand ways to show you I love you, Lady Cole."

"Start now, will you?"

"My pleasure."

EPILOGUE

July 1888
Cole Manor
Brighton, England

Ada ambled down the stairs in her slippers. The house was quiet, the five children still asleep this hot morning. She relished the idea of peace and quiet for her morning meal.

Victor had left her earlier this morning at six to walk the beach alone. She could not walk in the sand easily given her condition. He liked to stroll along the coast, forming verbiage for his speeches, this one about voting rights. She wanted only to read the papers.

"Good morning, ma'am." Goodings had stayed on as butler and ran a very orderly house. Indispensable, he knew her preferences for meals, her needs for a multitude of receptions and her tendency to entertain her large and growing family at a moment's notice. "Shall I serve you?"

"Yes, please. I'm afraid I'm not very agile this morning. I love being downstairs but hate being on my feet." She was pregnant with her fourth child. Or, declared the doctor after listening with his stethoscope, more likely her fourth *and* fifth. She was certainly big enough for two, she admitted as she inched herself into her dining room chair. Liv had advised her to take her breakfast in bed. Lily had seconded the idea. But no matter how many pillows she plumped up behind her, she was more crippled by the stay in bed than gratified by it.

The butler knew what she liked for her morning meal and he ran off downstairs to the kitchen to fetch her two poached eggs and salmon. By her place was the morning's Brighton paper. On the front page was a story about her husband, the Honourable Member for Brighton, who had officiated at the opening of the new orphanage facilities yesterday. On another page was an interview with him discussing life in the Chinese treaty ports and the need for control of substances containing opium. Many aligned with Victor on this issue, including chemists and physicians who studied the affects of opium and its derivatives. Women's groups, including those who wished to extend the franchise to women, also supported him. Laudanum for 'hysterical females' was, many said, simply another way to subdue them. With all this support, Victor had won his first and second elections to Parliament handily.

The article she skimmed told of the recent engagement of the marquess of Ridgemont to an eighteen year old American heiress. Richard continued to face financial problems and he'd changed much in life as a result. Or at least according to the gossip sheets this was true. She and Victor did not receive his brother, nor did the duke and duchess. Their estrangement was well known among society. And the old rumor that Richard had started that it had been Ada who seduced him was long since discredited. People saw who Victor and she really were and that their marriage, no matter its impetus, would have occurred because they loved each other.

She sighed, finishing her second cup of coffee when a

clatter on the stairs announced the arrival of one of her children. Deirdre, most likely, as she took her cues from Ada and rose early.

"Mama! Good morning!" Her little dog Bud, a spaniel such as King Charles had favored, scampered along beside her. Deirdre, now twelve, had sprouted up this summer, almost nearly as tall as her older sister, Vivienne. Both of them had variations of their father's and grandmother's auburn tresses. When they debuted, Ada was certain they'd have proposals by the dozens.

"Sweetheart, how are you? Well? Good. Has Bud gone out?"

"I'll take him down now." She kissed her on the cheek. "Are you finished with the papers?"

I am, indeed." Deirdre liked her news, too. "Shall I return to sit with you after I let Bud out or are you retiring?"

"I thought I'd walk out to the kitchen garden. Join me there when you're ready, will you?"

An hour later, shaded by the awning on the gardener's hut, Ada had a bevy of people bustling about her. Deirdre had been joined by thirteen-year-old Vivienne who'd lost herself in a novel. The nursemaid tended to the younger children, Ethan age four, Oliver, age three, and Michael who at two was sure to set the world on fire one day with his non-stop chatter. Her feet up on the stool, Ada sat facing the shade of the trees and admiring the height of her azaleas. They'd bloomed in a palette of roses and pinks last spring. Their blossoms gone now, their green leaves raised their faces to the sun. Beneath them, rows of her chrysanthemums grew tall and bushy. The number of buds meant the rich colors of autumn would be theirs when cooler weather came.

"Here's Papa!" Deirdre announced, skipping to take

Victor's hand. "And he's got Camille and Uncle Pierce with him!"

"Do not," said Victor as he came to Ada and bent to kiss her cheek, "get up. Look who I found on the beach this morning."

Her older brother Pierce, a replica of her father with his virile Black Irish good looks, strode toward her in his casual seaside attire. Camille, her step-sister, walked beside him swinging her large straw hat and pursing her lips.

Ada examined her brother, his silver eyes hooded, his ink-black hair windblown. Although he greeted her with a smile, it was tight. Camille looked no better. *Had they argued?* While that was nothing new since Pierce had arrived back in England a week ago from his latest trip to Shanghai, Ada speculated that Pierce had given her a piece of his mind about her latest beau. The new man in Camille's life had come to family dinner last night at her father and Liv's house. He was fair, handsome, heir to his father's barony, a financier, and from first glance it was clear to Ada...and she'd bet hard money others in the family, that Pierce did not care for the man.

Victor brushed a hand through his hair and took the white wicker chair beside Ada. "Feeling well?"

"Out here? With all of you?" She sent him an endearing smile. "You know I am."

She turned her attentions to her guests. "Are you staying for coffee? Or would you like breakfast?"

Camille plunked herself into the nearest chair and cast a derisive glance at Pierce. "I'd welcome breakfast. Arguing requires food."

Pierce shot her a narrowed look. "If you'd choose a man with a bit of gumption to him, I'd not have a problem."

Camille took inventory of Ada, Victor and even Viv and Deirdre's expressions. "Why do I put up with this?"

Why, indeed? Ada suppressed her grin.

All the Hannifords knew why. Except for Pierce. And Camille, who at twenty-four and an accomplished author, had entertained marrying nearly every eligible man in Britain.

Viv giggled, then extracted a small red ball from her pocket. Even Viv knew these two had more to say to each other than to constantly argue. "Shall we play ball, Ethan? Oliver, you come, too."

And as they marched off to the field, Michael fussed that he was being deserted. The governess, smart woman, took him off to toddle around among his siblings.

"Tell me about Shanghai," she said to change the subject into a topic more logical. "I've not really had a chance to hear you talk since you've arrived home."

"All's very well." He crossed his legs and pressed the crease in his navy trousers between two fingers. "We're putting the finishing touches to the new generators. We'll expand electrical service to the southern boundary of the city by the new year."

"And Wu-lai?" The young girl who had served them as the girls' nurse had returned to China with Pierce on one of his trips four years ago. In fact, she had become his housekeeper in the British sector.

"She is well. She'll marry one of the local governor's administrators next spring. Then she'll leave me. I'll need a new housekeeper when I return."

Ada had often wondered if the lovely shy young Chinese woman had become Pierce's mistress. But she was to marry a *literati*, so most likely Ada's fears were unfounded.

Victor's book published six years ago was now considered a classic, used by many who wished to do business in China. But it was Pierce who was the current expert.

"When will you go back?" Ada asked, always concerned for his safety with more and more peasant riots there.

"I'd like to stay here awhile. Six months, more?" He glanced at Camille and frowned. "Camille tells me that Madame Chaumont passed away in May. I'm sorry to hear that. I liked her."

"For many years," Ada told her brother, "she was a great help to us. Liv and Lily went to Paris to her funeral. Marianne and Remy joined them." From the Hanniford's first arrival more than a decade ago, the French countess had shepherded the Hanniford women through the rigors of European society. Always hoping she might find a man to marry her, she died in her little townhouse in Paris with Marianne holding her hand. "She was an asset to the end, even talking up our French perfume among her many friends."

The flower shipments that Victor had begun six years ago had been a boon to the fragrance industry. Today, half of their family prosperity came from the perfume companies in which Victor owned stock.

Then she had to ask the question few others would broach. She knew, as did all the others in the family, that Elanna, Julian's sister, the widowed countess of Carbury, corresponded with Pierce. Elanna had departed England a year after the death of her husband, the earl. The whispers about her relationship with him, her well-known hatred of him, and his mysterious death were on the lips of the gossips many months after his demise. Reclusive before his death, Elanna became a hermit afterward. So hateful of her husband, she had left her young son, Nathaniel, in Carbury's care. After the man died, she refused to take the child in. Instead, she drew up legal papers and handed the boy to Julian and Lily to rear. Born on the same day as the Setons' oldest son Garrett, Nate went to live with Lily and Julian. They raised him as their own, and they educated him to take on his inheritance as the earl of Carbury. A week after she'd granted them custody of Nate, Elanna had departed for Dublin. Leland,

Ada suspected, had gone with her. But no one spoke of him at all.

"What news of Elanna?"

At Ada's question, Camille studied the scarecrow in the garden.

"She's in Quebec," Pierce said, sounding nonchalant.

Yet Ada knew where his affections were. Had he loved her? Or pitied her? A madness or an obsession? She had no idea.

"Canada?" Elanna's newest location. She'd tried Dublin, then New York, now Quebec.

"I don't think she will ever stop traveling."

Running was the term that came to mind.

"She and Phillip Leland are to marry."

Camille turned to stone.

"That's long overdue," Ada said.

Camille simply stared at her with fixed umber eyes.

Oh, how she wished that she could blurt out the truth she saw here. But then, neither of them would believe her.

By ten, Pierce and Camille had departed, well-fed and nicer to each other.

"I wish they'd settle their differences," she told Victor as he took her arm and they strolled back to the house.

"People need time to see who they truly love," he responded.

"We didn't," she said and paused beneath a bower of fragrant purple wisteria.

"No." He kissed the tip of her nose. "We took only a day."

She smiled up at her darling husband. "And bad poetry."

The End

TRAVELS WITH CERISE

Here I am inside Park Monceau on my way to the Musee!

Serendipity!

I had a wonderful surprise recently when I went to an exhibit in the Paris Musée Cernuschi. This Asian art museum near lovely Parc Monceau exhibited a collection of items on the production of perfumes from China. I knew I would soon be writing this book in my series and that I wanted to describe the challenges faced by a Western *tai-pan* in the Foreign Settlement of Shanghai. This visit—and the description of development of perfume and incense—was one I was thrilled about.

We in the West think of porcelain, artistic screens, silks (and even beautiful multi-colored T'ang statuary of camels, horses and more) when we think of imports from China. But flowers were among the most prized imports, not only from China, but from Japan, too. (In fact, the imperial throne of Japan is called The Chrysanthemum Throne for the flower they love best.) Transporting these flowers by ship was delicate work.

Today, many of the most popular scents come from flowers...or the imitation of their fragrances. But fragrances have often been included in concoctions to adorn bodies—or refresh bodily odors.

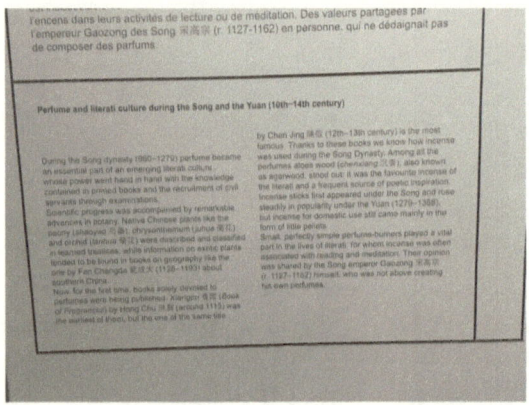

From the exhibit on perfumes and incense!

From China have come the fragrances of camellias and chrysanthemums, roses, jasmine, peonies, orchids and many more. In the Sung and Yuan Dynasty periods (approximately 10th through 14th centuries), perfume "became an essential part of an emerging *literati* culture..." The *literati* were the Confucian-trained government officials whose power was unchallenged politically and esthetically. If a Confucian gentleman and his family including his wives, concubines and daughters used fragrance, others sought to imitate them. As you read here, understanding the botanical life-cycle of plants meant that an industry rose up to service the Chinese population who could afford it.

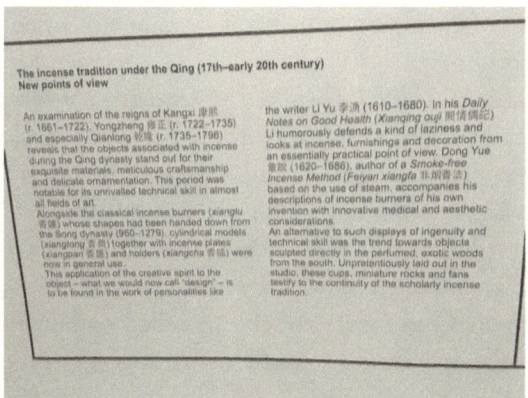

The incense tradition under the Qing (17th–early 20th century)
New points of view

An examination of the reigns of Kangxi 康熙 (r. 1661–1722), Yongzheng 雍正 (r. 1722–1735) and especially Qianlong 乾隆 (r. 1735–1796) reveals that the objects associated with incense during the Qing dynasty stand out for their exquisite materials, meticulous craftsmanship and delicate ornamentation. This period was notable for its unrivalled technical skill in almost all fields of art.
Alongside the classical incense burners (xianglu 香爐) whose shapes had been handed down from the Song dynasty (960–1279), cylindrical models (xiangtong 香筒) together with incense plates (xiangpan 香盤) and holders (xiangcha 香插) were now in general use.
This application of the creative spirit to the object – what we would now call 'design' – is to be found in the work of personalities like

the writer Li Yu 李漁 (1610–1680). In his Daily Notes on Good Health (Xianqing ouji 閒情偶記) Li humorously defends a kind of laziness and looks at incense, furnishings and decoration from an essentially practical point of view. Dong Yue 董說 (1620–1686), author of a Smoke-free Incense Method (Feiyan xiangfa 非煙香法) based on the use of steam, accompanies his descriptions of incense burners of his own invention with innovative medical and aesthetic considerations.
An alternative to such displays of ingenuity and technical skill was the trend towards objects sculpted directly in the perfumed, exotic woods from the south. Unpretentiously laid out in the studio, these cups, miniature rocks and fans testify to the continuity of the scholarly incense tradition.

The Chinese also developed incense to perfume rooms. Made into sticks or pellets, the product was distributed around homes and shops. They developed small burners to dispense continued fragrance into a room. Such essences became associated with poetic inspiration and for meditation. Westerners copied those uses and still do!

Lord Victor Cole's sudden financial success in Shanghai was not unusual. British, American, French and many others took advantage of the weakness of the Chinese imperial government and earned a fortune. Western control over the lives of Chinese in the treaty ports did create problems. Eventually, when the last Chinese emperor abdicated in 1911, the backlash and chaos that followed engendered riots, starvation and civil war. Four decades later, Mao Tse-tung and his communist comrades forced out the Western-backed Chiang Kai-shek and anti-western sentiment prevails to this day.

Opium features prominently in this novel. I have made Victor Cole's export-import company one of the few that did not traffic in it. As Ada says to him, opium in all its derivatives was used freely in syrups and tinctures to calm 'irritable' babies, to cure digestive problems and to soothe 'hysterical' women' with 'female problems'. It was sold in many forms as powders to be ingested or injected, or as liquids to be smoked in hookas or pipes.

A column, entitled *The Abuse of Narcotics*, appeared in the *London Daily News*, Monday, February 2, 1880. "Thus, grocers, and even village hucksters and hawkers can do safely sell chlorodyne, chloral, laudanum, by simply paying off...for a patent medicine (license) which the (?) give to anyone bringing the money....Pharmacy and Sales of Poison Acts would compel the makers of the so-called patent medicines to state plainly with each bottle or package the proportions such preparations contains..."

In this novel, my spelling of Chinese names may look odd to you. Today we use a new simplified version of transliterating calligraphy. But what was used in this period of 1880s and until approximately twenty years ago was this system, called Wade-Giles. Because this was used in this 1880s period (and because this was the system familiar to me when I was in graduate school majoring in Chinese and Japanese history), I used this here. You can look up on Google, for example, Li Hung-chang, the famous self-strengthener and *chin-shih* governor of Anhwei and Chih-li Province, and you will see his biography listed in Wade-Giles as well as the newer Chinese version.

Other little facts you may wonder about I list here. The home of Julian and Lily Ash, the duke and duchess of Seton, sits on Green Park not far from the Piccadilly home of Killian and Olivia Hanniford. I say many of the public would often come to the windows and try to converse with the inhabitants. This is possible and often occurred as the owners of Spencer House on the Park do claim.

What we would term 'yellow journalism' or 'editorializing' was not unusual in newspapers of the time. Dowries of American heiresses, such as that of Lady Randolph Churchill who was Winston's mother, were indeed listed. The amounts, who held them in trust and how they were to be dispensed to children or upon death, were usual topics.

This from *The Belfast Herald*, on her settlement: "Thomas Foote [of New York City] and George Charles Spencer Churchill, Marquis of Blandford, are made trustees, to receive an annuity of 10,000 dollars in gold. A portion of the 125,000 dollars is allotted to Lord Churchill, in the case of the death of his wife...and a further allotment of 250,000 is made for the issue of the marriage, in case of the death of both parties. The...Union League Club House is the security for this settlement."

In Britain in the 1880s, nobility did hold influence in boroughs and sponsored candidates whom they favored for seats in Parliament. Women did not have the vote, but many began to clamor for it. There was indeed a general election in Britain for Parliament in 1885 and a different party took power. (Another occurred soon after that.) Victor Cole could indeed hold his seat as a duly elected MP.

And as for the legal system in Britain at the time, a suspicious death such as the earl of Carbury's would require the attentions of a coroner to determine the cause of death. The Metropolitan Police should have been notified of Carbury's death and they would investigate the circumstances. The coroner would summon a jury for an inquest if the death was not a result of natural causes. The jury's responsibility was to determine place, time and circumstances of death. It was not their job to determine criminal intent or actions. How Carbury died is a mystery! Please write an email to tell me how you think he died!

I hope you've enjoyed this fourth book and return when famous gothic romance author Camille Bereston, Liv's sprightly daughter, tells the man she adores that he's a fool not to make her his mistress!

Although this is the breakfast room from Chateau de Cheverny in Loire River Valley, I see it as perfect for Ada's breakfast room in her Brighton home!

THOSE NOTORIOUS AMERICANS
CONTINUES!

WHO IS CERISE DELAND?

Cerise DeLand loves to write about dashing heroes and the sassy women they adore. Whether she's penning historical romances or contemporaries, she has received praise for her poetic elegance and accuracy of detail.

An award-winning author of more than 50 novels, she's been published since 1991 by Pocket Books, St. Martin's Press, Kensington and independent presses. Her books have been monthly selections of the Doubleday Book Club and the Mystery Guild. Plus she's won nominations and awards for Best Historical of the Year, Best Regency and scores of rave reviews from *Romantic Times, Affair de Coeur, Publisher's Weekly* and more.

To research, she's dived into the oldest texts and dustiest

library shelves. She's also traveled abroad, trusty notebook and pen in hand, to visit the chateaux and country homes she loves to people with her own imaginary characters.

And at home every day? She loves to cook, hates to dust, goes swimming at least once a week and tries (desperately) to grow vegetables in her arid backyard in south Texas!

ALSO BY CERISE DELAND

Regencies

Lady Starling's Stockings

The Stanhope Challenge, Regency Quartet, box set

Regency Romp Series:

Lady Varney's Risque Business, #1

Rendezvous with a Duke, #2

Masquerade with a Marquess, #3

Interlude with a Baron, #4

Christmas Belles, Series:

The Earl's Wagered Bride, #1

The Viscount's Only Love, #2

The Duke's Impetuous Darling, #3 (currently in Nine Lords for
Christmas box set)

Delightful Doings in Dudley Crescent Series:

Her Beguiling Butler, #1

His Tempting Governess, #2, *2019*

His Naughty Maid, #3, *debuts soon*

Erotic Regency Romances:

His Delectable Cook

Sense and Sensibility

Victorian Romances

Those Notorious Americans Series:

Wild Lily, #1

Daring Widow, #2

Sweet Siren, #3

Scandalous Heiress, #4

Miss Bereston's Last Beau, #5, *2019*

Medievals

Swords of Passion Series:

At Her Service, #1

For Her Honor, #2

With Her Kiss, #3

* * *

Military Romances

7 Brides for 7 SEALs Series:

You Were Always Mine, #1

No Getting Over You, #2

SEALs Going Hot, box set

Burning for Nero

Conquering Zeus

A Long Time Comin' (erotic romance)

Hard Drivin' Man (erotic romance)

Contemporaries

Is That a Gun in Your Pocket? (erotic comedic suspense)

Tall, Hard and Trouble, box set

Tall, Hard and Mine, box set, *Coming Soon!*

Tall, Hard and Fierce, box set, *Coming Soon!*

***

Sign up for Cerise's newsletter: <u>Cerise's Bon Bons</u>